FLASHFALL

FLASHFALL

JENNY MOYER

HENRY HOLT AND COMPANY

NEW YORK

Henry Holt and Company
Publishers since 1866
175 Fifth Avenue, New York, New York 10010
fiercereads.com

Henry Holt® is a registered trademark of Macmillan Publishing Group, LLC.
Copyright © 2016 by Jenny Moyer
Map on pp. vi–vii copyright © 2016 by Jon Chadjurian
All rights reserved.

Library of Congress Cataloging-in-Publication Data
Names: Moyer, Jenny, author. Title: Flashfall / Jenny Moyer.
Description: First edition. | New York : Henry Holt and Company, 2016.
  Summary: In a world shattered by radiation fallout, teenaged Orion and
  her climbing partner Dram, in exchange for freedom, mine terrifying
  tunnels for a precious element that keeps humans safe from radiation
  poisoning, but disturbing revelations force Orion to question everything
  she knows.
Identifiers: LCCN 2016008939 (print) | LCCN 2016035846 (ebook) |
  ISBN 9781627794817 (hardback) | ISBN 9781627794824 (ebook)
Subjects: | CYAC: Radiation—Fiction. | Mines and mineral resources—
  Fiction. | Government—Resistance to—Fiction. | Love—Fiction. |
  Science fiction.
Classification: LCC PZ7.1.M72 Fl 2016 (print) | LCC PZ7.1.M72 (ebook) |
  DDC [Fic]—dc23
LC record available at https://lccn.loc.gov/2016008939

Our books may be purchased in bulk for promotional, educational, or
business use. Please contact your local bookseller or the Macmillan
Corporate and Premium Sales Department at (800) 221-7945 ext. 5442 or
by e-mail at MacmillanSpecialMarkets@macmillan.com.

First edition—2016 / Designed by Liz Dresner
Printed in the United States of America by LSC Communications US,
LLC (Lakeside Classic), Harrisonburg, Virginia

10 9 8 7 6 5 4 3 2 1

For Jacob,
who wouldn't let me quit

ONE

297.84 grams cirium

CAVES MAKE GOOD hiding places. But this close to the flash-fall, they also make the most likely places to die. The creatures dwelling in the deep caverns are rabid by-products of the flash curtain, altered by radioactive particles. And they're starving.

Which makes them almost as desperate as us.

My boots scrape the cavern ledge, and a red marker illuminates at my feet. *Danger. Do not cross.* Behind me, Dram shifts, and in the soft jangle of climbing harness and anchors, I sense the questions he's not saying aloud.

My mother once told me I have magic. She didn't speak the words, nothing as dangerous as that. The day she guided me down my first tunnel, she simply pressed my hand to the cavern wall, and I knew.

I have magic in a place where it is outlawed.

My father would call it something different—bioadaptability. That's really what we Subpars are, adapted to the curtain's fallout and resistant to its elements in ways that Naturals aren't.

But he doesn't know what I feel when I'm down here.

I tip forward, and musty air caresses my face like the breath of a ghost.

"You passed the boundary marker," Dram says, his soft warning drawing me back.

I lean past the ledge, my heart thundering. My headlamp penetrates the first few meters of darkness.

"Secure an anchor," I command softly. "We're going down." When he doesn't move, I glance back. He studies me, blue eyes narrowing beneath his headlamp. "There's cirium down there, enough to earn more Rays."

"Rays don't mean much if we're no longer breathing."

My gaze slips to his arm, to the seal of our city-state and the two curving metal bars he wears pinned beside his designation. Each Ray represents 100 grams of cirium mined in service to Alara. If we earn two more, the director will pin them beside the others and then we will never have to wear these suits again.

"Step in my steps," I murmur. He sighs, loud enough for me to hear it through my earpiece, then kneels to anchor a line. I've invoked our cavers' creed, and there's not much you can say when someone commands you to follow blindly. Besides, there's more than that going on here, and Dram knows it.

At least, I hope it's more than me just being reckless. *And desperate*, my mind whispers.

"When you were little," Mom told me once, "I couldn't keep you from climbing the Range. You'd press your cheek to the stone and tell me it was singing to you." Her eyes had grown anxious then, so I didn't tell her that the cirium called to me so much stronger from beneath the mountains—that it reached for me like a hand in the dark.

"Use it to get free, Orion," she had said. A week later, tunnel seven swallowed her in a waterfall of rock.

Now, at sixteen, I'm the caver closest to earning a place in Alara, the city safe behind the cirium shield. As much as I want to live beyond the reaches of the flash curtain, far from the flashfall, I wonder how much of what I risk is for her. So that the part of her I carry inside me will know a place beyond this dust and ash.

I move my pickaxe to the holster on my back, watching Dram secure the bolt. We stand in a place where light filters down through cracks in the rock ceiling. I can almost pretend that it's sunlight, instead of fallout from a solar incident that occurred over a century ago. The flashfall is like this—hinting at the curtain's beauty, painting our excuse for a sky with luminescent clouds, quietly killing us while we're mesmerized.

"Anchor's secure," Dram says, giving the rope a tug. He knots the other end and throws it over the side.

"Be sure to mute your lights before you descend."

"At that depth, even muted lights will draw the gulls—"

"I know the risks." Tension pours from me, like I'm bleeding out with all the worry I've kept buried for days, and since despair will immobilize me, I lean into anger. I face Dram, trying to decide how to confront him.

Protecting Alara isn't the only reason we're down here.

My caving partner is keeping things from me, and while it's true I'm keeping things from him, my feelings aren't going to get me killed. His secret is a clock ticking down to death.

"Let me see your Radband," I say. In the sparse light threading past the flashfall, I see his face register shock. "Five years we've been scouting tunnels together—"

I grasp his wrist. "Did you really think I wouldn't notice when you started covering your Radband?" My fingers tighten over the biotech dosimeter we're all fitted with at birth—the band that monitors our radiation levels and sets us apart as Subpars. "How bad is it?"

"Orion—"

"Show me."

He mutters a curse and holsters his pickaxe, all the while meeting my stare. He flicks open a knife and cuts the cloth wound over his Radband.

"There." He holds his wrist in front of my face. "Satisfied?"

For the past year, I've watched his glowing green indicator dull to the muted shade of cave moss, but this gleaming light hits me like a kick to the stomach.

"How are you at *yellow*?" There are only two colors beyond it, and no one in the flashfall lives long with a red indicator.

He doesn't answer, and I know—*I know*—it's this cursed tunnel. Nine is bigger than all the rest, with the most potential for cirium. And the most potential for exposure.

"Why did you hide this?" I whisper.

"I got tired of looking at the damn thing!" His tone is hollow, but I hear the fear there. He's only eighteen, in prime health otherwise . . . but his body's cumulative radiation levels indicate yellow. It's the warning before amber, when you really start dying.

Subpars are resistant to the curtain's particles, but not immune.

He squeezes my hand. Some of what I feel must be showing on my face. "There's nothing I can do about it," Dram says.

"You can get to the protected city." And it's like I've dropped over the ledge; my blood pounds through me like I'm falling. "There's a vein of cirium down there," I say, pointing past the boundary marker. "I'm certain."

He studies me, as if he's listening for the words I'm not saying. Then he lights a flare, steps to the edge, and tosses it over. We watch it fall, red fire sputtering against the darkness. One second, two, three . . . the smoking flame grows smaller as it drops . . . six, seven . . . I know Dram's counting, measuring the distance to gauge how much climbing line we'll need, what it will take to get us down and back up again.

I barely watch the flare. In my mind, I've already made the drop. The truth is, I stepped off this ledge the moment I saw Dram's Radband.

"You understand the risks of going down there?" he asks.

"I understand the risks of not going." The statement hangs between us, but I don't look away, not even as his gaze locks with mine.

He threads the rope through my rappel device and secures it to my harness. I'm aware of his touch, his closeness, and I try to make my breaths sound normal, in case he can hear them through his earpiece.

"You're shaking," he says. I don't answer because he'll hear the emotions rioting through me—anger, fear, and something new that feels out of place down tunnel nine. A longing that probably belongs more with a Natural girl in the protected city who doesn't have an entire mining outpost relying on her. A normal girl who isn't trying to save her best friend with a pickaxe and a reckless disregard for boundary markers.

"Alara needs this cirium," I say. But it's not duty to our city-state that gives me the courage to grasp the line and lean back over the chasm.

"Careful," Dram says.

"Step in my steps," I murmur, thinking how many hundreds of Subpars have echoed those words. I'm not the first to scout the unknown, to face my fears and drop.

I'm just the youngest.

I rappel, my stomach dropping as I give in to gravity. The silence of the chasm presses around me, and I feel like that flare, tumbling through a void. Cold creeps in through my caver's suit, making me shiver as I descend. My heart beats in my ears, and it sounds like *too deep, too deep, too deep.*

But then another part of me comes awake.

Ah, yes, this.

The innermost parts of me—places I think of as distinctly Subpar—stir, as imprinted memory and sensation come to life.

My feet touch bottom. I free myself from the line and kneel, pressing my bare hand to the chasm floor. Humming. A faint vibration I feel deep inside. I stand, turning in a slow circle as my headlamp skips over walls wet with rivulets of water. Fear seizes me, a reactive instinct, but no orbies lurk in this water, piling atop one another to reach me, to taste me.

"Abseil clear!" I call, giving the rope a tug. The descending line is free. Safe to follow.

Moments later, Dram drops beside me. He pulls free of the rope and grasps a knife. "Lead the way."

As I mute my lights, his Radband glows in my periphery, a flash of yellow. I feel the color, an undeniable warning, pushing me on. We forge through a crevice, the rock so tight around us our Rays scrape the stone. I hear each one of Dram's breaths. Then, a sound louder than our sliding and scraping. Soft mewling, like the cry of an infant for its mother. But not a human mother.

I freeze.

"Orion . . . ," Dram breathes, so close I feel his breath against my ear. He says a hundred things in that one utterance, his tone confirming my worst fears.

Tunnel gulls.

I turn my head and meet Dram's eyes. We share a conversation in the space of a few shattered breaths. Survival instincts fire along my synapses.

There's a knife clenched in my hand that I don't recall reaching for.

"Right behind you, ore scout," Dram whispers. He turns off his headlamp and all his suit lights. We are going to cross beneath this gulls' nest blind, and he trusts me to lead the way.

I force myself to take one step, then another, and all the while we listen as the mother gull feeds her baby with a clicking of beaks and the dying sounds of some creature. We are soundless, holding our breath as we hug the wall and pass the rows of roosting father gulls, anxiously awaiting their turns to feast. I look up—just once—and the light of our Radbands illuminates the knife-point feathers of dozens of gulls. I want to cover my hair so badly. It would be the first thing they'd tear into—but I force my attention to the widening of this pass I can just see about ten meters ahead. After that, we'll at least stand a chance fighting back. Or running.

Five meters.

One.

I let my senses move beyond me, a part of me detaching and finding its home in the call of the caverns. Free of its bonds, the cavern creature within me stirs, listening from a place of bone and marrow.

Yes. This.

Slowly, impressions filter through my mind, and passages overlay my senses like the pages of a map. The vein of cirium is down here.

I just need to find it.

The youngling gull cries out for more, and talons scrape the stone. The mother is off to hunt.

And so am I.

TWO

297.84 grams cirium

WHEN YOUR NAME is a source of irony among the cavers of Outpost Five, you're motivated to work hard for a new one. Scout isn't an illustrious nickname, but it sure beats Orion in a place where you can't see the stars.

It's exactly this kind of musing that tells me my oxygen levels are dropping faster than I thought. I should be focused on not dying. I've earned the title of ore scout, but right now it's about to earn me a funeral pyre beside my best friend. I've led us too far off course.

"Read me our coordinates, Dram," I command softly, trying to keep the tension from my voice. Our mouthpieces pick up everything.

"Fifty-two meters southwest by thirty-three degrees, ten minutes," he says.

Not where we're supposed to be.

I close my eyes, straining my senses to pick up the vein of cirium I've been chasing. It's harder to do when your air's not a guarantee. I adjust the Oxinator I'm wearing over my nose and mouth.

Some people die on a sort of sigh, a shift of breath from one path to another. I doubt I'll go like that. Nothing in my life is peaceful—I don't expect death to be any different.

One thing is certain—I'm going to experience it for myself soon. My air tank hisses as my lungs reach for a breath that isn't there. When I go, there won't be any peaceful sighing, but a violent thrashing, a desperate wrestling with an invisible opponent. I refuse to die before I've had a chance to live.

I tap gloved fingers on my wrist monitor, hoping the readings there will contradict what the tightening in my chest is hinting at.

"Your oxygen levels are low, Rye," Dram says.

I look back at him through my lighted goggles. His brown hair falls into his eyes beneath his skullcap. Even with the Oxinator, I can hear the concern in his deep voice.

I glance at the cylinder looped over my shoulder. "Tank fifty-nine's always testy."

We duck beneath a dripstone, avoiding the water that drops from its sharp points like saliva from a monster's teeth. These caverns are always hungry, tunnel nine most of all. It's taken everyone on our scouting team. All but Dram and me.

I pull off my glove and set my hand to the wall. Cavern particles prick my exposed skin like the warning nip of a feral creature. Even the air bites down here. I listen for the call of tunnel gulls. Instead, I hear the flash curtain.

A hundred fifty kilometers long, one hundred kilometers high—even if techs hadn't told us its dimensions, I think I would sense its magnitude. Our outpost lies thirty kilometers west of it, behind a barrier of mountains, but I feel it, distant, pulsing with energy. It hums, and something inside me sings back.

My breath stutters.

"They issued you a compromised air tank," Dram says. "We should turn back."

I take a cautious sip of air and press on. Without cirium, we are all dead anyway. An element born of the flash curtain, it can be milled and refined into the only effective shields we have against the band of radioactive electromagnetic particles the sun sent crashing through our atmosphere more than a hundred years ago.

"Alara needs this cirium, Dram." A cough catches me off guard, breaking up my words. I steal a glance at my indicators. Worse than I thought.

"Our city-state doesn't need a dead ore scout," Dram says, unclasping his tank. He pulls a deep breath from his mask and switches the tubing to the valves on my tank.

"No, Dram—"

He pushes my hands aside as easily as he ignores my protests. The air hisses, and he takes a breath from faulty tank fifty-nine. I realize I'm holding my breath for every one of his, more concerned about the busted valves on that tank now that it's strapped to his back.

"Let's get what we came for," he says. "And get the hell out of here."

We tromp past a narrow river of water glowing with luminescent bacteria. It's strange how the beautiful things are often the most deadly. If the cavern is hungry, the water is ravenous.

"That's right," I say. "You promised Marin a date tonight."

"Just a dance."

"Uh-huh," I hum the word. Teasing him makes it sound like I don't care. I can't afford to care. These caves are too hungry.

The Congress of Natural Humanity gives the Subpars at Outpost Five one night and one day off each week. Since we're hemmed in by fences on the fringes of the Exclusion Zone, all sixty of us just end up around the fire pits, playing music and dancing. Food is still our rationed nutrition packets, but on Friday nights there is the addition of alcohol—lots of it.

My father says it's when the Congress lets the monkeys out of the cages and throws bananas at them. Too many bananas is not a good thing. His words, not mine. I take my bananas where I can get them. So does Dram.

"Stop," I say suddenly. I lift my palm light to a stretch of rock. Hope spins through me, more sustaining than oxygen. "It's up there."

"You sure?"

I don't bother responding. The air tank Dram gave me is having issues, and I need to conserve my breath. Besides, we both know I'm sure. They don't name a sixteen-year-old girl lead ore scout for no reason.

I approach the seam of ore, and Dram follows. He has mined 271.56 grams of cirium. We are both less than 200 grams from freedom—a nearly impossible goal. Until now.

"Marker, please," I say.

He slides a cartridge into his bolt gun and aims it at the cavern floor. "Mark," he says, and pulls the trigger. I cover my ears to block the sound. Yellow light fills the cavern, illuminating the wall. I hear his gasp through my earpiece. There might be even more here than we hoped.

A piercing cry rips through the dank underbelly of the cavern. We reach for our pickaxes at the same time.

"Tunnel gull?" Dram asks.

"Could be," I murmur. "Or a flash bat." Our backs nearly touch as we turn slowly, our palms and headlamps illuminating the shadows.

"Fire," Dram curses. "Let's hope it's just a gull. They don't usually attack."

"Unless we're near a nest . . ."

Dram curses again.

We stand in tense silence for a few moments. My hand hovers over my arm sheath and my double-bladed knife. I slowly let out a breath.

"Whatever it was, it's gone," I say. "Let's hurry and collect the sample."

Dram unhooks a rope and loops it through our harnesses. I feel his hands move over me, tightening straps, checking tension. Under the pretense of planning my climbing route, I tip my head back and let my headlamp flash over the silvery veins in the wall.

Dram and I have a system, a sort of wordless communication that's evolved from years working the tunnels together— which is why I have to work hard to conceal my panic from him now. Tank twenty-seven has a popped seal and at least one cracked valve. I can feel the cavern's particles slipping into the airstream, attaching to my lungs like microscopic leeches. But if we go back empty-handed, they won't let us come this far again. And we are so, so close.

"Will your axe hold?" Dram asks.

I glance down at my pickaxe, its worn handle split by a

narrow crack that has been widening for weeks, a fault line in the wood that threatens to send my axe head flying loose. But this axe is all I have left of my mother. I fit my fingers to the impressions hers left in the handle. When I grasp it, I feel like I'm holding her hand.

I imagine her with me now, urging me on. "It'll hold."

I tuck the axe in my holster and climb.

When I told our outpost director what I suspected was down here, he didn't believe me. Large deposits of cirium are rare. I told him he just wasn't looking in the right place. When you're bargaining for your life, you use whatever words are at your disposal—and whatever leverage. I have a surprising amount for a sixteen-year-old in a mining camp, but then, I didn't hang the sign above the lodge.

400 GRAMS CIRIUM = PASSAGE THROUGH FLASH CURTAIN

Dad says the Congress hung it there to motivate as well as mock us. Four hundred grams of cirium takes a lifetime to acquire. No one going down the tunnels lives that long.

The day after Mom died, I took up her axe and went down my first tunnel. Dad said nine was too young to mine; the director said I wasn't strong enough. The 2.38 grams I brought back with me told them both what they could do with their opinions.

But I'm afraid that sign is going to end up mocking me after all. The pain in my chest tells me I've already started dying.

"What's wrong, Rye?" Dram asks.

"I'm fine." I shoot a climbing bolt into stone and clip my rope into it.

"I don't have enough energy for your lies today," he says. And he's right—he sounds exhausted. I let go of the wall, and

Dram takes my weight as I sink into my harness and dangle beside the rockface.

"Let's get what we came for," I say. "Just enough to convince them." I slam my axe into the rock. Sparks flash as I chip away at the stone.

"Tell me when you're ready for the dust," he says, his words breathless.

"Are you all right?"

"I don't have enough energy for my lies, either," Dram mutters.

"Fine, let's hurry this up." I holster my axe and brace my legs against the water-streaked stone.

"Careful," Dram cautions.

My breath hitches, and I'm not sure if it's my restricted air supply or fear. The water flows, glowing with *Orbiturnus nocturne*—we call them orbies. My father believes they're drawn to the cirion gas released from oxidizing cirium. So I followed them, like a trail of bread crumbs. Bread crumbs that will just as likely eat me before I can use them to find my way.

"Rye?" Dram says. "You ready?"

All I can think is, *The water is hungry, and I am so, so close.*

The stone glistens near my face, swarming with orbies so dense I can't see the rock beneath them. But if this seam of ore is as big as I think it is, I can finally earn a life that offers more than darkness and death. I can get the people I love to Alara, safe behind the cirium shield.

If I think on that hard enough, I imagine it is worth my blood.

Time to test Dad's theory.

"Now!" I call.

Dram launches a pouch of dust at the wall, and it explodes against the dripping rock. I yank my flash blanket over my head and body. It sizzles, burning with the drone of thirsty, unsatisfied bacteria.

"Clear!" shouts Dram.

I toss the blanket away from me, holding in a scream as a few orbies burrow their way through my gloves. Then I see the wall.

"Holy fire," I breathe. Dad was right. The compound he made illuminates the cirion gas. The dust glimmers above the stone, revealing a massive vein of cirium. My eyes water like I'm staring into a Subpar's headlamp.

I've found enough to buy my way out of the Exclusion Zone—and Dad, Dram, and his sister, Lenore. There's more than enough here for 400 grams each. We just have to dig it out of rock covered in carnivorous bacteria. But not today. I'm running out of air, and so is Dram.

There's a tug on my rope.

"Rye . . . I can't—"

Dram's voice cuts out. My earpiece crackles, and I crane my neck to see behind me. He collapses to the ground, the belay line slipping from his grasp.

"Fire!" I swear, dropping, lurching for handholds as the tension goes out of the line. I cling to the rock, my feet dangling. "Dram!" I'm fifteen meters above the ground in a dark, wet cavern. The glowing water drips over my hands, deep orange and burning like lava. I scream.

Orbies are minuscule, but I swear I feel their teeth as they burrow through the layers of my gloves and skin. I drag in air, force myself to think through the pain. I'm starting to lose feeling in my hands. My grip on my handholds loosens.

I let go with one hand and reach for my bolt gun. I need to secure myself and set up a rappel, but the orbies swarm over my remaining hand, a mass of glowing orange. They travel past my wrist. My hand shakes. I am telling it to hold tight, but I'm not sure it can hear me anymore. I slip my rope free and bite the end with my teeth, threading it through the bolt. Tears seep from my eyes, blurring my vision behind my goggles. I shove them down around my neck and swipe my sleeve across my eyes. The orbies are eating through my wrist gauge. My radial artery pulses fast just beneath it.

My claw of a hand slips. I cry out, firing the bolt and falling. It sinks into an arch of rock, and my wrist nearly snaps with the force of the rope catching. I dangle from the line, swaying over the pool of orbies. I try to shake off the ones clinging to me, but they've dug in deep.

The pain is the only thing keeping me conscious. That, and my fear of falling into the water. The particles in the air float into my eyes, but I steal a glimpse of Dram, passed out beside the pool. One of his hands dangles over the water. Orbies pile on top of one other, forming a liquid ladder of want that grows out of the water toward his fingers.

"Dram!" I shout his name, even though he's got my voice right in his earpiece. I can't hear him breathing.

I tilt my head back and assess my situation. I start with the positives: not dead yet. I move on to the negatives: Dram needs air now. I can't climb one-handed. Can't lower myself to the ground because I'm directly over the water.

There's a loosening over my wrist, and what's left of my

depth gauge falls to the pool six meters below. The orbies on my wrist celebrate by digging into my epidermis.

"Flash me," I mutter. I'm out of time. There's only one thing I can think to do. Grasping tight to the rope, I bring my legs up and sway my body. When I get close to the wall of ore, I catch myself with my boots and shove off. Back and forth, I repeat the motion, building momentum. The third time, I push with all my strength and let go of the rope.

Air rushes up at me, and my stomach tells me I'm free-falling. I stretch my arms, willing my body to make it beyond the reaches of the orbie pool. I hit the ground and curl up, my protective padding slapping the ground as I roll. I gasp for breath, and the particles in my lungs scratch like grains of sand.

Groaning, I turn onto my stomach and crawl toward Dram. The orbies still swarm my left hand and wrist. As I push myself toward him, I pull a flare from my belt and ignite it on the cave floor. Red flames pop and hiss, and I hold it under my orbie-covered arm. I scream behind my teeth as the heat penetrates my suit and the holes in my gloves, but the orbies ignite, burning to bits of ash. They make a screeching sound before they flame up, and the ones that are deep burrow with renewed urgency. I still can't feel anything in my hand, so I dip it closer to the flame, grateful the synthetic layers of my suit aren't flammable. The flare burns out, and I toss it away.

"Dram!" I drag myself to his side and lift his head. His lips are blue.

I unstrap my Oxinator and press it over his nose and mouth. "Breathe." I tap the side of his face. "Open your eyes. Breathe." Tears prick my eyes.

He sucks in a breath, and his eyes slowly open, meeting

mine. The orange lights of the goggles distort their color, but I know they are blue with flecks of gold. Like I imagine the sky looks in places where there are no flash curtains.

"You are not allowed to go before I do," I say. "That was our deal."

"Other . . . way . . . 'round," he says. With a shaking hand, Dram presses the mask to my mouth. I breathe.

"Can't . . . do this . . . long," he gasps.

The air hisses through the tube. "Not leaving you," I say.

"So stubborn."

"We're not dying here." I lift my palm light to point to a narrow crevice carved into the rock face. "Air cave."

"Too far," he says.

"Thirty meters."

"Too narrow." Breath.

"Have to try." Breath.

The indicator light on his Radband begins to pulse, responding to the drop in his vital signs. If we hadn't already switched off the auditory alarms, it would be screeching at us by now.

I grasp him under the arms and half drag him to his feet. We stagger across the cavern like a couple of drunks. Halfway there, black spots fill my vision and I forget to pick up my feet. I stumble against the wall, and Dram steadies me with his hands at my waist. A second later, the mask presses against my face and I take a shaky breath. I can see the cave through the black spots. I turn and grasp Dram's wrist, force the mask to his face. We stare at each other, and I swear I can hear his thoughts over the sounds of the oxygen draining from tank twenty-seven.

If you go now, you'll still make it.

I'm not leaving you.

So stubborn.

He sighs behind the mask, grips my arm, and hauls me across the crevice toward the air cave.

Please, let it be an air cave. I've never been wrong about the hidden passages beneath the Range, but still, air caves are rare this far past tunnel seven. We stagger toward the opening. I have to squeeze in sideways. Once inside, I grip the rocks and climb up to give Dram room. His shoulders won't fit through.

Dram pushes the tank through the crack. "Take it!"

"Not without you." I drag in a breath and shove the respirator over his mouth.

He clasps the mask and scans the crevice with his palm light. A whine vibrates through the cylinder. Dram and I meet eyes. I bang my hand against tank twenty-seven, hoping it's just being temperamental. It protests with a whir and goes silent. I bang it again. Nothing.

In the space between breaths I wonder at the coincidence of both Dram and me being sent down with faulty air tanks. Then my survival instincts kick in.

The air pocket is trapped up against the ceiling of rock. I crack a glow stick and toss it on the ground. The green light illuminates the walls. The air cave's about two arm lengths wide and twice my height. No water, no gull nests, no flash bats. Shoving my feet into cracks, I grip narrow handholds and scale my way up as best I can with injured hands. Toward the top, there's a shift in the air, like it's lighter without the particles that infiltrate the rest.

Heading back down, I don't bother with handholds. I drag in air and drop. The force of the impact jars my legs, but I lurch for the crack where Dram is trapped. I cup his face in my hands, point to my mouth and mime taking a breath. He nods, and we reach for each other at the same time. His lips press mine, and he draws a breath from my mouth. I'm sure I will think about the intimacy of this moment later, but for now all I can think is *Breathe, Dram. Don't die on me.*

We yank off his harness and bulky outer layers. I unzip his suit and peel it down to his hips. He gasps as the air pricks his skin and my fingers tangle in the synthetic mesh cloth of his undershirt, working the buckles free. The dark rises up. I need air. Now.

There's no time to spray skin barrier over Dram's chest and arms. The particles in the air frost his torso with slivers of crystal. He groans as they adhere, but without the protective layers, he can squeeze through the opening. He falls into my arms, gasping and trembling. My hands slip over his torso, and I feel the hard ridges of muscle he's carved from years mining and trolling the tunnels with me.

"Have to climb," I gasp, pointing to the shadows above us.

He leaps for the nearest handhold and drags himself up. I'm smaller but faster, and we reach the ledge at the same time. We brace ourselves in the air pocket, letting the clean air fill our burning lungs.

He shudders, and I let my palm light shine over him, head to toe. His Radband lets off its pulsating glow. Someone back in Central is seeing the alert and passing along the message.

Dram Berrends is dying.

They will study our coordinates. Down tunnel nine, far from where we're supposed to be.

I wrap my arms around him, and he shakes against me. "We

made it," I murmur. "We're going to be okay." I watch the mineral burn spread over his skin. He is far from okay.

I unzip the emergency medical supplies from a pouch in my suit. Serum 38 is a vaporized spray. I empty the canister. His skin rises up in angry red pustules, but he doesn't seem to feel it anymore. I uncap a syringe of Serum 129 with my teeth and push it into his arm. A shock inhibitor, though I'm sure it's late for that. I can't cover his skin, or risk flame to warm him, so I turn up the heater in his suit and clasp his gloved hands in mine.

"What . . . happened . . . your hands?" he asks.

"Made some orbie friends. Introduced them to my flare."

He grunts, and reaches for a syringe in the pocket of his suit.

"What are you doing?" I ask. "That's adrenaline—" He flicks off the cap and holds the needle above my thigh.

"Old . . . caver trick." He slams the needle into my leg and presses the plunger.

I take rapid breaths, my eyes tearing from the pain. "My blood pressure," I gasp. "Those orbies will explode—"

"That's the . . . idea," Dram murmurs, dragging my glove from my hand.

Adrenaline pulses through me, and I suppress the urge to run, my breath hitching from my mouth. "Dram, what—" A scream cuts off my words. The orbies burst under my skin, illuminating my veins in splashes of orange.

"I'm sorry." He drops the syringe and pulls me against his side. "They would've . . . gotten to . . . arteries."

Tears stream from my eyes, but the adrenaline is a barrier

against the pain. As we huddle at the top of the air cave, our legs start to shake from the effort of bracing ourselves up. Dram slips off his goggles and turns his head. I think he's afraid I'll see the pain he's hiding from me. As the minutes tick by, his skin swells, until every needle-like puncture looks like a spider bite. We have to get him out before they burst. There's nothing in our medical kits for that.

I've seen only one person die from mineral burn. His death was no gentle sigh.

"What . . . did we . . . find?" Dram's head is still turned away, his voice shaking more than his body.

"Enough cirium to earn a place in the protected city."

"Something more than . . . cirium in that cavern."

"Yeah, orbies." I feel them, even now, pushing against the current of my bloodstream.

"Two . . . bad tanks." His words penetrate my haze of pain. The idea that someone tried to sabotage our ascent wedges a knot of fear in my stomach. He turns, and his eyes bore into mine. My good hand clenches my arm, above the seal of our city-state, where black stitching marks my designation. Lead Ore Scout.

What have I led us to?

I remind myself that the Congress needs our cirium. Generations of Subpars have served at this outpost, hunting the caverns for cirium ore to protect one of the last remnants of civilized humanity—the city on the other side of the flash curtain.

Help will come. If not for us, then for the vein of cirium we discovered.

My eyes stay fixed on the rhythmic pulse of Dram's rescue tracker.

"Help is coming," I murmur. "They'll find us soon."

Surely it's true.

I'm not ready to die. Not when we've found a way to finally live.

THREE

305.82 grams cirium

NEWS OF OUR escapade down the tunnel spreads through camp. I can tell by the number of people gathered near the mouth of nine as we stagger out. I think it has less to do with our near-death rescue, and more with the seam of ore we found. Someone in Central must have let it slip. Hardly surprising in a place where cirium is everything.

I lean into the man supporting the bulk of my weight. "I think we missed the monkey party, Owen." He gives me a pitying look that tells me the drugs in my system must be talking again. I've never reacted well to shock inhibitors.

"Hang on just a bit longer, Scout." He smiles, his teeth flashing white against his dark skin.

"We'll have to dance another day, girlie," says Graham Jorgensen, breathing hard under Dram's weight. He always calls me girlie and Dram boyo. Since our mothers died and he taught us how to swing their axes.

The other two members of the retrieval team follow close behind, dragging our discarded Oxinators. By now, the fires around camp have burned to embers. Someone plays a waltz on a fiddle, and a few of the cavers stagger toward us in an alcohol-induced haze. They're probably more coherent than I am.

Dram missed his dance with Marin, but she is waiting for him anyway, a draft of ale in hand. I have people waiting for me too, but they wear guns instead of smiles.

I feel Dram hesitate beside me, and his eyes skip past Marin to the group of guards circling me. "Flash pistols," he whispers.

My gaze swings to the metallic cylinders projecting from the sides of their guns, reservoirs for flash dust. Only Alara's elite are issued weapons that harness the energy of the flash curtain. Mined in the cordons, flash dust is an even more precious commodity than cirium.

"Orion Denman?" A man steps past the unfamiliar guards. Tall, younger than my father, but with a bearing that feels ageless. His uniform bears the seal of Alara on his arm like we all have, but his opposite sleeve carries five red bands for the five outposts, and five black bands for the cordons.

"Flash me," I whisper.

"I'm Commissary Jameson." He shows the chain at his neck—his badge of office, as if I needed further proof he's from the Congress of Natural Humanity. His gaze flicks to Dram, then back. I feel us being assessed and weighed, like the ore in our pouches. "Are the reports true?"

His cultured tone sets me on edge, reminding me that he comes from a place behind a shield.

"I brought proof, as requested." I barely stop myself from saying "ordered." Subservience is always an effort for me. I pull away from Owen's support, swaying slightly. I will meet this man on my own two feet, even if they're wobbly.

"I'm here to inspect your ore," he says.

Dram grips my arm. I think he's afraid I'll make some derogatory reply, and I bite my lip to keep it in. Subpar humor is usually lost on Naturals.

The commissary's features swim before me, and some part of my addled mind orders me to stand up straighter and dig deep for some respect. This man is the Congress's own representative, overseeing all the outposts and cordons. It's hard to imagine one person in charge of the entire Exclusion Zone, but he carries himself like he owns whatever land he stands on.

"Come this way, Scout," Mull Cranston says, striding forward as if he wants to take my arm. Or grab me by the hair.

I drag my goggles off my face and let my gaze skip over the director all us cavers refer to as Cranny. He wears an ill-fitting, rumpled gray uniform. "I didn't realize you owned a uniform, sir."

Definitely grab me by the hair. His eyes narrow over his beaklike nose. I can't help it. I'm angry about the faulty tanks. Dram and I almost died.

Cranny stands off to the side, an inconsequential planet inhabiting the commissary's solar system. He glares at me as if it's my fault a man of such importance is striding about his domain reminding him he's inferior.

"I want you to describe how you located the vein of cirium," Jameson says.

I pull off my skullcap, and my hair tumbles out. I need to get out of my caver's gear—the cavern particles are irritating my skin like tiny slivers. A stricken look crosses the commissary's face, as if a weapon unexpectedly lodged in his chest. Maybe he's realizing how bad the exposure is down nine.

"Come with us to Central," he commands. I look past him, to the command center that dominates the outpost, the gated mansion that houses all the Natural techs and guards. As far as I know, no Subpars have ever gone inside.

"Huh." Not what I intended to say, but my brain's struggling to connect the dots.

"She needs the infirmary," Dram says.

I start laughing. Dram's words, spoken from someone who looks like death warmed over, strike me as terribly ironic.

"My sh-shock inhi-hibitors are w-wearing off," I announce. The smile on my face feels out of place; my body's having a hard time matching my expressions to my emotions. I feel Serum 129 evaporating from my system, like a blanket sliding from my body. Pain penetrates the haze, and I cry out, clenching my teeth to hold in the sound.

"What's wrong with her?" Jameson demands.

"I b-brought you your ore," I murmur, lifting the samples. It's like I've finally remembered I have hands, and they're not in good shape.

"She's infected." Cranny eyes my burned, chewed-up gloves as if I'm aiming a weapon. I suppose in a way, I am.

"Get the physic!" Jameson calls.

Marin gasps. I suppose my glowing hand is something of a stunner. She drops the mug of ale and dashes off.

"Director, the boy is worse off," Graham says, supporting Dram with an arm around his waist. "We did what we could for him down the tunnel, but he's got the burn bad." He slides aside the silver shock blanket draped over Dram's torso.

This time, it's Cranny who gasps. "How is he still standing?"

"You'd be surprised what p-people with the will to live can

do," I say, too loudly. If Dram had any strength at all, he would've clamped his hand over my mouth. Apparently Serum 129 breaks down the brain-to-mouth filter, and mine was questionable to begin with. I try to bite my lip, but my mouth is growing numb.

"Get them to the infirmary," my father calls. He runs to Dram's side and gives him a cursory scan, palpating his torso gently. "Good, we've still time." He looks at Graham. "Get him on the table and start an IV."

"Hi, Daddy," I sing. A giggle bursts past my numb lips. "Owen gave me Serum 129." My words still sound like a song.

He tears off my remaining glove. A couple orbies have chewed through the fabric and burrowed deeper. They move slowly beneath my skin, twin black dots. Full orbies don't glow. Not once their bodies begin to swell like ticks.

"I need to remove these at once, before they chew through an artery," Dad says. He looks at Jameson. "Whatever business you have with her will have to wait."

The commissary looks equal parts horrified and fascinated. Then his features blur, and I can't tell which way is up and which way is down. He reaches out to assist me, and it's an unexpected sight. Naturals tend to keep their distance from Subpars—and none of them touch us when we are fresh from the tunnels, with particle dust coating our suits. He catches my arm, and his dosimeter flashes red at the contact, in case there was any doubt I've been crawling through radioactive elements.

Now it's Cranny's turn to look poleaxed. Naturals protect themselves from the flashfall, and that includes us.

"Commissary, you're breaking Protocol," he says, his tone carefully neutral, though I see shock in his eyes.

The ALARA Protocol, the rule our city-state was named for, an acronym for As Low As Reasonably Achievable. A philosophy of radiation use and exposure, borrowed from the time before the flash curtain. Everything in our society is based upon this principle: exploit the resources of the flashfall, but limit radiation exposure and preserve human life, particularly the most vulnerable of our society, the Naturals whose genes remain uncorrupted by exposure.

My thoughts suddenly break apart, whirling from my mind's reach like ash on the wind. Someone stuck me with more Serum 129. The night sky tips up and spins. My father breaks my fall. I focus my last remaining energy trying to interpret the expression on Jameson's face.

The commissary who crossed the flash curtain to inspect my ore.

Who broke Protocol to keep me from falling.

———

"Explain to me again how both your Oxinators ceased to function," my father says.

"Coincidence," I say softly, watching him tie off the bandage on my hand.

"Funny thing, coincidence," he muses.

"Hilarious." I hop down off the kitchen table and pace. There isn't much space, just this room beside a bedroom and a small loft, but my steps carry me across the worn floorboards again and again as I work through what happened down nine.

Dad rinses his hands in our rationed water, his thoughts churning like mine. I watch him across the kitchen—both the room and the word itself a remnant from the days of the first outposters, when Congress still transported food into the camps, before techs developed nutri-pacs. I trail my fingers along the wall, a mix of wood and metal. With the exception of Central's mansion, everything here is like this—a blend of tech bracing up the original buildings. "Archaic," Dad calls it, but that's only because he's seen a picture of Alara.

I pick up one of his slides and peer at it. "What did you find?" I ask.

"How do you know I found anything?" He drops into his chair and adjusts the focus on his microscope.

" 'Cause you've barely looked up from those slides since I gave you the sample."

"Who else has seen this?"

I shrug. "The retrieval team and Cranny. Oh, and the commissary who came all the way from Alara."

His gaze narrows. "It's likely they still don't know."

"What?"

"This isn't typical cirium."

"I don't care what kind of cirium it is as long as it measures four hundred grams."

He looks at me over his glasses.

"What now?" I ask.

"You need to take me down there. I need to see this for myself."

"Too dangerous. Tunnel nine's not like the others."

I can practically see the wheels turning in his mind, assessing, shifting variables in equations I will never understand. He sighs and settles back in front of his microscope.

"Eat this." He hands me a nutri-pac.

I glance at the blue foil packet. "I'm not taking your rations."

He eyes my empty red packet, the half-size "children's portion" we're given until we turn eighteen.

"You're not getting enough," he says, pressing it into my hands. "Take it." I don't tell him that Dram shares his larger portions with me each day, because he's right—I'm starving.

I rip open the packet and squeeze some of the nutrient gel into my mouth. Dad told me it used to be flavored when he was a child. Berry, I think he called it. I don't know what berry tastes like, but the slick texture is similar to the water posey down nine, if not as bitter.

"The orbies covered this vein of cirium?" he asks.

"More than I've ever seen before."

"So they've been down there . . . absorbing the cirion gas, and taking . . . nutrients from the cirium for the past hundred and fifty years." I know better than to answer. He's not looking for my response. He scribbles a series of numbers and letters on his notes, staring hard, like he's waiting for them to rearrange themselves. "This cirium is altered," he murmurs, one eye peering through the microscope. "Fewer radioactive isotopes." He shoves his notes aside and grabs a beaker. "Orion. Grind this ore. I need to see something."

"Dad?" I grip the pestle and set myself to pulverizing the ore.

"Our ancestors drank the water down the tunnels," he says. "Those who didn't die adapted." There's urgency in his actions as he lights a burner. "They ate water posey and tunnel gulls— the only things available to them. They absorbed trace amounts of cirium and built a tolerance to the curtain's electromagnetic particles—like drinking small doses of poison until you eventually develop immunity to it." He looks at me—hair mussed, glasses askew, and fire in his hazel eyes. "Do you understand what I'm suggesting, Orion?" His voice is as soft as a whisper, and I feel his words move over me. I can only nod.

He takes my bowl of crushed ore and pours it over a burner. I know what he means to do, and part of me is wishing I'd never found this vein of cirium. He goes back to his notes and slides, and I stare at the beaker, where this new, altered cirium is beginning to liquefy. I wonder if he plans to inject it or ingest it.

"Please don't do this." I cannot lose him too.

He looks up, surprised. "If I'm right, a compound made of this cirium could boost our resistance to the flash curtain. We could survive in places without cirium shields. I'm talking about freedom, Orion."

Freedom. The word shivers through me. "But if you're wrong, then it's just poison."

There's a knock on the door, and Dad yanks the slide from the microscope. I cut the burner flame and whisk the beaker into a cabinet. The door opens, and Cranny steps into the dim light of Dad's desk lamp.

"I saw a light on," Cranny says. "You know how important our energy rations are."

"Yes, of course." Dad switches off the light. "I was bandaging Orion's hand."

"We have an infirmary for that, John," Cranny says. He walks toward me, his focus so sharp I feel it cutting through the haze of pain and exhaustion. "You need to be more careful next time, Scout."

A tart reply forms on my lips, but then I catch sight of

something through the open door. Indicator flags, red with three yellow stripes. Something in my expression must reveal my horror. He follows my gaze.

"We've just raised the alert. Techs have traced patterns of instability in the atmosphere. They've warned us to expect anomalies and fluctuations in the flash curtain. A flash storm's coming." He tosses the words out as if they don't weigh anything at all. As if they don't invoke memories of deaths so violent, I still have nightmares of it.

"When?" Dad asks, his voice rough.

"A week at most. You'll need to begin prepping the infirmary."

"There's not a lot that gauze can do for radiation poisoning," I say.

Dad throws me a warning look, but I can't seem to help myself. My three-year-old brother died in the last storm.

"Fortunately," Cranny says, "the cirium shields over Central are larger now. We shouldn't have as many casualties."

I snort. "Fortunate, indeed—that the guards and techs will be safe while the rest of the *entire camp* scurries under the rocks."

Cranny's gaze narrows, and he gets that look on his face—like he'd feel better if he were squeezing my neck between his hands. "The lodge has a steel roof—"

"Which worked so well before." Images of Wes, the last time I saw him, tear through my mind.

"She's right," my father says softly. "The cavers down the tunnels were safer that day."

"Then I guess it's lucky your daughter was taking her mother's place down there." Cranny taps the cord I wear around my neck—the pendant I never take off. His fingers brush the blue glass that contains Mom's ashes.

This time, I'm the one to restrain my father. His arm tenses under my bandaged hand.

"You understand I must maintain order," Cranny says. His gaze slips to our empty ration packets. He picks one up and idly passes it through his fingers. I want to ask him what size his rations are. I doubt anyone at Central is going hungry. "If Central falls, the outpost falls." Cranny gifts me with the paternal look he uses on Burning Days. "Subpars are helpless without this vital connection to Congress.

"If you don't care for me, or the guards, or the technicians"—Cranny leans in, like he's sharing a secret—"at least have some concern for the city this outpost protects."

My teeth clamp my lip. But the words won't stay put. "*Concern?*" I throw the word back in his face. "I risk my life every day for *the city this outpost protects.*"

Cranny's expression hardens. "You went past the boundary marker."

I can't immediately speak past my shock. "I found a vein of ore!"

"Whatever you found has brought the commissary breathing down my neck!"

"I'm supposed to protect Alara—"

"Not without *compliance,*" Cranny growls. "There are boundaries for reasons, Scout."

My heart pounds like Dram just shot me with adrenaline. I know this tone. There is punishment coming.

"Two weeks, half rations." He turns toward the door. "And, John—prepare for the storm."

The door bangs shut, and I tremble in the darkness. My unsteady breath fractures the stillness as Dad folds me in his arms. His memorial pendant presses against mine.

"I'm going to get us free," I whisper. The flash curtain will not take one more person I love.

Dad doesn't answer. I know he's thinking of broken air tanks and coincidence that likely wasn't coincidence.

"Me too," he says after a moment, and even in the dark, I can tell he's looking at the cupboard. At the place we've hidden the altered cirium.

I shiver again, and he holds me tighter.

I'm out the door before most cavers have stirred from their alcohol-induced sleep. Daylight—or what passes for that around here—lightens the sky like it's as reluctant to emerge as the rest of the outpost.

Frost coats the ground, but I wear only my undershirt with my shirt tied around my waist. When you spend most of your life beneath stone, in darkness, the wind on your skin feels like a gift. I tear open my red foil packet and eat my rations—just half—and tuck the rest in my pocket. Thoughts of Cranny and his angry warnings fill my mind, but I push them away.

Today belongs to me.

I pass the tunnels, ignoring their yawning entrances, pretending that my feet haven't carved a path into the ground between my house and this place. I'm a Subpar by birth, but for the next few hours, I don't have to be a caver. I'm no one's ore scout. I'm not a potential meal for orbies, flash bats, or tunnel gulls.

I have no idea what girls my age do on the other side of the cirium shield, but I have never shied away from imagining it. I know only that sixteen-year-old girls in the protected city are safe from the flash curtain. They don't fear storms, and they never, ever pick up axes.

I set my foot on a ledge of rock and push up, my fingers skimming the stone and finding handholds. Outpost Five is bordered along its east side by giant heaps of rubble that fused with the mountains when the flash curtain fell. We call it the Barrier Range because it provides a natural shield, separating us from the burnt sands of the cordons, which stretch all the way to the curtain. As bad as things get at the outposts, things could be worse. We are the fortunate ones.

My bandaged hand loses hold, and I hang from my other fingers. Breath saws from my lungs, filling the air with tiny clouds. I shake feeling into my injured hand and reach up, my toes sliding into familiar footholds. I've been climbing here since before I started down the tunnels. I guess that, even as a child, I looked for something beyond Outpost Five.

No one here climbs like I do. They call me the mountain goat, which I think is funny, since none of us have seen such a creature. The flash curtain killed most nearby animals and vegetation. Except my ancestors. They eked out a means of survival beneath the ground and emerged when the worst of the radiation dissipated. Subpartisans. Not a grand name for a new kind of people, but I suppose they weren't really concerned with how it would sound to their great-grandchildren.

I push myself over the final ledge and lie on the ground a moment, catching my breath. I imagine the air this high up is truer to what it once was. It's not, but this is a place for pretending.

"Fire, you've gotten fast," Dram says.

My head whips up. Dram reclines on a projection of stone that overlooks the cordon.

My stone.

I can count on one hand the times he's come here with me, and none within the last year. We tend to give each other space when we're not partners beneath the earth. Especially since Marin.

"You going to keep lying there?" he asks. "I thought the point was to look out at the . . ." Dram stretches his gaze toward the pseudo-horizon. "The nothingness."

"It's not nothingness." I climb to my feet and join him on the rock.

He looks toward the flash curtain. The view is hampered by the orange and red sulfur clouds over Cordon Five.

"Okay," Dram murmurs. "The view of hell."

Hell is climbing a kilometer beneath the ground with orbies digging through your skin.

"I like it," I say.

"That's because you have a good imagination." He turns to face me. I imagine the sight of Cordon Five reminds him of his father and his exile to Cordon Four.

"I thought you'd take the day to heal up," I say. "How's your skin?"

"Healing." He lifts his shirt. Small red bruises cover his chest and abdomen. I look away before he can see the heat creeping into my cheeks. He does this to me lately—confronts me with reminders that he's eighteen and not the boy I've been hunting ore with most of my life.

Fire, my hands are sweating. I wipe them on my pants and

stare toward Cordon Five. The image is still emblazoned in my mind. The curve of his muscles, the smattering of hair—

Ergh! Why did he have to come here? Seeing his bare chest reminds me I touched him mere hours ago, that our lips pressed together. Yesterday, all I could think about was saving him. Today, far above the tunnels, with plenty of air—it makes me breathless.

"How's Marin?" I tease, even though I'm sure he spent most of the night in the infirmary.

He grins. "Marin's good." The look he shoots me makes me think that maybe he wasn't as incapacitated as I thought.

"I imagine she was worn out from pouring those pints all night long."

He lifts a brow. "Jealous?"

"Of her proximity to the ale? Yes."

He grins. "Of her?"

"Am I jealous of the lodgemistress's daughter? Of tending the lodge and looking after the orphans and unmarrieds? No."

Dram smiles.

"Why are you here?" My tone holds more bite than the air, and I pick at the bandage on my hand. My nails are broken, and the skin peels away from where the orbies chewed their paths. I'm sure Marin holds nothing more dangerous than a cleaning cloth. I doubt she even has a callus.

Dram studies me a moment. "How's your hand?"

"Tiny glowing organisms exploded inside it less than a day ago. How do you think it feels?"

Dram grins. "You *are* jealous."

"I'm irritated. There's a difference." I spear him with a look. "You're intruding on my time."

His smile fades. "I won't stay long." He looks toward Cordon Five, then quickly away. "I wanted to talk to you about our descent yesterday. I'm concerned about the faulty Oxinators. That shouldn't have happened."

I should tell him that my dad said practically the same thing. I look toward the cordon, to the place where orange clouds block the towering, radioactive curtain we're trying to earn our way past.

"Then a representative from the Congress shows up," Dram continues. "Something's off."

"It makes sense they sent the commissary," I say. "It's a massive vein of cirium, probably more than anyone's found before."

"You're *too good*, Orion." Dram looks at me, his gaze shuttered, but I hear the warning in his voice. "What happens when you have to explain how you found it?"

"I'm lead ore scout—"

"No, Rye. It's more than skill. You . . . sense the cirium somehow. I'm your marker—I watch you more closely than anyone. You're *listening* when you're down there."

I break eye contact, but it's too late. There's nothing I can hope to keep from Dram. Not about the tunnels. Not about cirium.

"I'm right, aren't I?" he asks. There's anger in his tone now, mixed with a hint of fear. "What the hell is it saying to you?"

I cannot tell him what I've never understood myself—that when I first swung my mother's axe, I felt something in the stone respond. A pulse, like blood in veins, a hum that's more than vibration. And it's not just the cirium I hear, but its source . . . the flash curtain. And it doesn't speak to me.

It sings.

He curses long and low. I wonder how much he can read on my face. I'm suddenly wishing for the barriers of Oxinator and goggles, the darkness of tunnel nine. But this is Dram— even with all that, he still reads me.

"If they find out," he says softly, "they'll never let you go."

"I'm almost to four hundred grams—"

"No." He shakes his head. "They need cirium more than they need to give you a place in the city."

I lurch to my feet, as if I can physically combat what he's suggesting. "Congress won't go back on its word. That's the deal they make with us—Subpars do their part to protect Alara, and if we do really well, we're granted passage through the curtain."

"Maybe," he says, looking out over the cordon. He wears the pensive gaze of his father, like he's seeing something more than the ash-filled sky.

"We're not prisoners here, but protected." I nearly choke on the words. I have seen too many people die to ever call this outpost safe. "Maybe the commissary is here to reward us. Congress knows we're close to earning four Rays . . ." But even as I speak, my chest tightens, the ghost pain of lungs screaming for air that won't come.

Dram turns toward me with a shake of his head and a smile that puts a dent in his cheek. "I'm overthinking things. Guess I expected the man in charge of the outposts to greet us with gratitude and a handshake, instead of a contingent of guards with flash weapons." His dark hair blows into his eyes, his lips lift, and I realize suddenly how much of him is muted down the tunnels. Maybe this is why I avoid him aboveground.

Something in him sings to me in ways more powerful than the flash curtain.

Maybe if I wasn't a girl who needed ninety-five more grams of cirium to be free, I might sit beside him, set my hand next to his, and see if he touched his fingers to mine. I'd reach and see if Dram reached back.

"Orion . . . ?" he says, drawing my name into a question.

I feel like Roland's fiddle, my strings plucked hard, humming. But it's more than this moment. I sense the flash curtain stirring me. My head whips toward the horizon. I can just make out faint waves of iridescence rising above the clouds of the flashfall—same as it always looks. But I feel its approach.

Something stirs above the cordon. Dozens of shimmering projections sail toward us. They're beautiful, like the shooting stars Mom told me stories about.

"Dram, look." He turns, and his face pales.

The wail of an air siren pierces the stillness.

"What is that?" I ask.

"Cordon breach," Dram says.

"A what?"

"Energy shifts in the curtain," Dram says, "strong enough to kick up rocks and debris." He drags me down behind the ledge of stone. "I was only six, but I still remember the last one."

The balls of light make a sound as they approach, a whistling so loud I can hear it over the siren. Two of them arc over us. The flames of the cordon ignited the metal ions in the rocks and they burn with different colors—purple, gold, and aquamarine.

It's like the flash curtain is attacking us, hurling flaming missiles past the cordon, mocking our shelter. It is spellbind-ingly beautiful. In a place that is so many shades of gray, the colors mesmerize me. The shards arc over us, pulsating with a vibrant, searing intensity. They are alive.

They are death.

Screams rise from the camp. Too many shards have found their mark in homes, in paths. Dram squeezes my leg, and I realize he's pulling me back, that I've worked half my body over the side.

"Stay here!" He drags me closer, hauls me to his side.

"We have to get below!"

"Too late." He wedges me into a wide crack in the stone just large enough for my small frame. He's torn open a cut above his eye. It drips blood, and he swipes his arm across it. His arms bracket the walls of rock on either side of me as he pushes his body tight against my burrow. It blocks my view of the soaring projectiles; it's dark as a cave.

He's dampened the sound of the screams, but I hear his breath punctuate the quiet. Everything in me yearns to get deeper. We are too exposed up here. Sounds of shattering rock break into my refuge, and Dram's body tenses.

This is not the air cave. I can't pull him in with me where it's safe. "Dram?"

"I'm okay," he says.

Another minute passes with my pulse pounding out the seconds. The rock beneath us stops trembling.

"I think it's over," Dram says.

"Let's go." I push past him and reach the mountain's edge in three strides, sliding to my knees and pitching myself over.

Dram joins me. Neither of us speaks as we climb down,

both hampered by our injuries. The air siren cuts off, and I hear cries for help from camp. I swing away from the wall and jump. My feet hit the ground, and I pitch to the side, stumbling to my knees. Dram hauls me up, and we both run.

"I've got to check on Lenore," he says. Then: "Flash me." He staggers to a stop. Half the lodge is missing. Its splintered walls poke up through the wreckage like broken matchsticks.

He doesn't say her name, but his face screams his fear. Marin.

"Go to the lodge," I order softly. "I'll check on Lenore. Most of the homes seem intact."

He nods and takes off running.

I rake my eyes from the rock and rubble of the lodge and pray that Marin-of-the-soft-hands is not beneath it. Dram has already lost too much.

As I sprint past the tunnels, I see the cavers emerging. Face by familiar face appears, and I breathe in gratitude. Their eyes widen, reflecting their shock, when they see the lodge. Then I hear a shout.

"Tunnel three's been hit!" A bleeding caver comes running from the south end of the tunnels. "Get your axes—they're buried in there!"

Half the cavers run for the Rig, for caver's suits and equipment to help save whoever sought refuge down three. The others head toward the lodge, where there might actually be a chance at saving someone.

Yellow containment dust spews from pipes that run the length of the outpost. Even Central's stalwart fortress is being showered with the radiation barrier. So far, it seems to be effective. As I trudge through the mixture, I don't see anyone showing signs of radiation poisoning. Maybe this isn't as bad as a flash storm.

I give my two-room house a quick glance as I pass. Dad won't be there. He's either at the lodge or infirmary, saving as many people as he can.

Nine houses later, I reach the Berrends'.

"Lenore?" I push into the tiny cottage Dram shares with his older sister. The kitchen and loft are spotlessly clean. And empty. A sense of foreboding works its way into my thoughts. It tangles in my stomach until I feel I may lose my meager rations.

"Lenore!" The silence jabs me in the gut. "Fire, oh fire." I dart through the door.

My eyes comb the dirt pathways between the houses, looking for straight brown hair the same shade as Dram's. Every person gets a second look—my hopeful, desperate appraisal. At nineteen, Lenore's just a year older than Dram, but she's cared for him since the day after their mother died and their father was sent to the burnt sands. She is all he has.

Well, he has me. But if I were him and I had to choose, I'd want Lenore. She is kindness, where I am tough. She is thoughtfulness, where I am action. She's compassion. I am survival. We both love Dram, but her love is tender and mine is like an axe forged in fire.

"Lenore!" I scream, not caring who sees my fear. Most people are screaming, anyway. They hardly notice me.

I can't get near the lodge. Our outpost is only sixty strong, but they're all here, gathered beyond the bones of the building. I search the faces, my heart pounding out a rhythm.

Please, please, please.

My chest heaves, and I skirt the crowd. There's Dram—he's with Marin. My heart gives a leap of gratitude, then:

Please, please, please.

Lenore has to be here. Alive.

"Is she safe?" Dram shouts to me over the sounds of the crowd. He's helping to drag away broken timber.

He reads the uncertainty in my eyes. The wood pylon hangs from his grasp, forgotten. Then he drops it and pushes through the people.

"Len!" he shouts. "Len!"

"She's fine, son," calls Foss, a quiet caver with muscles the size of boulders. He sets a broken beam aside and strides toward Dram. "She's helping at the infirmary."

Dram visibly relaxes, and tears stream from my eyes. I sit down right where I am, in the middle of the chaos. My legs shake so hard that it filters up through the rest of my body. Containment dust coats my hands, so I can't wipe my eyes.

"Do you need the infirmary?" A guard crouches beside me, his voice distorted by a rebreather. They are beginning to stream from Central, pouring onto the yellow-coated path in hooded Radsuits.

I shake my head.

"Then clear the area. We need to make room for the forfeit."

A weight lodges in my chest. The forfeit.

We're worse off than I thought.

FOUR

305.82 grams cirium

GUARDS IN HEAVY Radsuits draw their guns, and the locked gate barring the entrance to tunnel four grinds open. We rarely see the forfeit—the prisoners who have been permanently denied the rights of Subpars. Once they pass beyond those bars, it's easy to forget they exist at all, men and women scrabbling out a life in utter darkness. Cranny stands with Jameson at the entrance, bracketed by guards. He clangs an enormous iron bell.

"Wonder if they know they're being called?" Ennis says beside me.

"Why are they doing this?" I ask. As the oldest caver, he's most familiar with outpost customs.

"They're going to get the forfeit to move the cordon stones." He nods toward a boulder coated in particle dust.

"Won't the radiation kill them?"

"Maybe, maybe not. It's a chance for them to earn their freedom."

The bell clangs and clangs, and people begin murmuring.

I think we're all starting to suspect the forfeit are not going to make an appearance. Maybe they don't realize their opportunity to earn back their rights.

Maybe they're hoping we all just rot from radiation exposure.

My Radband still glows a steady green. I steal a glance at Dram's. Whatever we've been exposed to hasn't changed our levels. Yet.

The bell clangs, and I look back at Cranny. His lips are pinched together.

"When was the last sentencing?" Jameson asks, loud enough to be heard through the clear hood of his suit.

"Four years ago," Cranny answers. "A young man tried to stow away on a hover."

"Reeves," Dram says beside me.

Reeves Stram, the impetuous orphan with the wild blond mane, a few years older than Dram.

Shame grips me. I haven't thought about Reeves in months, not since the last time I distracted a guard so Lenore could stash a bundle of clothes and medicine inside the bars. I find her in the crowd. She stares at the gate like it's the entrance to the protected city. Her Radband glows yellow.

"I'll go after them." The words leave my mouth without waiting for my brain to give permission.

Dram scowls at me, and my dad shakes his head. Fire, I'm going down the prison tunnel to search for violent and desperate people who aren't even Subpars anymore.

But I forgot about Reeves, and he has a chance to come up out of that cave.

"Let me suit up," I say. Cranny eyes me like I'm a species he's not encountered before. Jameson looks stricken.

"It's not safe, girlie," Graham says.

"I'll have my axe." My mouth is a runaway ore cart with more bravado than I actually feel.

"Fine," Cranny says, handing the bell to a guard. "Hurry and suit up."

"I'll go with her," Dram says.

"So will I," says Lenore.

"That won't be necessary," a low voice says from the other side of the bars. The man's hidden in shadow, but his voice carries as he emerges slowly. Four years older, less a boy and more a man, but I'd recognize that wavy blond hair anytime.

"Reeves," I whisper. He's alive.

"Name?" Jameson demands.

"None," Reeves says. His gaze narrows on Cranny, and a dark smile lifts his lips. "My existence was wiped from Outpost Five."

Dram shifts beside me, his hands flexing. I wonder if he feels the same shame I do. Reeves was his friend.

"Where are the others?" Cranny asks. He consults a ledger. "Three males and two females."

Reeves's gaze shutters. "Where do you think?"

"You're telling me they're dead?"

A cold light hardens his eyes. "They weren't as resourceful as me." His gaze slips over the crowd and swings back to Lenore. "I'm the only one down here."

"We have a proposition for you," Cranny says.

"So I guessed by the clanging bell."

Looking at him now, I'd never guess he'd been living beneath a rock. The guy is remarkably clean. There's water down four. Of course, he would have had to search for it in the dark. Well, not total darkness. One of the first things Lenore sneaked him was a headlamp that Dram swiped from the Rig. And a battery charger.

Reeves is resourceful. He almost made it away on that hover. No guards saw him stow away in the hold—one of the cavers gave him away. I search the crowd, trying to remember. Foss. The burly caver with a tender heart. A good man who probably thought he was saving Reeves's life.

Foss stares at the ground. Whatever shame I feel, it's multiplied tenfold in that man. He stands hunched, as if his massive frame can't bear the weight of it.

"There are cordon shards all around the camp," Cranny says. "We will provide you with a Radsuit and a cart. You will haul the shards to the catapult and launch them back over the cordon."

"Then you'll no longer be forfeit." This from Jameson, who studies Reeves like he'd like to get him under a microscope.

"The radiation exposure could kill me," Reeves says.

"It might." Cranny shrugs. "It's your choice."

"What if I can't lift some of them?" Reeves asks.

"Then you will return to four."

Reeves tucks his hair behind his ears. He walks forward, and the Subpars part to give him room. Congress told him he wasn't a person anymore, but he defied them—in darkness and isolation, through sickness and death and fire only knows what. As a boy, he risked everything to get free. That same spirit wasn't broken by four; it was honed.

Reeves looks over the crowd, his gaze lingering on Lenore. "I'll do it."

I want to thump my axe into the ground. It's how a caver

tells another they're worthy. I understand why I let myself forget Reeves Stram.

It hurt too much to remember.

————

They offer him a Radsuit and rebreather like those the Naturals are wearing. If I ever break into Central, it will be to steal one of those things before the next flash storm. I glance at Dram and see that he's thinking the same thing. His eyes narrow, and his head tilts thoughtfully—but there's a reason no Subpar has ever breached the Protocol-protected command center. The mansion's external security sensors would alert guards in seconds, and even if we somehow made it inside, our biotech Radbands would set off the internal alarms. The idea of breaking into the mansion suddenly loses its appeal. I don't want to have to leave clothes and serums inside the bars of four for Dram.

Reeves crouches and hefts the first few shards. The entire camp gathers, hanging back to stay clear of the radioactive particles, but close enough to send an unspoken message of support. Dram slips him rations he palmed off a guard. Lenore gives him a tie for his hair.

But it's not enough. As strong as Reeves is, the day wanes into evening, and there are so many shards left—the largest and heaviest.

A pale haze, the color of bleached bone, hangs over the outpost. Beside the Alaran flag, new indicator flags slap the air with warnings, declaring the higher-than-normal Radlevels.

"I'll help him." Dram strides forward, wearing his caver's suit dusted with yellow powder.

Lenore grasps his arm. "You don't need to do this."

"Yes, I do." His eyes hold Reeves's as he moves to his side. He crouches and sets his shoulder to the enormous rock. "You've grown since I saw you last."

Reeves grins. "And you don't have little-girl arms anymore." Together, they heft the cordon shard and drop it in the cart.

"And yours are wide as doors," Dram mutters. "What have you been doing down there, wrestling bears?"

"Flash bears." Reeves laughs and tosses another huge rock onto the cart. "There are all kinds of things deep in those tunnels." His gaze shifts to me. "Isn't that right, mountain goat?"

I smile, pleased to see that four didn't steal his humor. "I beat your record."

"That so?" His eyes search the board posted on the lodge. "Well, well, looks like the littlest caver grew up. Lead ore scout, huh?"

"Three hundred five grams."

"A Third Ray caver," Reeves muses. He and Dram heave another boulder into the cart, which sags under the weight. "No more help, Berrends—it's not safe." He nods toward Dram's Radband. "We're resistant, not immune." He puts his shoulder to the cart and pushes.

No one says anything about the two shards pointing up out of the lodge like a couple of incisors. They are enormous. Deadly. From where I'm standing, I can feel the radiation pouring off them.

Even if Reeves could move them, he wouldn't survive long after.

I begin to see the other Subpars arrive at the same conclusion—in the way Marin's mother sneaks Reeves a pint of ale and how Graham talks to him, slipping in words of wisdom he'll need to survive a lifetime down tunnel four. Dram's palmed so many things off the guards, I'm surprised they haven't caught him. Dad slips Lenore a wrapped bundle, and she disappears toward the prison gate. Everyone's preparing for the inevitable moment when Cranny forces Reeves back down four.

Reeves loads another shard into the catapult. Then he nods to Owen, who releases the catch. The arm swings, hurling the shard back out over Cordon Five.

"Everyone back!" a hoarse voice commands. We all turn as Foss approaches, his shoulder to a cart. Every muscle in his body bulges, straining against the weight. "Clear out!" Cavers dart away, every one of us aware of the danger he's towing.

Reeves stands frozen, with his mouth open.

"Move aside, boy," Foss grunts. His eyes are yellow, and he swipes blood from his nose. The exposure has permeated his system. I don't know how he's still standing.

"How did he lift that on his own?" Dram murmurs.

"Physics," Dad says beside us.

Foss lifts a long metal girder from the cart. I recognize it from the rubble of the lodge. He climbs into the cart, wedges the girder beneath the shard and levers it onto the catapult.

A guard strides forward. "No one gets close. Director's orders."

Apparently, there's a limit to how many of us Cranny's willing to lose in this endeavor.

"Release the lever, son," Foss calls. His breath heaves from his lungs in unsteady gasps. Sweat streams down his body. Sweat and blood.

Reeves pulls the release. Wood groans as the catapult strains against the weight of the shard. The arm tips forward, sending the boulder sailing over the Range. It's so massive, we see it catch fire over the cordon, a blaze of blue and green, before it plummets.

"Foss," my father says. There's a warning in the way he says the caver's name.

"I know what I'm doing, John." Foss grips the empty cart and tows it back toward the lodge. "Keep everyone clear."

The guards push us back until we can barely see him ply his lever of twisted metal. But we can hear him. He cries out, straining against impossible weight, while his body begins to shut down.

I steal a glance at Graham. Tears slip down the old man's face, and that grips me like nothing else. Graham is a rock—as steady to me as my heart hammering against my ribs.

"Graham . . ." All at once, I'm nine and following him into darkness so deep I can't breathe.

He doesn't look at me. Instead, he raises his axe high above his head. Beside him, Ennis does the same, and suddenly every caver is holding an axe in the air. I don't have mine, so I just raise my arm.

It's what we do to protect the head of the caver standing next to us when there's a cave-in. It is too late to save Foss, but we are here, showing our support in silent salute.

Foss tips the shard into the cart with a grunt and staggers to his knees. Something, maybe the sound of crying, makes him look up. His eyes widen when he sees us. Slowly, he smiles. There is blood on his teeth, and conviction in his eyes like I've never seen before. The indicator on his Radband glows red.

He pushes himself to his feet and drags the iron girder from the ground. With agony in his eyes and that smile on his face, he thrusts his arm toward the sky.

The cavers shout. It's not a cheer, but a roar. The guards pull their weapons, holding us back, but they can't keep Foss from hearing us.

He staggers to the front of the cart, settles the yoke over his massive shoulders, and leans forward, muscles straining. The cart wheels turn, splashing up yellow mud as he guides the shard toward the catapult, never taking his eyes off Reeves.

The boy whose freedom he's buying.

He stumbles twice trying to climb into the cart. His bloody hands slip on the girder, but eventually, the final shard tips into the catapult. The arm swings and the shard flips, end over end, toward its home. Foss collapses. Reeves leaps forward and lifts him in his arms, and Dram runs to help.

"To the infirmary!" Dad shouts. "Lenore and Orion, you come too."

As we run after him, I glance at Lenore, trying to think what possible help we'll be to a man dying from radiation.

"You're not here for Foss," Dad says. His gaze shifts to Reeves, standing white-faced with the caver in his arms.

We settle Foss into the Radbed, a glass-enclosed case that sends oxygen and vaporized Serum 60 over an exposed patient. Dad injects him with Serum 129, twice the dose he'd give normally. He doesn't even start an IV. He's doing what he can to make Foss comfortable and limit our exposure to him.

"You shouldn't have cleared the lodge," Reeves says.

"Four years ago . . . made mistake," Foss murmurs. His eyes

drip blood. "Would've . . . traded places . . . with you." Patches of his hair have fallen out. His red, inflamed skin rises up in open sores.

I bite my lip and will the serums to work faster.

"Will you . . . wear my ashes?" Foss gasps.

"I'm forfeit," Reeves says. "I'm nobody."

"You're . . . Subpar," Foss says.

Reeves sets his palm against the glass and his eyes fill. "What color?"

"Black." Foss chokes the word out. "Like cave you . . . survived. You're . . . survivor."

I think of the memorial pendant I never take off, a shell-like swirl of blue glass surrounding Mom's ashes. Dram and Lenore wear green for their mother.

"When you . . . get past . . . curtain," Foss whispers, "bury it. Put my ashes in ground . . . of free men."

Tears slip down my face.

"Ore scout—" Foss's eyes shift and find mine. "You'll help him get there, I know it."

"Yes." I say it aloud. A dangerous word if the wrong person were to hear. My heart wants to shout it.

He struggles for breath, and I press both hands to the glass, trying to suppress tears. I lost my brother this way. It is agony to stand here.

I like to think I am brave, but I could never do this.

Even if I have to mine his 400 grams myself, I will make sure that Reeves sees the other side of the curtain. And I will see Foss buried in free soil.

That much I can do.

Foss's eyes widen now, and he gasps. I tell myself he caught a glimpse of something beyond the curtain—maybe the sky, with sunlight that is kind, and a breeze against his skin that feels like a gift.

His eyes glaze, and then he's gone.

FIVE

305.82 grams cirium

WE CAVERS HAVE many secrets, most of them preserved down the tunnels where Congress will never see.

Dram and I climb over twin lumps of stone—markers, for those who know what they're looking for. Past the stones lies the first pool, but this is a puddle compared to our destination.

Cracks dent the cavern ceiling, like someone punched holes to the outside. Someone probably did—back when Conjurors worked the tunnels alongside Subpars.

When Mom first told me of the Conjies, they seemed even less believable than the stars she named me for, but proof such people existed is illuminated in the glow of my headlamp. Gnarled roots twist up through stone, forming a ladder. I climb the underground tree, trying to imagine the ability to manipulate matter, to touch rock and make plants sprout up through my fingers. We weren't the only ones the flash curtain altered.

Like magic, Orion, Mom would say.

But then Conjies rebelled and the Congress punished them, taking away their abilities through a process called Tempering.

Not magic, after all.

"We're getting close," Dram says.

I scan the walls for chalk marks. "There—" I point to a V tipped on its side.

A whining sound echoes off the cavern walls, like the drone of an unnatural insect. Dram grabs my shoulder and hauls me into a crevice. A second later, a tracker whines past.

Guards don't have to risk themselves down the tunnels in order to look after us. Years ago, Alara developed pulse trackers; fist-sized, hovering monitors that can detect and monitor human heat signatures. Techs use them to locate cavers when a transmitter's damaged.

And they use them to expose Subpars who are breaking rules.

The fact that they're down six tonight tells me that Cranny must suspect we're up to something, but he won't find us.

Trackers don't register us when we're in water.

Dram cracks a light stick, and we follow the cavers' marks as the tunnel winds and widens into a cavern. Blue, luminescent light glows so brightly from a pool I have to squint until my eyes adjust.

A band of cirium shimmers at the bottom of the basin, but Subpars will never mine it. We will not carve this place up, not even to buy ourselves freedom.

Reeves and Lenore step from the shadows.

"Did you bring it?" Reeves asks. I hand him Foss's axe.

They have churches in the protected city. Faith, for us, is

something less tangible—raw as these cavern walls. Graham says that "sacred" is what you carry with you in your heart.

We move toward the pool, and blue light bathes our faces, mimicking the sky beyond the curtain.

"The guards have set pulse trackers," I say.

Reeves nods. "Let's hurry and get in the water."

I hear the sounds of belts unbuckling, and axes and knives clinking on stone. Beside me, Dram drops his boots and zips off his caver's suit. The air is kind, warm even—a pocket of grace on the fringes of hell.

We leave everything on the side and slip into the water in only our underclothes. The only thing we bring of Outpost Five is Foss's massive pickaxe, held above the pool in Reeves's clenched hands.

I spread my arms and lie back, floating, weightless. This place doesn't have a name, but in my heart I call it the Sky.

We brought Foss's axe here, where he will never be forgotten.

"You should be the one to do it," Lenore says to Reeves.

"It should be all of us." His low voice echoes in the cavern, filling the space, filling my bones. Reeves extends the axe, his arms flexing from the weight.

Dram clasps the end of the handle. I take hold just above, the edge of my hand pressing his. Lenore fits her hand beneath Reeves's.

"Ready?" Reeves asks.

We hold our breath, and he lowers the axe beneath the water. I take the image of Foss with me as I'm drawn deep, the weight of the axe pulling me down, down. Our bodies brush as we glide to the bottom, each holding tight to the handle as the pick clinks against the cirium.

The last swing of a caver's axe is one of beauty.

We kick to the surface, letting go until Reeves bears the weight of the axe once more, then we swim to the other side, toward an expanse of rock covered in white markings. Water flows over Dram's bare back as he climbs out of the pool.

"Hurry now." He reaches down and clasps my hand, lifting me from the water. It cools our body temperatures, making us less detectable to the trackers, but no one wants to get caught down here.

Some secrets are sacred.

Reeves nestles the axe in a crack in the cavern wall. I slip a watertight pouch from my undershirt and withdraw a piece of chalk. Lenore does the same. The chalk scrapes over the wall as I write Foss's name, and beside it, the flash date.

Took the cordon shards so the rest of us didn't have to, I write.

Gave a forfeit his life back, Lenore writes, dragging her chalk in a circle beneath the words. Before techs in Alara developed light bolts, Subpars marked caverns with an X for danger and a circle for safe.

All the inscriptions bear this caver's mark.

"He is free," Lenore whispers.

"He is free," we echo.

Sometimes I forget the date, in a place where time is measured in grams added to the Cavers' Log, but then I step back and glance over other inscriptions, some reaching back fifty years. My eyes catch on one of the newer ones.

Ferrin Denman, 142:03:07

I touch the date when seven claimed my mom. March 7 in the 142nd year since the flash curtain fell. The words are faint in places, written in a child's scrawl. Lenore's.

Loved John, Orion, and Wes
Held her axe over my head so I could live

Lenore swam my mother's axe to the bottom of the Sky, but she didn't leave it here. She brought it back to me.

Tears slip down my cheeks, the only things I have to lay at my mother's memorial. I trace my chalk over the circle beneath her inscription. "You are safe," I whisper.

We never stay long. Soon, others will filter in, staggering their comings and goings so the guards don't notice. Cavers will come throughout the night, slipping in and out like shadows.

Burning Days are for all Subpars, but this ritual is for us.

Not even my father knows about this place.

Lenore and Reeves dress beyond the ring of light, preparing to leave.

"I stole something," Dram announces softly. "From one of the guards. This is the only safe place to show you." He crouches beside his suit and slips something from one of the pockets—a narrow, rectangular piece of tech the size of his palm. "When the guard first pulled this out, I thought it was a flash wand—"

"You stole a *flash wand*?" Reeves asks. Even he looks horrified. I've never actually seen one of Congress's most powerful weapons, but I've seen what they can do. Tunnel nine was blasted open with flash wands.

"It's not." Dram grins ruefully. "I wouldn't have risked stealing a flash weapon. This is something different." He touches the device, and an image projects across the cavern.

"A map . . ." I'm relieved, but part of me is oddly disappointed.

"This is more than a map," Lenore says. It moves as she moves, as if it senses her presence.

I walk forward, and the three-dimensional image shifts so that I'm crossing the five outposts bordering the Barrier Range. On the other side of the Range, the cordons stretch all the way to the flash curtain. Beyond it are more cordons, and the tapped-out tunnels of the first outposts, now an abandoned strip of the Exclusion Zone. Congress calls this area the Overburden, the name given to land above depleted mines. All around me are elements of the flashfall—shifting clouds and the fractured radiance of the curtain I've known all my life

I step beyond it.

My breath catches. I know it's just tech—an illusion only—but as the towering peaks of the provinces rise up around me and the first forest I've ever seen enfolds me like a lush green secret, I want to take hold of it. I want to grasp at bark and pine needles and seize this life for myself. Living things. Life-giving, natural things. A life of my own choosing.

This isn't real, this isn't real, I keep telling myself.

But, fire, I want it to be.

Everyone stops moving, and I look to see what they're all staring at. The cirium shield rises up before us, arcing around the city like an enormous silver wing.

The shield our ancestors died to put in place. And beyond it, the place we're trying to earn our way into, a gram of cirium at a time.

"Ready?" Dram asks. We step forward, and the shield shifts past us. We stand inside the protected city.

The jewel.

The Prime Commissary called it that once, during a transmission she sent to cavers. I remember her smiling when she said it, her accent lending precise corners to her words. *The protected city is the jewel in the crown that is our city-state.*

I see so much water and so many green, growing things—not rugged, like the provinces, but tamed. I reach toward buildings glowing with light, thinking, *jewel.* In the distance, waterways bisect parks and roads. Transport devices whir by, and I'm saddened by how small-minded I was all the times I imagined this.

Dad is right. We live a rustic life here in the outposts. Now I understand the way he half laughs, half cringes the word when he says it. *Rustic.* I want to spit it out like a sour taste. No wonder Cranny and the other Naturals spare no smiles for us. Who would want to leave this to go serve in the outposts? I can hardly imagine more different worlds.

I'm standing in sunlight that does not wish to consume me, with the arc of the shield casting part of the city in shadow. There is no hint of the flashfall. Above me the sky—

Ah, the sky—

Clear. Not a cloud in sight. And blue, like Mom always told me it was.

Blue, like her glass memorial pendant around my neck.

The thought brings me back to this cavern, my bare feet on smooth stone, the grit of memorial chalk on my fingers.

I glance at Dram, but his eyes aren't fastened on the jewel. They're on me.

"You climb the Range like you keep hoping to see beyond Cordon Five," he says softly. "So when I saw the guard use this . . ." His lips lift in a half smile.

My eyes fill, blurring Dram and his gift.

"They'll tear the outpost apart when they find out this is missing," Reeves says.

"I'll return it tonight."

"You're mad, Dram. If you're caught, they'll send you down four."

"Some things are worth the risk," Lenore says, and she crushes Dram in a hug. I'm not the only one who longs for a life beyond this outpost. She breaks away, darting a look toward the shadows. "I think I hear a tracker."

"We need to leave," Reeves says.

Lenore fastens her skullcap, her eyes locked on Dram. "Stay by the water. We'll go first." She reaches for the rest of her gear.

"Hurry, Len," Dram whispers, his concern as evident as hers. The air fairly hums between them, like there is a special tension reserved for siblings who have only each other left in the world. Reeves stoops to help Lenore, and it occurs to me that he has *no one*—not a single person in the world with shared blood. But as he and Lenore duck from the cavern, he clasps her hand, and I think maybe shared blood doesn't mean as much as love.

I've never been more aware of the chalk circles in this cavern.

Dram slides his finger over the device, and the image cuts out. Now it's just us two beside the luminous blue pool. He sets the device with his gear, and our gazes collide and bounce away. With Reeves and Lenore gone, this space feels smaller, and I'm suddenly aware that we are wearing almost nothing. Wet almost nothing.

But now, when I close my eyes, I can call up an image of a forest, and the sky, and they are more than my imaginings of them ever were before. No one has ever given me such a gift.

"Thank you," I whisper. The words aren't enough, but I don't know how to say what I'm feeling.

He starts to respond, but then whirls toward the cave entrance. We hear the whistling at the same time, louder than usual, and throw ourselves into the water just as they hum into view. Not one, but four trackers.

"Dive!" Dram says.

I kick to the bottom of the pool, my chest squeezing for lack of air. I've never seen trackers working in tandem, and some instinct tells me it magnifies their sensors. I press my hands to the cirium, willing my body to stay down.

Dram's beside me, staring up toward the surface. We breathe out air, working to keep our bodies submerged. The bubbles lift, where we can see the trackers hovering still.

I need air. Panic flutters beside the pain in my lungs. These aren't black spots clouding my vision, but a red wave of pain. One set of trackers leaves.

My body is having a war with my mind. I'm telling it to stay under, but it's showing me it intends to live, and I realize I'm kicking to the surface.

Dram grabs my leg, and I cry out, losing my last bit of air.

One second . . . two . . . three. The trackers leave. And now Dram's not pulling me down, but pushing me toward the surface.

We gasp, treading water, and I lie back, letting the Sky hold me in its embrace again.

Dram dives deep, and I watch him stretch his hand along the cirium basin. The water moves in eddies as he breaks the surface, droplets shimmering over his chest and arms. He looks different with his hair slicked back from his forehead, more a man, less a boy.

"If you're going to look at me like that, it's only fair that I get to stare back."

I blink. "Oh. Um." I duck beneath the water. Flash me, what am I doing? I stay under longer than my lungs tell me they're comfortable with.

When I emerge, Dram's waiting. A smile lingers in his eyes.

"We should go," I say. But I don't swim to the edge. The levity fades from Dram's eyes as he watches me. "What is it?"

"I just had this image of you—taking my axe to the bottom."

"Our axes will *never* hang here." I swim to him, grasp his shoulders. "We're getting free."

He studies me as if he's judging how sure I really am. "What does it sound like?" He speaks so softly, but I know what he's asking.

All Subpars sense the elements in the earth—to some extent. We are born with an innate connection to the curtain that is honed down these tunnels, where our families have mined for generations.

But it is different for me.

"I don't hear it with my ears." I take his hand and press it above my sternum. "I feel it here. Like a sort of vibration . . ." I hum and watch his face. "Feel it?"

He looks down at his hand, pressed above my heart. "No."

I lift his hand so it cradles my jaw. His fingers brush my skin, and there's a question in his eyes. "Sometimes it's stronger, like this . . ." I hum, and his breath stutters.

"Felt that," he says.

Then there is just the sound of Dram's breathing and mine, and the water lifting us, so that everything feels impossibly light. I feel things that scare me, that threaten to take what

Dram and I have together and trade it for something altogether different.

"I have an idea," Dram says suddenly. He pulls away and swims for the pool's edge.

"What are you doing?" I heave myself over the side and follow him.

"We're both about to reach four hundred grams, so this may be our last time here." He fishes some chalk from his suit pocket and writes *Orion* on the blank stone wall. And beside it, *Dram*. But he doesn't draw the caver's circle. We're not safe yet. Instead, he scrapes two parallel lines, tilted at an angle. It means—

"The way out," Dram says. He and I will be the first cavers of Outpost Five to earn our way beyond the curtain without dying. "Maybe one day this wall will be filled with more names—other Subpars who mined enough."

I touch the expanse of dark stone, and something stirs in me, too big to name. A promise that beats above my heart, in the place where the cirium sings.

We rarely see hovers at Outpost Five. The few times a year Congress sends us supplies and collects our cirium, the machines drop down behind the walls of Central, usually in the dead of night. But a cordon breach must break all kinds of rules. Cranny released a forfeit, and the day after, a craft lands beside the lodge.

I nearly drop the hammer I'm clasping in my blistered hand. Nails hang forgotten from my mouth as I watch the craft settle with a hiss into yellow sludge and ash. We were given the day free from caving, to honor the dead, but we've spent the remaining hours of this Burning Day salvaging what we can of the lodge. Because I'm the "mountain goat," Cranny has me perched in the eaves, banging shingles into place.

I spit out the nails and scurry down the roof. My mind is racing so many places at once, I nearly fall. All I can think is that a hover like this will be coming soon for Dram and me, Lenore, and Dad.

I make my way to Dram's side, where he watches the craft, grim-faced. He saw this sight the day his father was forced aboard. I can barely picture the hover that day, but I remember Dram clearly. His shirt had a tear, and I kept thinking that Lenore was going to have to learn how to sew. And I wondered about the new memorial pendant he wore for his mother—if it felt as heavy to him as mine did to me.

Technicians unload the craft, revealing crates of nutrient packs and wooden beams to rebuild the lodge. There are also new cavers. Congress sent us replacement parts and, apparently, replacement people.

Ashes from the funeral pyres lift on the wind, mingling with the smoldering remnants of the cordon breach. Even now, there's a burn in the air. It irritates my exposed skin and makes my lungs work a little harder for air.

People are pouring from the hover. Four women, six men, and two I can't quite believe. A little girl, maybe eight years old, and a boy who looks about eleven. I watch the children through the smoke of nine bodies.

"Looks like they're planning the future repopulation of Outpost Five," Dram murmurs.

"No Radbands," I say. "They're not Subpars." These new people aren't transplants from another outpost. They're Naturals.

"Cave fodder," Ennis huffs at my side.

I look at Dram. His jaw clenches so tight I see a muscle twitch in his cheek. "Why wouldn't they just send more Subpars?" I ask.

"Maybe there aren't any," he says.

Outpost Five has never lost so many. Not even in the last flash storm. It's safe to assume the other four outposts would have been impacted, too.

The little girl tips her head back, like she's looking for a familiar landmark. She's discovered the night is darker this close to the curtain, where we have only ashes for stars. Her dark hair hangs down over her yellow dress. She is the only splash of color in this gray world.

My eyes sting. From grief, from ash, the remnants of the curtain—it hardly matters. Congress is going to send this child down the tunnels.

"Fire," I whisper. I have this horrible image of flash bats seizing her through that yellow dress.

"We'll keep her safe," Dram says.

I curse again and turn on my heel. I can't listen to any more empty promises today, so I run past the infirmary, the Rig, and the weigh station, unsure where my feet are taking me. We tell ourselves we're serving the city in some noble way, but the truth is so ugly, and it's getting harder and harder to believe what they tell us.

"Evening, Scout," Barro says as I turn into the forge. He glances up from his bellows just long enough to nod his head.

"Can I just . . . sit here awhile?" I ask.

His eyes shift back to mine, and in their depths I see a deep sorrow. This man gave me the memory of my mother that hangs around my neck. Barro is the only artisan at Outpost Five, but I've always thought of him as a magician because he takes all the death and gives back some precious bit of beauty. Something that reminds us that the tunnels don't take everything—not the memory of the person we love.

I sit beside the furnace, absorbing its warmth, hoping it will thaw the ice within me. I close my eyes and imagine that I'm on the other side of the flash curtain—but it's difficult with smoke burning my nostrils and the ache of Foss's death pressing my chest like a stone.

———

"Found you," Dram says quietly. The firelight plays across his face, bathing his stubbled cheeks in flickering shadow. He sits beside me and watches the glassblower pour ash into his tube. "They are free."

It's what we say on Burning Days to comfort the grieving. Today it just makes me angry. "Do you think Naturals have Burning Days?" I ask.

"Naturals aren't as strong as us," Dram says. "I'm sure they mourn even more dead than we do."

"They call them 'funerals.'" A young man steps into view. He has almond-shaped eyes and fair skin, and I remember seeing him emerge from the hover. His black hair hangs to his shoulders. "I'm Gabe," he says. "Gabrielein, actually."

He has an inflection to his voice I've never heard before. It makes me think that the language we speak is not the only one he knows. I stare at his hands—or rather, the metal palms and fingers that have taken the place of his hands.

"Not seen these before?" he asks.

"Sorry. I didn't mean to stare."

"It's fine. I still catch myself looking at them." He flexes his hands. The hinged phalanges and metacarpals make a pinging sound.

"Were you in an accident?"

His eyes narrow, like he's weighing his words. "No. I had two perfectly great hands. The Congress gave me these."

"Why?" I can't keep the shock from my voice.

"Have you never heard of Tempered Conjurors before?"

Conjuror.

I glance at Dram. His eyes are as wide as mine. "There hasn't been a Conjie here for fifty years," he says.

"That you know of," Gabe says with a wink. "We're a sneaky lot." He lifts his hands. "Have to be, these days."

"So you could . . . *alter* natural elements?" Dram asks.

Gabe watches the flames dance in Barro's forge. "Our talents vary, but I could build shelters from rock, make shrubs produce berries—that kind of thing. Before my alterations, anyway." He waggles his fingers.

I imagine weaving a vine from rock and letting its twisting arms carry me up and out of Outpost Five. But that's ridiculous—there's nothing out there but wasteland, outposts, and the cordoned zones on the other side of the range.

"I once knew a free Conjie so skilled he could form fire in his hand," Gabe says.

"A free Conjie?"

Gabe gives me a smile, like I'm a child asking if the boogeyman is real. "How much do you know about the world beyond Outpost Five?"

"You mean the protected city?" Dram asks. "Are you from there?"

"I get to keep my hands—or what passes for my hands these days—if I limit what I say to you Subpars. That's the deal your director made with me. So, in the interests of keeping my fingers—"

"Why are they sending Conjurors to the outposts?" Something isn't adding up, and my own talent is telling me something that's impossible.

Gabe smiles, but his eyes darken. "Stay safe in your ignorance, young ore scout. I intend to keep my hands this time." He stands and walks out of the forge.

"Wait!" I jump to my feet and follow. "What's it like—beyond the curtain?"

"Like nothing you can imagine. My people live in the mountain provinces—in places where you can still see the sun rise." He's right. It's hard for me to imagine such a sight. His gaze sweeps the shadows. "I'm really not supposed to talk to you."

"Your hands . . ." I reach toward him, needing to confirm what my scout's senses are telling me. "Holy fire," I breathe, clasping his metal wrists. "Cirium."

His eyes widen. "You're mistaken. It's not even the same color—"

I scrape my fingernail across a joint seam. "Paint," I whisper. "Why would they—"

He yanks his hands away. "Not a word to anyone, Subpar."

"Why cirium?"

"It's the only substance we can't conjure." He moves his fingers. "Or conjure through."

The element hums along my senses. Purest cirium. It would take every gram I've ever mined to create just one of these hands. "Is this rare? What they did to you?"

"I can't—"

"How many?" My voice is a bare whisper. "How many Conjies get cirium?"

Pain fills his brown eyes. "All of them."

His answer stuns me into silence. "I thought . . . I thought cirium was used only to protect the city."

"If I tell you what you want to know, they won't just take my hands."

Dram coughs, over by the forge. A guard is walking toward us. When I look back, Gabe is gone. Gabrielein. The Conjie with secrets too deadly to tell.

I came here hoping the heat of the forge would thaw the ice inside me, but now I'm on fire. A lifetime of mining nine to produce shackles for another human being?

"Five minutes to curfew," the guard says.

"Thank you," Dram says, cutting off my reply that wasn't as polite. He touches my elbow. "I'll walk you home."

Silence stretches between us as we pass the mill and thread the dirt paths between the houses. My mind is a storm, as if I'm seeing through new eyes.

"Talk to me," Dram says as we reach my door.

I want to tell him. My teeth ache because I've clenched my jaw so tightly, holding back the words. Congress disguised the cirium used for Gabe's hands. They want the truth hidden, and they have no idea I don't need to see cirium to know it's there.

What Gabe told me is enough to incite rebellion. Subpars have served at the outposts for over a hundred years, dying in our efforts to mine the one element that can preserve Alara.

I mustn't tell anyone, not even Dram.

"Rye?" he studies my face, trying to read me as usual, but I'm getting better at hiding secrets.

"What if my dad's right, and we really are all prisoners here?" I muse, looking toward the boundaries of our camp.

"It's been a long day, Orion."

"They took your father away, Dram!" I hurl these words because I can't say the ones I want—and I need him to feel the same sense of betrayal I feel.

He looks like I sucker punched him. "We each have a role," he says after a moment. "My father refused his." There's hurt in his eyes still, but confusion too. "What did Gabe say to you?"

For a moment I can't answer him.

"He said there are places you can see the sun rise," I say. The diversion works, and Dram smiles.

"We're going to see it," he says. "The new vein you found will get us to four hundred grams."

My gut twists. We are so close.

I want to be free, like the Conjies.

Instead, I mine the element that Tempers them.

SIX

305.82 grams cirium

THE TUNNELS STRETCH the width of our camp. Some, like tunnels one and two, are wide passages in the Range, tall enough for a man to walk into. Others, like three and six, are just holes in the ground. Nine was blown open with flash wands. It is the deepest of them all, and the most unstable. It is mine.

Dram and I suit up in the Rig with the other cavers. Since we go farther than the rest, we require more equipment and protective gear. We stand beside the rigging wall in our own corner of the windowless wooden structure, double-checking each other's packs and gauges. The other teams eye us from across the room. They treat us with a sort of reverential awe, but I think they're just grateful we're still alive so they don't have to be the ones going down nine.

Their suits are varying shades of yellow, and light up inside the tunnels. They're tagged with transmitters that emit a pulse on a frequency the techs can track. Dram and I wear black to blend into the dark caverns. Light-up suits would help us see, but we can't take the risk, nor do we wear transmitters. The creatures down nine can track the transmitter pulse even more effectively than the techs at Central. All cavers carry knives, but ours have double-bladed tips for splitting open the skulls of flash bats. Only people die easily down nine.

Dram slides a freshly sharpened blade into my arm sheath. "What are you thinking about?" he asks.

"Freedom."

"That sounds dangerous." He draws my hair aside to check my tank.

"Don't you think about it?" His fingers brush my neck, and I try not to notice how good his hands feel. Lately it's been getting harder.

"I think about the caves and the work. And Friday nights," he says.

"Don't you want more from life?"

"That is our life, Rye." I shuffle back a step and realize he's hiding a grin. "Of course I think about leaving this place. You think I'm going down nine just for fun?" I must still wear a disgruntled expression because he clasps my Oxinator strap and pulls me so close our noses touch. "We're almost there, ore scout."

"Almost free," I whisper, but I can't seem to find the certainty I felt before.

"Cavers up!" Owen calls. He thrusts open the doors, and we all shuffle out toward the sign that proclaims our Subpar motto. I put my hand on a wooden sign support, worn from the touch of hundreds of cavers before me. Dram lifts his arm, and the weight of his extra belay devices and climbing lines shift with a jangle at his belt. I know the moment he taps the beam because I hear his soft exhale—a habit he doesn't know he has.

He touches it twice. Once for him and once for his mother, who should be here too.

Other cavers emerge from the Rig, tap the wood, and head to their tunnels, flowing around us like we're rocks in a stream.

"Orion . . . ," Dram says, his voice low.

I don't answer. He knows I need this moment, here, where we spread the ashes of our fallen. I stare up at the metal sign, and it creaks in the breeze, as if it's speaking the words it holds.

WE ARE THE FORTUNATE ONES.

Our daily reminder before we descend into darkness and danger. Most people didn't survive when the flash curtain fell. It is our duty—privilege—to secure a better future for the generations to come. Every gram of cirium we bring up is another bit of protection against the radiation Mother Nature hurled down upon us more than a century ago.

At least, that's what they tell us.

Tunnel one's team wanders over, their suits as clean as when they were first issued. They brush past me, tapping the wood with gloved hands. Steady hands. One's nothing like the other tunnels.

"*Nos sumus fortunati*," a woman murmurs. Maybe our motto's easier to believe in Latin, as if it holds power, like a spell or an incantation. If we say it enough, perhaps it makes it true.

"*Nos sumus fortunati*," I whisper.

We've been betrayed. The realization burns through me, a fiery ember drifting over dry tinder. I want to tell Dram, but he would confront Cranny. He'd challenge the commissary and be on the next hover to Cordon Four. And Gabe, the poor Conjie, would likely be sent with him—along with me. Dad and Lenore would never be free of this place.

My silence protects us all.

We will mine 400 grams. We'll earn our Rays and forge lives for ourselves on the other side of the flash curtain. I tell myself this over and over, but the flames still spark inside me.

I draw my glove over my hand, recalling the hinges of Gabe's mechanized fingers—the faint hum of cirium I sensed. The fire in me blazes.

"Do you think the rumors are true," I murmur, "that the tunnels are nearly depleted?"

Dram looks at me hard. Cranny penalizes this kind of talk with ration cuts and even, one time, striking a miner's week's worth of ore weight from the Cavers' Log.

But Subpars can sense the presence of cirium . . . and the lack of it. Late at night around the fire pits, when the fires have burned low and the ale has numbed all sense of caution, we speak of it. Of what will happen to the outpost when there's nothing left. Of what will happen to us.

"You sense it better than anyone here," he says softly. "So you tell me—do the tunnels still have cirium?"

"Nine does."

"Then we'll find it." He buckles a strap across his chest. "Why are you thinking about this?" Suddenly he curses. "Flash me, here comes Cranny."

"Scout, Marker," calls Cranny. "The commissary wants to see you and the team before you descend."

Jameson strides toward us, framed by two of his guards.

"Sir," I say, nodding to the commissary. I lift a hand toward Dram. "You've met Dram. I'm afraid the rest of my team is the ash you're standing on."

His mouth drops open, and I see Dram shake his head. Cranny bristles in his too-tight, wrinkled uniform.

Jameson recovers his composure. "How unfortunate. So it's true, then—tunnel nine is the most dangerous."

I hold his direct gaze. "They're all dangerous."

"Well, then, I commend you for your bravery. Given the choice, a lesser person might turn away."

"Given *the choice*, Commissary, I'd never go down another tunnel again." I slide my axe into my holster, nod curtly, and stomp toward nine.

"What the hell was that?" Dram says, falling into step beside me.

"People have *died* to keep him safe in his protected city, and he pats me on the head like an obedient dog. Fire, he's lucky I didn't punch him in his perfect, shiny white teeth!"

"I think he was trying to be kind."

"Kind?" I whirl to face Dram. "This isn't kindness!"

"They give us food, shelter, protection from the flash curtain—"

I rip my axe from its holster and point at the tunnels. "This is *slavery*, Dram."

"It's our way to serve honorably, Orion. It's what our people have always done."

I snarl out a curse and leap for the sign supports. Wood creaks beneath my weight as I climb and hoist myself astride the top beam.

"We are the fortunate ones," I call. Dram narrows his eyes on my face. My voice is too loud, and I'm drawing all kinds of attention up here on my perch. The sign sways beneath me, and I give it a tap with my axe. Iron pings against the dented metal, and I long to hammer at it till the sound carries across the outpost.

"Two days ago, I watched a man *melt* from the inside out. Where was our fearless director then? Hiding with all the rest of them behind the cirium-plated walls of Central, while we Subpars dodged cordon shards and waded through containment dust."

The look on Dram's face shifts from frustration to fear as the crowd of cavers grows beneath me. He stiffens, his gaze bouncing from one face to the next, gauging the threat like he's walked into a gulls' nest. Anger pumps through me, like a heart that is too big for my chest.

A caver blows his whistle. One blast. *Stop. Not safe.* It's Graham. He stands in the midst of the others, eyes fierce in his wrinkled face, the whistle still gripped between his teeth.

But I am remembering the screams of my team when the gulls tore at them, and the memory drives me past caution. *I'm afraid the rest of my team is the ash you're standing on.*

"Congress sends us to our deaths and calls it duty. They post a sign outside hell and call it privilege." I can't look at Dram. I know he's begging me to stop.

But last night I met a man with cirium hands that weigh more than Dram and I will mine in our lifetimes. More than our mothers brought up before seven claimed them. Subpars are dying, and it's not to protect a city.

"We are the fortunate ones," I call, louder this time, thrusting my axe at the sign. "This is what they tell us, over and over till we believe it." I stretch across the beam and swing my axe at the chain.

Twang! The piercing metallic sound rings out across the

outpost and the sign breaks loose, dangling from the weathered beam like a useless limb.

I'm going to pay for this later, but right now, I welcome the flush of elation, the adrenaline singing through my veins.

When I look down, I see every caver gathered beneath the broken sign. Owen pulls out his axe and hammers the handle against the ground.

Pound. Pound. Pound. I feel it like a heartbeat.

Graham does the same, and it's just like the way we applaud our dead on Burning Days.

The others join in. Reeves slams his handle down again and again. Beside him, Lenore thumps her axe, a twist to her lips and a hardness in her eyes I've never seen before. I imagine it's the look her father wore when he stood in this place and told Cranny no.

People stream out of the lodge to see what the commotion is. I watch Ennis pound his axe with gnarled fingers that should have earned rest by now, and Roland, whose father was sent to Cordon Four a few years after Arrun Berrends. More and more cavers join in, till the wooden sign supports creak beneath me. The enormity of what I've done settles over me like lead weight.

I find Dram in the crowd, but he's not hammering like the rest. His gaze is fixed on the man with a rumpled uniform and hard lines bracketing his mouth. Beside Cranny, Jameson stares at me with an expression I can't read.

The adrenaline that hummed along my veins freezes instantly.

I knew I would pay for this act of defiance.

But now I know that they will, too.

I read off coordinates to Dram. "Marker, please."

"Mark." He aims his light gun at the floor of the cave and presses the trigger. The sound of steel on stone rings out, and a bolt of yellow light glows in the darkness.

The passage narrows, and I have to crawl through on my stomach, holding my palm up in front of me to light the way. It penetrates the dark for about two meters, but the rest is pitch-black. This is the neck of tunnel nine—a tight passageway that opens into the vast caverns beneath. Through my earpiece I hear Dram breathing heavily. He is staving off panic. Tight spaces mess with his head, especially this tube of rock.

"So I guess this is as good a time as any to talk about what happened earlier," I say—more to distract Dram and cover the sound of his fear than because I want to have this conversation.

"Still not talking to you," Dram mumbles.

"I was mad," I say.

"I think you made that clear."

"I didn't know the others . . ." I sigh, trying to sort my rambling thoughts.

We push ourselves through the passage, our suits scraping over stone. My axe catches. I'm pinned in place, my arms stretched out before me. Panic squeezes my chest. I clench my eyes shut and count, one . . . two . . . three. Dram's headlamp moves over me as he pries his fingers around the edge of the pick. He tugs my axe free, his movements painstakingly slow in the confined space. There is no one to free him if his axe catches.

"Do you remember my father?" he asks.

"Of course." Everyone at Outpost Five remembers Dram's father. You don't forget the ones who are made examples.

"When our moms died down seven," he says softly, "he went to see Cranny. Told him he was through with caving. He didn't want that kind of thing to happen to me or Lenore."

"You had just started down five," I murmur, remembering that brave, lonely boy. Dram's breath grows more even, and we move slowly forward.

"Cranny gave us their Burning Day free," Dram continues. "The next day, he personally walked my father to the tunnels. 'Remember,' he told my dad, 'we are the fortunate ones.'"

The tunnel widens, and I push myself to my hands and knees.

"You weren't the first person to take an axe to that sign," Dram says.

I realize I've stopped moving. "I didn't know." All they say is that Arrun Berrends refused the tunnels. I didn't realize he was the one who put the dents in the sign.

"A day later, they sent him to mine the burnt sands."

That part I know. The poor man probably didn't last more than a few days out there beside the curtain.

"We really are the fortunate ones, Rye. It could be so much worse."

Now my breathing's ragged, but it's not from fear. Anger, maybe—or perhaps grief. My chest is seized in the grip of an emotion I don't have a name for yet.

I vow right then to take the sign down for good.

I'll do it for Dram's father.

And for Dram.

SEVEN

305.82 grams cirium

THE STINK OF sulfur pinches my nostrils, and I draw my neck cloth over my nose and mouth. We're not deep enough to need our Oxinators yet. I steal a glance back at Dram. He stares past me at the deepening darkness of the path. I sigh and press forward. He's still upset with me.

A breeze teases the hair at my temples. I lift my hand, and Dram stops behind me. Turning my head, I close my eyes and stretch my senses. A draft of air indicates another passage to the outside—a passage that gulls and bats travel. I don't hear the rustle of feathers or younglings, so we've not stumbled upon a nest. I tug my neck cloth down and sniff the air. The acrid stench of bat guano fills my senses.

My heart pounds. The echo of the light gun is going to reverberate to every bat in the vicinity, but it's a risk we have to take.

"Marker," I say quietly.

Dram loads a red bolt into his gun, points it at the ground, and waits, his eyes lifting to mine. I draw my knife and slowly nod.

"Mark," he says. He fires, and the bolt anchors to stone with a piercing ring. He reloads his gun. Red again.

They come at us all at once.

"Dram—"

"I see it." He lifts his arm and fires at the nearest bat. The creature cries out, a piercing screech that I feel all the way to my toes. It flaps above us, its torso impaled with a glowing red bolt light. Flash bats swarm in the illuminated cavern. There are less than ten. We may survive this yet.

"Just a hunting party," Dram says, lunging with his knife. He spears a bat, and the furry brown body writhes on his blade, jaws snapping.

The snout and teeth of flash bats are overly large, jutting out beneath their extra set of eyes. Their jaws are like spring-loaded traps that snap over their prey with enough force to break skin and bone. Dram stabs his double-bladed dagger into the creature's skull and twists his wrist. Its glowing yellow eyes slowly dim.

Two more drop, and our backs brush as we move into a defensive position. I thrust my knife at the nearest bat. Miss.

It careens toward me again, and I lash out, skewering it through the belly. Wings flap wildly, and I tighten my grip as the bat pulls me forward a step. It makes a clicking sound with its teeth as it gnaws at my blade. I shove my boot over the creature and drive another knife through its head, staring up at the remaining bats above us.

Dram works his blade free from a carcass. "I don't think any more will—"

Another bat dives. I lurch back, but it tangles in my hair, thrashing, twisting, and flapping its wings.

"Dram!" I cry out as its claws scratch my face. I reach for it—

"No, Rye!"

Two rows of teeth clamp down on my forearm, and I scream as they penetrate the layers of my suit. The thing must be a baby, because my arm isn't broken, but burning pain radiates through my veins. Venom. Only the females are venomous.

Dram has his hands in my hair. He's wrestling the flash bat while I concentrate on not passing out. A second later, I hear a thunk and a crunch. He cuts the creature out of my snarled hair and lowers my arm in front of me. I steal a glance at the bat's cloudy blank eyes, faintly glowing still. Its mouth grips my arm like a vise.

"Lean into me," Dram says. "I'm going to pry its jaw open."

I sway against him and force myself to just keep standing. He cuts part of my sleeve away. I feel his blade, cool against my forearm.

"Ready?" he asks. He levers his knife, and the bat's jaw lifts. His arms shake as he forces it wide enough for me to pull my arm free. I shut my eyes against the sight of my streaming blood and sink to the ground, dimly aware of the bat bodies nearby. The pain eclipses everything. Dram kneels beside me where I quiver on the floor, moaning.

He draws my arm across his knees. I know what's coming, and I shake, knowing it hurts as much as the initial bite. Dram meets my eyes, but then seems to decide against whatever he was going to say. Nothing he could say will make this next part any easier.

He presses his lips to the wound and sucks. A fractured cry bursts from my mouth. Dram hands me a piece of rope, and

I bite down as he continues to draw the venom from my arm. He spits blood and green poison on the ground beside us, over and over, until my voice is hoarse and my cries have dissolved into a whimper.

"It was shallow," he says, wiping his mouth. His voice sounds strained, like he's been yelling along with me. "Come on." He grips my arm and hauls me to my feet. "Let's find some water posey."

I stumble along behind him, trying to shut out the pain.

As much as it hurts, it doesn't warrant Serum 129. There are too many perils down here to risk dulling my senses. We are too deep. I need to be able to climb hard and fast—impossible with shock inhibitors buzzing through my system.

"I hear water—" I point to the left, still too hoarse to speak.

Dram lets go of my hand to use his palm lights, and I stare down at the place where his hand was, trying to understand the sense of loss. When did his touch become so important to me?

"Stay with me," Dram says, cupping my cheek in his gloved hand. "We'll find some posey for the pain. Hang in there."

We pass an outcrop of stone, and blue light fills a cavern, glowing up from a massive pool. Blue is not an orbie color. This water is safe. Dram jogs toward it and reaches into the water for the plants growing up toward the surface.

"Found some," he calls. He's not wearing his mouthpiece, but the cavern carries his voice. I sag against the wall. It will be bearable soon.

Dram cuts a frond of water posey, a plant that soothes skin and numbs pain. He slips his knife through the middle of the leaf, dividing it into two glistening green halves. Gently, he lifts my arm and draws back the torn sleeve. A ring of bruises surround the bite wound, from the force of his mouth pulling the poison out.

"I'm sorry," he murmurs, his thumb brushing the purple marks.

"Wasn't your fault," I say, watching as he wraps the leaves over my forearm. "It's not like that bite is from your overly long teeth."

"I was just following orders," he murmurs, binding the wrap with gauze. "You were the one who led us past that tunnel."

I look up with surprise. "It was your light gun that drew them."

He raises a brow. "You're the one who ordered the marker."

"That's my job!" He bites his lip, and suddenly I see what's going on. "You're arguing with me on purpose to distract me from the pain."

"Maybe." He ties off the bandage and pulls my sleeve back into place.

"Oh no." The cavern is spinning, so I close my eyes. I can still picture the vibrant blue pool.

"Do you think the sky is as bright as that?" I murmur.

"We'll find out," Dram says, pressing a kiss to the top of my head.

My heart stills. Maybe the venom reached it after all. His touch tingles down through every nerve ending. It pulses behind my sternum, like a secret.

"Posey-wosey," I mumble. "Posey making me woozy." It takes all my concentration to speak.

He grins. "We might as well rest a bit."

"Wait." The posey works fast. My mind seems to be heading up the tunnel without the rest of my body. "The venom burned your lips." I run my finger inside the posey leaf and touch it to Dram's mouth. He holds still as I smooth the juice along his bottom lip. He's not wearing his goggles, and his blue eyes glow like the pool behind him.

"Rye," he whispers. He reaches to take over the job himself, but I shake my head.

"Let me." I spread posey extract along his top lip and feel his breath against my hand. It's as unsteady as mine.

"You need to sleep it off." He guides my hands back to my sides and unpacks a thin metallic blanket from his pouch, then he leans against the cavern wall and slides down.

I drop down beside him. He helps me unfold my blanket, and we huddle side by side, wrapped in the synthetic warmth. The sound of the water trickling into the pool lulls me until my eyelids feel as heavy as my axe. My head tips back and finds its way to his shoulder. The fabric of his suit rubs my scratched cheek, and I hiss with pain.

"Here . . ." Dram draws me across his lap and cradles me in his arms.

It's like I'm floating again, far above my body, a kite with no strings. I wonder how much of it is the posey and how much has to do with Dram's closeness. I savor the feel of his arms around me, of being held so close to his chest that I feel each one of his breaths.

"Sleep." His voice sounds gruff.

"We can't keep doing this," I murmur. "Barely surviving nine."

"We're not out yet. We could still die in a variety of ways."

I smile. We are morbid, the cavers of Outpost Five. But my smile fades as the reality of my life sinks in. Tears prick the back of my eyes.

"I want to live in a place where . . . don't have to cut . . . flash bats . . . out of my hair."

"Shhh, just sleep." He threads his fingers through my tangled blond strands, as if he's replacing the memory with something new. Something good. His voice rumbles against my ear where it presses against his chest, so I close my eyes and let myself drift.

Dram pulls me closer, lowering his head until his lips are beside my ear. "I won't leave you. I won't let anything steal you away."

I am just far enough gone with posey to believe him.

EIGHT

315.82 grams cirium

THEY ARE WAITING for us when we emerge.

I've never seen so many guards assembled at one time. The commissary stands at their apex, his gaze fixed on something above us.

Someone repaired the sign. It hangs in place above the tunnels, like my act of defiance never happened. WE ARE THE FORTUNATE ONES.

I want to take my axe to it all over again. Instead, I cradle my injured arm against my chest and force myself to think of words like *consequences*.

Cranny stares at me. His eyes slip down my hair, a mess of tangles streaming from beneath my skullcap, to the knives strapped onto my arms, the harness that buckles across my suit, down to my boots. Dram takes a half step closer to me.

"We've been waiting for you," Cranny says. "I've summoned the cavers for an announcement in the Rig." His words fill me with panic—more than I felt when the bat caught in my hair. He smiles, just at me, and my breath freezes in my chest.

"Let's go," Dram murmurs. He stares at Cranny, too. But he isn't smiling back. He looks like he wants to see what his axe would do to Cranny's body.

We follow the other cavers into the crowded house. Benches fill half the room, most of them full. Cavers still wear their suits. Some hold bandages to bloody injuries. Cranny is in a hurry to give us this news, whatever it is.

He strides to the front of the room. Jameson follows like a shadow.

"The food that fills your bellies," he says, scanning the faces of the cavers. "Who provides it?"

"What's a full belly?" I mutter. Dram kicks my foot.

The cavers remain silent except for a few coughs of those still clearing their lungs of particle dust.

"I will ask you again," Cranny says. "Who gives you food?"

"The Congress," a man says.

"And the clothes you wear?"

"Congress." A few others join in.

"What about your homes? Your serums? Your light and warmth? The *only* thing standing between you and the flash curtain *is this outpost.*"

A tense silence fills the Rig.

"Your lead ore scout raised her axe in anger, lashing out at the government that protects us. She doesn't consider Subpars at Outpost Five fortunate. But then, she's never set foot in a cordon."

The word hangs in the air. *Cordon.* I feel it like a draft on my neck.

A few cavers glance at me, some angry, most with pity in their eyes. They know Cranny will make an example of me.

"Do you feel her actions should go unpunished?"

Dram slowly draws his axe from its holster.

"Not one of you stopped her," Cranny says, letting the implication hang in the air. The cavers look at each other, and I see mostly alarm. This isn't just about me anymore.

Cranny watches us with a look of satisfaction, apparently pleased we're all finally catching on. "You will all share in the consequences of her actions."

Beside me, Dram tenses. I can't breathe.

"Tomorrow you will all descend tunnel nine, and she will guide you to the new vein of ore. The three cavers who mine the least will be sent to the burnt sands of Cordon Four."

Silence descends over the crowd—except for me. I'm making a sound like another flash bat just clamped onto my arm.

I lurch to my feet. "Director." Cranny's dark eyes fasten on me. "I was the one who damaged the sign." I wipe my sweaty palms on my thighs. "I take full responsibility. Please don't make anyone else suffer for what I did."

"Since the cavers are so eager to follow you," Cranny says, "you will guide them down nine."

My stomach drops. I think of Gabe with his non-hands, Ennis, who is the oldest of us, and—my gaze shoots to the little girl—Winn. She probably has no idea what Cranny's talking about. She doesn't know she will be sent to her death. She can't swing hard enough to mine the dense walls of the deepest tunnel. And if nine doesn't take her, the sands will.

"Give us time to form another team," I say. "Dram and I will bring up the cirium."

"Her last team was attacked by tunnel gulls!" a man shouts.

"That wasn't her fault!" Dram twists in his seat.

"This is outrageous!" Blaine Cresley jumps to his feet. "I've done nothing." He tosses a look in my direction, like I'm an orbie he found on his arm. "You can't force me down nine— every caver you've sent with them has died!"

Cranny's hard gaze gleams like obsidian. I want to yell for Blaine to stop, to shut his mouth now, before—

Cranny nods to the guards at the back of the room. Two of them stride forward and grab Blaine under the arms.

"What are you doing?" he cries. The crowd parts as the guards drag him toward the door.

"Tunnel nine," Cranny says curtly. "Minimum descent of four hundred meters."

"No!" Blaine cries. "I haven't charged my lights, I don't have any rations—"

"You're going to get acquainted with tunnel nine," Cranny says, his eyes alight. "Maybe then you won't be so scared come the morning."

I realize my hand is wrapped around Dram's. I've never seen him so angry, but he's not afraid. He grips the bench so hard with his free hand that I see the whites of his knuckles.

"What are you doing?" I whisper.

"Keeping myself out of an impossible fight."

I hold his hand tighter and wonder if I have the strength to hold him back.

Or if, perhaps, this is a fight I've already pulled him into.

———

My father sends the summons in the dead of night. It passes secretly from house to house, until every caver slips through our door, silent and undetected. Even little Winn arrives in the care of Dram and Lenore.

No one speaks, except my father who explains, in a hushed undertone, the plan we've devised. Cranny's plan is flawed, and we intend to exploit it so no one has to die.

"If you agree to this," he says softly, "every caver will have the same amount of ore. There won't be three lowest-producing cavers to send to the sands."

"You're assuming we're going to survive the tunnel in the first place," Roland murmurs.

"Yes, I am," Dad says. "Dram and Orion will each lead a team. Anyone injured or older, anyone who can't fit through the neck of nine, will go an alternate path with Dram."

"If there's an easier path, why don't we all go that way?" Gabe asks.

"It's not easier," I say. "Just more accessible."

"It's riskier," Dram says. "Orion and I have marked gull nests along that path."

They stare at him blankly, and I realize that most have no idea what a tunnel gull is. I put my hand on Dram's arm before he can explain. It's probably best they don't know.

"There's nothing we can do about the transmitters in your suits," I say, "but on your way to the tunnels tomorrow, dust your suits with the cinders from the fire pits. It will give you better camouflage and help cover your scent."

"From what?" Winn asks.

The cavers remain silent. They've seen enough of my and Dram's injuries to have a fair idea of some of nine's predators.

"Don't worry," Lenore whispers. She squeezes Winn's hand. "Just stay close to me."

"The ore is fifteen meters off the ground," I say. "The best climbers among us will be belayed by a ground team.

The rest will collect the ore and deflect the water from the climbers."

"The water?" Owen asks. "What kind of water?"

"The water that flows down the stone," Dram answers. "It's filled with orbies."

Owen curses.

"Why don't we just devise something to kill them?" Roland asks.

"Anything strong enough to destroy the orbies would harm you," Dad says. "Dram and Orion will bear the brunt of the danger. I've coated their suits with tar to give them another layer of protection."

"The rest of you need to wear two pairs of gloves," I add. "You'll use your flash blankets like splash guards."

"We're out of time," Graham whispers, glancing out the window. "Guards will be making the rounds any moment now." His eyes narrow. "Here comes Ennis, with the boy from the lodge . . ." He breaks off as the two slip through the door. Even in the sparse light, I can see their faces are pale.

"What's happened?" Dad asks.

"Roran and I passed the tunnels on the way here." Ennis glances at the boy. "The guards were dragging Blaine's body from nine. Gulls got him."

I shut my eyes, picturing it all too clearly. Foolish man probably had every light on his suit lit up. And his transmitter, calling to the birds like a dinner bell.

Winn starts to cry. Roran walks over and sits beside her. Something in my heart twists.

"No lights on your suits tomorrow," I say softly. "Speak only when necessary. You'll usually hear the danger before you see it." The cavers nod. A few stare, wide-eyed—mostly tunnel one's team. Roran's eyes focus on me like my words are the key to his survival and he intends to live. He holds a rock in his hands that he flips over and over. "Conserve your air," I continue. "You're going deeper than you ever have before."

"Keep your knife close and be ready to use it," Dram adds. "Don't hesitate. Kill anything that gets close." Cavers from one are shaking their heads. They've never used their knives on anything but climbing line. Roran's gaze settles on Dram. There's no fear in his expression—about killing or things getting close down the tunnel. He seems . . . resolved, and I can't imagine what in Alara prepared him for this. Winn's small shoulders shake, and without even looking at her, he leans closer.

"Subpars are really good at caving, Winn," I say, wishing there was some way I could spare her this. "We do it every day. Just stay close to Lenore." I can't tell her stay close to me. I will be where the danger is worst. "Never go past a red light."

She nods.

I search the crowd of cavers. "Where's Reeves?"

"Here."

"I need you to go with Dram's team. He's marked gull nests along that route." Reeves survived four, facing down the creatures in utter darkness and, if the rumors are true, ate what he killed. As a former lead ore scout, his senses are tuned to his surroundings like mine, and he's the best defense Dram's team has.

"Ennis?"

"Here." The oldest caver lifts his hand, his Radband glowing dark amber.

"You're in charge of weighing the ore. Make sure everyone brings up the same amount."

He nods. Ennis can judge ore weight at a glance.

"Owen?" He shifts from the shadows.

"I have some thoughts about bringing down the ore. I need you paying attention to structural support."

Owen nods. "I'll make sure we don't get buried down there."

"Guard's coming," Graham says.

Dad pinches out the candle, and everyone leaves, soundlessly bleeding into the night.

Except Dram. Our shoulders brush as we sit in darkness, whispering through the details of tomorrow's descent.

At some point Dad squeezes my shoulder. "Take this," he says, handing me his nutrition packet. "You need your strength tomorrow."

"Lenore and I will share with her," Dram says. "Even if everything goes according to plan, we're going to need you when we come up. You need your strength as much as we do."

Dad nods and leaves us to find his bed. My stomach growls.

"Tell me again why you're on half rations?" Dram asks.

Remembering Cranny's after-hours visit makes my stomach knot.

"I was noncompliant," I murmur. At Dram's raised brow, I shrug. "I scouted past the boundary marker."

He makes a scoffing sound and shakes his head. "*Glenting* Cranny."

"*Glenting*?" I ask. "What is that?"

"Conjie curse word. A really bad one."

I'm wondering how Dram learned a Conjie curse word and, more importantly, why he hasn't shared it with me before now.

Glenting. I consider its uses. *Glenting Cranny. Glenting tunnel nine.*

Thinking of nine effectively kills my appetite, so instead of focusing on my hunger, or my fear about all the things that could go wrong tomorrow, I traverse the tunnel in my mind, going over each obstacle with Dram. His deep voice steadies me now as it does beneath the earth.

The director is sending us down nine to teach us a lesson. He expects cavers to die completing a nearly impossible task. If we pull this off, it will say more than breaking the sign ever could.

It will show that we are more than what the Congress tells us we are.

NINE

315.82 grams cirium

I HAVE NEVER feared nine more. As lead ore scout, the burden of protecting the cavers falls to me, and it feels heavier than the twin Oxinators on my back. The guards were so distracted herding the cavers to the mouth of nine, no one noticed when I swiped a second tank. I will have to push it ahead of me through the neck of the tunnel. At least we'll have filtered air if someone else's tank proves faulty.

Dram lifts a brow when he sees the extra Oxinator, and I almost laugh—he stole one too. My eyes slip to Cranny's, practically daring him to say anything about it. I shift my body so he doesn't see the two extra bolt guns swaying from my belt. Dram will be leading the second team, so today I will have to anchor my own markers. And fire my own bolts through flash bats if necessary.

Fire, I hope it's not going to be necessary. This is going to be hard enough without flash bats.

Dram and I wade to the front of the Rig in our tarred suits.

Already the weight of it makes every step a chore, and I'm sweating beneath my layers.

"We'll split up just before the neck," he says.

I nod. We went over the plan so many times I lost count. We fell asleep leaning against each other on the kitchen floor.

"I'm not sure how long I'll have you in my earpiece once we separate," he says quietly.

My hands skim over his shoulders, checking for tears in his suit and tightening his harness. He turns and pulls me close, on the pretense of adjusting my Oxinator. "I'm worried about Ennis," he says. "The depth is a struggle for us, and he's fifty years older."

"If he's the only one you're worried about, you're doing a lot better than me."

He grins ruefully. "Hey, I'm just happy I don't have to squeeze myself down the neck of nine for a change."

I tighten my goggles. "Right, because tunnel gulls are always a treat."

"Just try not to make so many orbie friends this time, okay?"

I tap my finger on my tarred suit. "Dad says it's orbie-proof."

"It's also breathing-proof," Dram mutters. "I may not even make it to the orbie pool. This suit might just kill me first."

I smile and he grins back. My fears linger still, but they're not in control anymore. I face the entrance to nine. "Just remember our deal."

He switches on his headlamp. "Of course. You can't go before I do." He steps into darkness, but not before I see his smile.

I let the image linger in my mind, a talisman in the face of danger, then I turn on my headlamp and palm lights. My team lines up behind me. Their fear hangs over me, as heavy as my tarred suit.

"Step in my steps," I say to Lenore. She drapes her arm around Winn, whose eyes are fixed on me.

"Don't go past any red lights," Winn murmurs. She grips an axe to her chest. An axe I'm certain Lenore will end up carrying for her before long.

"Step in my steps," Dram says to the man behind him, and the cavers repeat it back, a quiet ripple of words.

Reeves shuffles into place at the back of Dram's team. Dangling from his belt is a chain with twisted barbs of metal. A long, jagged piece of metal sticks up from his boot. He wears his hair tied with the leather cord Lenore gave him. I turn back, but not before I catch Lenore watching him.

"You should tell him," I say.

She pulls her eyes away. "If we make it through this, maybe I will."

Just before we head inside, Reeves glances over at Lenore. Raw emotion carves his features. The expression I was not meant to see tells me he already knows.

Lenore has only one palm light because she threw her other into tunnel four, tucked inside her extra pair of socks the day after Reeves was sentenced. She told Cranny her flash blanket fell into an orbie pool and filled it with nutrition packets from countless meals she'd skipped. On her birthday each year, when Congress issued her a new pair of clothes, she sneaked out at night and set her old ones inside the bars, wrapped around syringes and vials of serum.

She may not have said the words, but her actions spoke loud

and clear. And, judging by the look on his face, Reeves loves her just as fiercely.

Dram guides his team away from our usual path.

"How come you stopped?" Lenore asks behind me.

"Sorry," I murmur. I force my feet to move, even though I feel like I'm separating from a part of myself. The last caver on his team turns the corner, and I see the flash of Reeves's chain reflecting from his palm light.

"You haven't ever done this without him, have you?" she asks.

"No. It feels . . . wrong."

She smiles.

"What?"

"I'm glad." Her smile widens.

"You're glad I feel all wrong about this?" I mutter.

"Something like that." She holds Winn's hand. The girl's axe hangs tucked in her belt beside her own. Sometimes I forget how strong Lenore is.

One of Dram's markers comes to life, glowing yellow beside the neck of nine.

I turn and face my team. "This is where it starts to get hard—"

"Rye . . ." Dram's voice cuts in through my earpiece. "Worried . . . neck . . . ORUs . . ." His voice crackles in and out. I'm losing him.

"I'll take precautions," I say, hoping he can still hear me.

I look up. The cavers' eyes are wide behind their goggles. I suppose it's not reassuring to hear that Dram and I are worried about something.

"It's the added gear," I say, pointing to the pack beneath my Oxinator.

Each of us wears a collapsed ore retrieval unit on our back. We haven't used them in years, not since Roland's father tried to escape Outpost Five on one, but it's the only way to move large amounts of crude ore quickly. When activated, the units ascend the tunnels a bit like hovers, following the wire laid out by the ore scout.

Dram and I have never worn them down nine, and I'm scared they will catch us in the tube of rock like corks in a bottle.

"Give me a head start," I say to my team. "I need to see how we'll fit with the ORUs. Our mouthpieces tend to cut out in here, so I'll blow my whistle to signal you. One blast for danger and two for follow." I stick the whistle between my teeth and crawl in.

It's tight. The tunnel scrapes against my ORU, but it's a chance we must take. I blow my whistle—two short bursts.

The tunnel narrows slightly—enough that I have to hold my breath to squeeze through. Dram would never have fit with the added equipment. I'm suddenly grateful he's guiding his own half of the team the other way down.

Our earpieces pick up every scrape of our axes and the ORUs along the walls, and I begin to wonder how much our noise might be noticed by tunnel nine's inhabitants. As we clear the neck, I hold my finger to my lips, calling for silence. Half the cavers illuminated their suit lights, and I stomp toward them, gesturing angrily. They mute their lights and step back into place as I grip my bolt gun and take the lead once more.

"Slow down, Scout," Roland says.

I look back and realize I can't see half the group. I forget that they aren't used to my grueling pace—that they usually plod through their tunnels, instead of attacking the caverns like Dram and I.

I wait for them to catch up, scanning the rock for a flash of wing or the telltale glow of yellow eyes.

An hour later, we stop again, long enough for me to demonstrate the use of Oxinators for those who've never needed one. We spray skin barrier over any uncovered areas before I guide them onward—more slowly now—giving them time to adjust to the depth and increased particle exposure. I am so focused on getting my team of twenty-five to the cavern safely that I'm caught off guard when the light bolts come to life at our feet and we're suddenly standing before it.

"The vein is in here," I say, ducking beneath an archway of rock. "I'll dust the cirion gas, and you'll see it clearly."

"Already did it," Dram says. He hangs suspended before the water-soaked wall, axe in hand. He holds my gaze, and for a moment, the other cavers fade away.

Lenore gasps, drawing me back. She lifts her hand, shining her palm light over the vein. Her headlamp sweeps the line of ORUs, half filled with chunks of ore.

The murmurs from the cavers grow so loud, I pull my earpiece away. Most of them have less than a hundred grams to their names—a vein of this size is beyond comprehension.

I walk toward Dram. "How long have you been here?" I ask.

"Two hours. Gull route is faster." His axe sparks against the rock with each swing, and bits of cirium ore break off into his pouch. "And since we weren't eaten by gulls, we managed to get a lot mined." He adjusts his grip and smiles at me.

I smile back. "We made it."

"We still have to mine it out from under these little bastards and then get it all back up."

My smile widens. "Save some for me, caver. I'm getting to four hundred grams today." I reach for my climbing line, and exhilaration spins through me so powerfully my hands shake.

Dram watches me, gripping his axe. A wordless communication passes between us, even as the other cavers haul on belay lines and hammer at stone, their excitement tangible as particle dust.

We're getting to 400 grams today. We're going to live, Orion.

I pass the rope through my harness, my gaze locked with his. This may be my last climb. Our last descent. The last time we are ever defined by only cavern walls and cirium ore. My eyes prick with unexpected tears. Dram tilts his head, like he's sensing the shift in my emotions.

"Still with me, ore scout?" he calls.

Always. I want it to be true, I realize suddenly, and it occurs to me that freedom from Outpost Five means the end of our partnership. Without the tunnels binding us together, will we still step in each other's steps?

A man yells. It's so loud in my earpiece, his voice distorts.

"What's wrong?" I search the faces of the cavers. Another voice cries out. I run to the edge of the orbïe pool as the climbers reel back from the wall, twisting on their ropes.

"Flash me," Graham grumbles. "Ore mites. Haven't seen them in years." He points to the wriggling white masses erupting from cracks in the cirium vein.

"They bite!" Roland swings away from the wall, shaking his arm.

"Probably their claws you're feeling," Reeves calls, sliding down his rope. "Let me help you. You don't want to pierce their skin."

The mites pour from the newly exposed rock.

"Pull your flash blankets up!" I shout. The writhing creatures bounce off the cirium fabric and fall twelve meters to the water.

Roland ignites a flare and holds it toward a wave of mites erupting from the stone.

"NO!" Reeves shouts. "Douse that flare! They explode in flame!" He maneuvers across the wall, from caver to caver, detaching the creatures with a skilled flick of his blade.

"You're saying they're combustible?" Gabe asks.

"I'm saying we used them to blow an entire gulls' nest down four."

"You're lucky you didn't bring the cavern down on your heads," Owen says.

"We did," Reeves says. "It was the lesser of two evils."

Dram hoists himself to the indentations where mites burrow in smooth lines. "They can't attach to my suit," he says, drawing back his axe. "I'll take this seam." The ore mites drop as Dram chisels at the cirium. Their legs writhe, tiny claws scraping along his tar-coated suit as they slide off him, rippling over his body like a waterfall.

A sense of unease tingles along my spine. "Dram, I'm coming." I stride toward the wall.

Winn screams, and I whirl toward her. She just summoned every carnivore around.

"Hush," Lenore says, reaching for her.

The white, wriggling mites cling to Winn's sleeves. More cavers gasp as the insects dig into their suits.

"Turn up the heat in your suits," Reeves calls. "They don't like heat." He unclips from his rope and leaps down, then swings his chain across his back, catching the end and dragging it down. The sharp points of the mites' legs catch on the chain, and they release their hold.

"Don't kill them!" Reeves calls. "They're filled with parasites you can't see. If you destroy the host mite, they'll attach to you, only you won't know until it's too late."

"Stop!" Lenore cries suddenly.

Winn shoots past, her eyes wide. A red light bolt illuminates at her feet.

"Winn, come back," I call.

But she's not listening to anything except the voice in her head telling her that mites are climbing her body. She cries, stumbling past another red marker. I untie from the climbing line and run after her. A third red bolt glows at her feet, but she runs away from me into a cavern. I lift my Oxinator and breathe. Bat cave.

The darkness swallows her, and I force myself to slow, to catch my breath so I don't give us away. I switch off my headlamp and mute my palm lights. I step past the bolt light and duck into the cavern.

"Winn!" I hiss her name.

"They won't come off!" Mites climb her arms as she shakes and spins.

"Hush!" I get to her in five strides and point upward. Dozens of flash bats hang suspended from the dripstones. Her eyes widen. I switch off her headlamp.

I turn the heater in her suit to full and slip one of my knives free. With shaking hands, I pierce a squirming mite. As soon as the blade penetrates the dense skin, tiny black dots spill out of the slit. I bite back a scream and fling it away. The knife scrapes stone with a clatter that is too loud.

Wings flutter at the corner of my eye, but the bats remain dormant. By some miracle we haven't roused them.

Mites drop from Winn, deterred by the heat of her suit. I pry the others off with my knife, careful not to prick them.

"Follow me. Slowly," I whisper, easing backward from the cavern. I have one hand clenched on her harness; the other grips my knife. I steal a glance over my shoulder. Dram stands in the shadows, his bolt gun aimed upward.

We're ten steps from the others. Nine. Seven.

Winn's transmitter beeps. We freeze. Yellow light illuminates the cavern. I clamp my hand over her transmitter and glance up. Hundreds of glowing eyes stare down at us.

My hand tightens on my knife. The bats drop.

"Run!" I grasp Winn's arm and sprint for the opening.

Dram fires. A bat screeches. Red light glows above our heads, but the swarm descends in front of us, blocking our exit.

"Orion!" Dram shouts. Even with my earpiece, I can barely hear him, the screeching is so loud. His knife flashes on the other side of the mob. The other cavers follow his lead. Knives and axes fly beyond the cloud of flapping wings.

It won't be enough.

"Get down." I drag Winn to the floor and kneel in front of her. She is crying hysterically, but it hardly matters now. I take aim with my bolt gun and shoot everything that moves. The cavern fills with the flickering light of impaled flash bats. "Stay behind me. Don't let them bite you," I say. I fire the last bolt and draw my knife, but there are too many.

"Hang on!" Dram calls.

I've bought us as much time as I could, and we both know it.

A flash bat clamps down on my knife arm, and Winn screams. Through the shock and pain, I grasp a knife in my left hand and drive it through the creature's head, wrenching it upward until the skull cracks.

"Rye!" Dram shouts.

"No venom," I gasp.

Another bat lands on my shoulder. I pull a blade and drive it into the space between the rows of eyes.

Winn shrieks. It's like a siren call to the bats, and they pour over us like a waterfall. I tuck Winn beneath me, covering her until only my body is exposed to the swarm. A third bat clamps its jaw onto my back, and another lands on my skullcap. My Oxinator cracks. Air hisses from the tank, and the bat screeches. More seize onto my back, their teeth scraping my Oxinator and ORU. They dig through the barriers, rooting for flesh.

I scream.

"I'm here." Dram's voice in my ear.

Reeves scoops Winn into his arms, and Dram drags me over his shoulder. He has a bat clamped around his wrist. A knife protrudes from its skull.

"Did it break the bone?" I ask.

"I'm fine." Dram carries me from the cave. "Male bat. No venom."

He lowers me onto my stomach on a ledge of rock and presses an Oxinator over my nose and mouth. I choke down the air. A few breaths in, I recall the bats dropping onto my back, biting into my tank. There are still some on me. I suddenly realize why my mind is spinning out across the cavern like a handful of particle dust.

"Subpars!" Dram shouts. "Watch me. This is how you kill them." He thrusts his knife into one bat's brain and extends the second blade. I hear a crack, and the pressure on my back lessens.

He pushes a piece of rope into my hand, and I thrust it between my teeth.

"This is how you remove them," he calls. I squeeze my eyes shut and bite the rope as he levers his blade against my skin, cracking the jaw and easing the teeth from my flesh. "Only the females are venomous. They have a black underbelly." He sighs. "This one's male." He tosses it to the ground. "Females will kill you inside of ten minutes if you don't get all the venom out."

The cavers curse and shout commands. Dimly, I'm aware they're still fighting the swarm Winn and I stirred from the cave. Another caver—Reeves maybe—works the dead bat from my arm.

"Brown belly," he says.

"Let me see," Dram says. Then: "Fire, you're lucky, Rye."

I was bitten by males. Only males.

"She could still bleed to death," Ennis whispers.

Dram hisses a breath. "Quiet, old man. She's still with us." He knots a tourniquet so tightly around my arm, I cry out. Lenore grasps my hand.

"You're wasting your time with me," I murmur. "I can't climb—"

Dram curses and presses cloth to my back. I want to tell him to leave me and help the others. There is so much they don't know; nine holds so many dangers. But I can't get the words out.

"She's still got one on her," Winn whispers.

Yes. The other flash bat. The one they didn't see.

Dram rolls me over. A twitching bat gnaws the inside of my thigh.

"Flash me," he breathes. He stakes it with his blade, and I cry out. The pain is piercing through my shock.

"I need help over here!" Dram calls. I've never heard that desperation in his voice before. "Reeves, put pressure on the wound, I'm going to pry it off of her!" He's breathing so rapidly, I start to think he'll pass out.

I hear the crack and pop of the jaw and then my head floats away. Something warm seeps down my thigh. It's warm, and everything else is so cold.

I shiver so hard the rope falls from my lips. Was I still biting that? I taste blood in my mouth. I want to laugh. The rope didn't work.

"Dram?" Graham's voice. He has that same fearful tone. The one that tells me I'm in trouble.

Dram doesn't answer. He sucks in a shaky breath. Fire, is he crying?

"Female," he whispers.

Now I understand. Tears seep from my eyes, warm like blood. Like the venom coating my wound, pumping through my veins.

Dram tears my suit open and cavern particles prick my exposed skin. "This is how you save someone from the venom," he says, and sets his mouth to the wound.

My mind goes as black as the tunnel.

I'm conscious again. Cracking one eye open gives me a view of the tunnel floor and Dram's feet. He's carrying me over his shoulder, placing each foot carefully as he tries not to jar my body. Foreign sounds leak past my lips. I try to make them stop, but Dram moves, and pain lances through me.

"Roland," he says, "another dose of Serum 129." He shifts my weight in his arms.

Roland spears me with a syringe. "She's fading fast," he murmurs.

"We need to get her up," Graham says.

"Impossible," Roland whispers.

"Boyo, stop for a moment and let me help you," Graham says. "You've still got that carcass sunk in your arm."

Dram huffs out a breath and extends his arm. There's a shuffling of feet as a handful of cavers move in to pry the flash bat loose. I smell Dram's blood before I see it drip into the dirt. He stifles a moan, and a moment later, a furry body flops to the ground. Blood patters, then flows in a steady stream.

"Did you see the teeth on that thing?"

"It might've broke bone—look at his arm."

"Bandage it, fast!" Graham says.

"Prep her ORU," Dram murmurs as Reeves helps him ease me to the ground.

I can't stop my tears. The movement feels like knives pressing into me.

"Winn?" I ask.

"Safe," Lenore says. "You saved her in that cave."

I let Serum 129 pull me a little closer to oblivion. Cool air brushes my bare shoulder where my suit's cut away. The sulfuric smell of Serum 38 coats my skin. The bite was deep, but they've saved me from mineral burn.

I don't even want to think about my leg. I can't feel anything below my waist on my right side.

Something Graham said sticks in my mind. Serum clouds my thoughts, but there's an idea I'm trying to puzzle out. He said Dram still had the flash bat in his arm. They just removed it to tend his injury.

Dram would have been the one to show them the proper way to disengage a flash bat's jaw from my shoulder. I try to imagine him stabbing the bat in the head, cutting away my suit, prying the teeth out, and treating my injury, all with a bat stuck in his own injured arm.

My eyes slide over him. He watches me intently.

"Hang on tight," he says. His lips are cracked and bleeding, the skin around them peeling. Through his goggles, his reddish eyes reveal that he's fighting flash bat venom. "I'm sending you up." He tightens the belt holding me to the ORU and engages the unit's transmitter. I flinch. It reminds me of Winn's transmitter the moment before the bats descended.

"I can't believe I'm putting her in an ore cart," Dram murmurs.

"It's the best chance she has, boyo," Graham replies.

Reeves clamps his hand on Dram's shoulder. "Send her up."

Dram's bloodshot eyes bore into mine. "If there was any other way, I'd do it."

He tips his forehead down against mine and whispers something. They replaced my earpiece, but I can't hear what he says.

"What?" I murmur.

He looks at me, and suddenly I know exactly what he said.

He engages the unit, and it jolts forward. I am towed behind it, my feet dragging the tunnel floor as it gains momentum. Then it rockets upward, and I'm grateful for Dram's tight belt, holding me secure. For the first time, I understand what Roland's father must have felt when he rode his ORU away from Outpost Five—in the moments before guards seized him. Possibility. Exhilaration. Hope.

The ORU scrapes along the tunnel neck, hitting the sides in a shower of sparks. The unit hovers above the wire, rocking me side to side, and I think of Wes, when he was a baby and I rocked him as he cried for our mother. Our mother who couldn't hear him because she was down seven. And later, when she couldn't hear him because she was dead.

The tunnel dips, and the cart veers right, my limbs swinging out behind it like a pendulum, cracking against the cavern wall.

Ding-dong. Like the gears in a clock. Counting down minutes. And seconds. And lifetimes. I can't hold on any longer. My arms flop loose, bouncing and dragging like dead weight.

But I can't die now. I made Dram a promise. Something about him before me, or me before him, or neither of us, ever. Not like this. Not on this side of the flash curtain.

The rocking cart lulls me to a place outside myself, and my thoughts scatter like cavern particles. All but one.

I'm returning without a single gram of cirium. And I'm going to be sent to Cordon Four.

TEN

315.82 grams cirium

I WAKE TO the glow of infirmary lights.

Cranny sits at my bedside.

"You're a special girl, Orion." He smiles like a bully pulling his fist back for a punch.

"So you've said." My head feels like it's stuffed with rags. I'm in the back room, isolated from the rest. My father must be in the main room, the infirmary aides with him. I'm hooked to an IV, and there's a catheter tube running from between my legs to a bag of urine hooked to the side of the bed.

"How long?" I murmur. My voice sounds rusty.

"Since you came up nine strapped to an ore cart? Three days." He sets a used syringe on the bedside table. "I used Serum 61 to wake you. I'm impatient to talk to you."

That explains the sting in my hand. How like Cranny to use a needle when his voice would have been enough.

"These must have been a surprise . . ." He picks up a vial from the bedside table. Inside, a wriggling ore mite claws against the glass.

I shrink back. "Why is that in here?"

He tips the jar, flipping the mite onto its back. Rows of pronged legs kick the air. "A reminder that, no matter how bad things seem, they can always get worse."

"That sounds ominous," I mutter, forcing myself to sit up. Every muscle in my body is tensed, though I doubt I could run if I wanted to. I'm not even sure I can walk.

"Graham is crippled," Cranny says.

"What?" My thoughts collide. What does Graham have to do with me?

Cranny shrugs. "He refused the treatment that would dispel the mites on his leg. The parasites worked their way into his tendons and knee joints."

"Why would he refuse treatment?" Cranny doesn't answer. He stares at the ore mite wriggling on its back. "What do you want?"

"A confession," he says.

My stomach knots. There are many things I could confess. "About what?"

"Whose idea was it? For you all to bring out the same amount of ore?"

"I don't know what you're talking about." My heart slams against my chest, like it wants to escape as much as the rest of me. "I came up with nothing."

"Actually, Scout, you had a hundred fourteen grams' worth of cirium in your ORU. Same as the rest."

"I don't know how that happened." That, at least, is no lie. Ennis must have weighed and loaded it just before Dram sent me up. I wasn't empty-handed after all.

He tilts the jar, and the mite wrestles itself right side up.

"I think you're a schemer and a troublemaker. Tell me what I want to know."

"I have nothing to tell you."

Cranny's lips twist. On an animal, I'd read it as a sign it's about to attack. "Stand up."

"I can't stand," I murmur breathlessly. "There's a . . . a catheter—"

Cranny lifts the bag, and I hiss with pain. He pulls it toward him, and I stagger to my feet, holding on to the bed for support. A sob breaks from my lips.

"Please," I whisper. "It hurts. Everything hurts."

"Like I said," Cranny murmurs, "things can always get worse." The light is back in his dark gaze. It reminds me of the hunger of flash bats—creatures who will die just to keep their teeth in their prey as long as possible. "Give me a name."

I can't believe this is happening. If I call my father, he will attack Cranny and be sent to the burnt sands. If I tell Dram, he will kill the director. He will become ash that I wear around my neck. My eyes dart to the closed door. No one can find us like this. I can't risk having the people I love retaliate against the director.

Anger replaces my fear. A rage so powerful that, for a moment, I think I might just murder Cranny myself. All the lies they've told us. All the brainwashing about what we're really doing here.

"Last chance, Scout," he says.

"I have nothing to tell you."

He hooks my catheter bag back, and I nearly cry out from the pain. Tears prick my eyes as I crawl back onto the bed.

"You disappoint me, Orion." He unscrews the vial.

Fear gnaws a pit in my stomach. "I'm the best ore scout you have."

"Maybe you're too good," he says softly.

"I've done everything the Congress wants!"

Cranny's eyes trace the scrapes and bruises on my face. "Poor, naive girl, you have no idea what the Congress wants." Glass clinks as he drops something inside the vial.

He sets it beside the bed. At the bottom of the glass, beneath the mite's clicking claws, lie four curving metal Rays—the symbol of how much ore I've collected.

"The Congress revoked your Rays." He drops the words like a bomb, and I feel the shock and then the utter annihilation of my hopes. Without my Rays, those precious 400 grams, I will never, ever leave this place.

Cranny walks from the room and pulls the door shut behind him.

I press my battered face into my pillow and scream.

———

"Wake up, Orion."

My eyes fly open. An anxious infirmary aide hovers over me. "You've been summoned to the Rig," she says. "All the cavers have." She doesn't meet my eyes.

"Where's my dad?"

"Your father's been detained."

"What?" I push myself up, wincing with pain. The wound in my thigh throbs like it has its own heartbeat.

"The commissary has questions about the cirium you mined." She lifts the bandage, and I see a row of stitches pulling together swollen skin streaked purple from remnants of venom. She sprays a numbing serum over the area. "The stitches will dissolve in a few days." She finally looks me in the eye. "You were lucky to survive this."

"My dad—"

"The guards are on their way to escort you. I need to remove your catheter."

I gasp and squeeze my eyes shut as she pulls the tube free. "I'm not sure I can walk that far on my own."

"Someone else already thought of that." She turns toward the door. "Dram, you can come in now."

Dram steps through the doorway and freezes when he sees me.

"Tunnel nine and I had a bit of a disagreement," I say. I try to smile, but my face is too bruised to pull it off.

He doesn't say anything as his gaze travels over my face. His lips press together, and his jaw tightens.

The aide slips past him. "I'll stall them as long as I can, but you need to hurry." She shuts the door softly behind her.

Dram walks toward me, and I drink in the sight of him, though he's battered and bruised, his left arm bound. He hands me a folded bundle of clothes and turns his back. "Do you need help?"

I slip my feet over the bed and start to stand. "No, I can—" I gasp and clutch the back of his shoulders. No one's told me the extent of my injuries. I'm discovering them one move at a time.

"Rye . . ."

"Just give me a second." I manage to drag my gown off. The effort leaves me shaking. I feel every stitch in my back.

"I've seen your body," Dram murmurs. "In the cavern, when we treated you—and times before that. Let me help you."

"All right," I whisper.

He turns. "Just like suiting up in the Rig . . ."

I stand still, like the doll I made out of old socks for Winn. He guides my arm into a sleeve, his hands tentative—more gentle than I ever am with myself. He maneuvers the cloth around my bandaged arm and draws the shirt closed in front.

"I brought you my clothes. I figured they'd fit over the bandages better."

I nod, unable to breathe, much less speak.

He struggles to get the buttons through the holes with one good hand. His fingers brush my skin, soft as the fabric of his worn shirt. His scent envelops me.

Dram kneels and slips the pants up my legs. He touches the bandage covering the bite on my thigh, and it takes me back to that moment—when he rolled me over and saw the bat. His eyes lift to mine.

"I was so scared," he says. "I didn't know if I'd be able to bring you back."

My throat tightens. "You did."

"Ashes, Rye," he whispers, drawing the pants up. "A few moments longer with that venom in your veins—you'd be ashes around my neck."

It hurts to lift my arm, but I do it anyway, reaching to wrap my arms around his neck. He curls his injured arm tight about my waist and pulls me to him.

A knock at the door breaks us apart. A guard steps in.

"All cavers to the Rig," he says.

"We're coming," Dram says, glaring at the man. He helps me into my boots, and we follow the guard. Six more flank us as we exit the infirmary.

I try to make sense of their unease. "I don't know where you think I'm in danger of running off to."

"Director's orders," says the guard beside me.

The guards herd us through camp. Every few steps I wince from the pain. My senses reel, and I fight to stay on my feet.

"Slow down," Dram calls. "She can barely walk." He slips his arm around my waist, and I lean into him. I realize he's got his bolt gun loaded and tucked into the back of his pants.

"Planning to mark a route to the Rig?" I ask.

"Just a precaution. Everything's changed."

"What's changed?"

His gaze slips to the board outside the lodge. The caving roster has been burned, but that's not all that's different about it. Between lines of charred wood, I can just make out my name at the top. When I last descended nine, it read 315.82 grams cirium. Now it says 429.21 grams.

I stumble, and Dram hoists me to my feet. Beneath my name is Graham's: 426.17 grams. And Ennis with 410.26 grams. The last name on the board is Dram: 402.86 grams.

The last trip down nine pushed us past 400 grams.

But that doesn't mean anything now for me. "Dram, the Congress revoked my Rays."

"I know."

I study his face, trying to interpret the odd tone to his voice.

"Four hundred two grams," I murmur. "You've earned your freedom—you should be celebrating!"

"No one's celebrating," Dram says darkly. A guard throws us an uneasy glance.

"What's going on? What happened to you while I was out?"

"Cranny's placed me under probation." His eyes meet mine. "These guards aren't for you. They're for me."

ELEVEN

429.21 grams cirium

GUARDS LINE THE walls of the Rig. The hooks that hold our axes hang empty.

"What did you do?" I ask Dram as he helps me onto the bench beside him.

"He spent two nights down four," Graham says behind me. His lips are pinched in a face that's whiter than my bandages, and one hand's clamped on his knee.

I lean in close. "Why didn't they treat your leg?"

Graham grunts. "Cranny thinks I have something of his."

"Do you?"

A smile cracks the lines on his weathered face. "I just might."

"But your leg—"

"These old bones have been aching for years. I'm thinking it's about time I quit the tunnels." He knows as well as I do that there's only one way to leave Outpost Five.

"What exactly did Dram do?"

"Set fire to the caving roster." My eyes widen. While I lay unconscious in the infirmary, my tunnel partner went mad.

Dram stares hard at the front of the room. "I was outside the infirmary the first night—after they weighed the ore. They wouldn't let me in to see you, but I overheard them talking about your Rays." The expression in his eyes is bleaker than I can bear. "You were right, Orion. We're prisoners here. They're never going to let us go, whatever we do."

The commissary steps to the front of the room, and tension descends. He holds a massive, aged book used since the first days of this outpost—the Cavers' Log, the record of every gram of cirium Subpars have mined.

I shift closer to Dram. "What aren't you telling me?"

"The Congress has been debating whether or not to count the ore we brought up from nine."

His words shatter something deep inside me, maybe the last bit of faith I held in our government.

"Subpars," calls Jameson, "I've received a response from the city." He slides his finger over a metal sphere, and an image flickers to life. The room falls silent as we take in this rare glimpse of Alara's technology.

A woman—the Prime Commissary—sits beside three other commissaries, all dressed in formal robes, with the seal of Alara on woven chains around their necks.

"Subpartisans of Outpost Five," she says, her voice deep, a match for the implacable look in her dark eyes. "The Congress of Natural Humanity thanks you for your service. Our city-state is indebted to you for the cirium you retrieved from tunnel nine . . ."

Dram stares at the image, jaw tight, anger burning in his eyes. "And your valiant efforts ensure the preservation of—" The image flickers, and for a moment it's just us and Jameson again, the image of Alara lost somewhere between here and the flash curtain. "We have conferred with Commissary Jameson about recent events at your outpost. Some of you have earned the distinction Fourth Ray, having mined four hundred grams. However, those Subpars will not be granted passage to the protected city."

In my mind I see that cavern wall beside the Sky, where Dram wrote our names. But now I know for sure—we're never getting free of this place.

None of us are. It was all a lie.

"Your descent down nine was a disciplinary action," she continues. "As such, any ore retrieved will not be counted."

Protests ricochet around the room like stray bullets. From the tone of them, I think Cranny was wise to take away our axes.

"You can't do this!" Lenore shoots to her feet. "Commissary, please." She strides forward, heedless of the guards raising their weapons. "My brother earned passage to the protected city. He mined four hundred grams."

Jameson opens the Log, revealing lines of crossed-out numbers. "Minus one hundred fourteen grams, Subpar."

Lenore's eyes fill with angry tears. "You set an impossible goal and call it opportunity." She stabs her finger at the book. "You are *liars*."

Cranny moves toward her, and Reeves stands, violence radiating from him. "Step back, little man," he calls, his voice deadly calm. "I don't need my axe to hurt you."

At Cranny's signal, four guards descend on Reeves and drag him toward the back of the room. Two more flank Lenore. I feel Dram tensing beside me like a coiled spring.

"I will have order," Cranny says, his dark eyes panning the

room. I think he's hoping more of us will object. He wants an excuse to order bloodshed. My hands fist at my sides. Cranny finds me in the crowd and gives me a knowing grin.

Things can always get worse.

"What the hell is that about?" Dram mutters.

I won't give Cranny the fight he's itching for, so I lower my eyes like he's beaten me, but I'm as angry as Reeves inside.

"I told you that the three cavers who mined the least would be sent to Cordon Four," Cranny says. "Since you all mined exactly the same amount"—he shoots a dark look at my father, hunched over in the front row—"we've come up with an alternate disciplinary action."

The commissary sets aside the Log. "One caver from each tunnel team will volunteer for service at Cordon Four. Tomorrow, a hover will come to collect that group of Subpars."

A deadly hush settles over the room. I can't form a clear thought—I'm simply numb.

Then my world implodes.

Nine tunnels. Seven teams. One from each active tunnel. Seven cavers are being sent to Cordon Four—to burn for something I did.

A woman's crying. Another person shrieks, but I can't make out her words. Graham and Dram sit, silent, staring at the place where Jameson announced the end of us.

My father drops his head in his hands, his shoulders shaking. I've only seen him cry once. The day Wes died.

Before I connect my thoughts to my actions, I'm halfway to Cranny, to the guards that bracket him and Jameson.

"It was me," I announce. "I told Ennis to distribute the ore weights evenly."

Cranny studies me with his predatory gaze. "You're bargaining with the wrong person. These orders come down from the council."

My gaze skitters to the commissary, who watches me with a look I can't decipher. "Please don't do this."

"I'm afraid you set something in motion," he says.

I realize dimly that Dram stands beside me, and the other cavers are on their feet, shouting, arguing. Everything is chaos. We've been taught to fear the burnt sands our entire lives. We thought we were mining cirium to protect people from the merciless radiation of the flash curtain. We thought we were the fortunate ones because we survive here, and no closer.

Cordon Four is so much nearer. It is death.

I can't save them now. I can save only one.

"I will serve," I say, my eyes riveted on Jameson. "For my team. Dram stays."

He shakes his head, and there is a weariness about him I didn't notice before, like the bands on his sleeves are exceedingly heavy. "Since you were the instigator, you are going regardless," he says softly. "And because that leaves Dram as the only possible representative of nine, he will go too."

"No." I never realized screams could be quiet.

Dram touches my arm, protecting me from myself. But this time it's too late. The damage is already done.

"Dram, Orion—in here," Dad says. He crosses his arms and leans against the kitchen table. He wears his physic's expression.

I prepare myself for a grim diagnosis.

"Much of this is speculation, but I'll share what little I know about the cordons. There are fences and rudimentary shelters. The boundary fences between them are electrified. But if you manage to escape, you *can* survive," he says. "Long enough to make your way north, to where the curtain ends and its energy bands diminish enough that you could get to the shield."

He doesn't mention how we'd get past the shield. Or what would happen to two escaped Subpars if we did get inside Alara.

"Urine. Don't drink it—the process your body uses to filter it will dehydrate you further. But it *can* be used as an antiseptic."

He's talking about pee in front of Dram. Us *drinking* pee. I should be mortified, but I feel only terror. The cold truth of what we're about to endure settles over me.

"Blood is a food source," Dad continues. "Whatever you kill in the cordons can be eaten. Few plants grow in the burnt sands, but there are cacti, and some of their fruits and pads are edible. They can be a water source, if you have something sharp enough to cut them open. Chew the pulp inside, drain the water from it—but don't eat it. And—this is very important—you have to make sure it's the *right* cactus, the one with yellow flowers—they're called miner's compass." He smiles sadly. *Miner's compass.* I can only wonder at the Subpars before us who gave it that name.

"Most lean toward the sun," he says, "so they'll also help guide you. Stay away from the ones with red fruit or gray, twisted spines—drinking from those leads to severe diarrhea and eventual paralysis."

I meet Dram's grim look. *Red fruit bad.*

"The flashfall may carry embers for fire . . ." Dad hands me a small magnifying glass. "When it doesn't, you can use this lens to direct light onto dry brush."

"How do you know all this?" I ask. "The miner's compass and everything?"

His expression changes, and he's no longer John Denman, physic, but Dad. "I spoke to someone once, who had seen things."

Most Subpars were born here, their families having worked this outpost for generations. Very few transfer from other outposts.

"Who?" I ask.

Dad sighs, and it's like the last breath holding closed a lock. "Your mother."

———

Come and find me, Orion.

Mom used to play games with me. I don't know how she managed the energy for it after a day spent mining, but I used to wait for her, watching through the window beside my loft bed.

There weren't many places to hide in our house, but I never got tired of looking for her. We'd always end up under the bed— the wide wooden frame left us plenty of room to squeeze beneath—talking, dreaming together of places beyond the outpost. It was there she taught me about constellations, and my own ironic part in the universe.

I just never knew that she herself had come from someplace beyond the outpost. That's the real irony. I feel betrayed. She told me made-up stories instead of sharing what was real. She should've told me herself about miner's compass and desperate people in the cordons—maybe then I wouldn't have leapt atop the Congress's *glenting sign* with my axe.

"She transferred here from another outpost when she was eighteen," Dad says. "She didn't deceive you, Orion. She just didn't like to talk about it."

I make a face beneath his bed. It's where I lie now, reaching up to trace the marks Mom drew across the underside of the wooden frame. This was the other game we played. She'd let me wear her headlamp, and together we'd spend hours drawing.

Draw what you see in your mind, Orion.

I used chalk, so each time I'd erase my pictures and make something new. She used a sort of dark greasepaint and only occasionally erased her markings. I stare up at the lines and marks, my mind whirring. I haven't thought of this for years— not since Dad's revelation. Mom kept secrets, apparently, and the ones she shared involved places none of us has ever seen.

I gasp suddenly. "Dram—come here!" I see his legs uncross from where he's been waiting beside the bed.

"'Come here,' like *under* here?"

I snatch his arm and pull him down. He bends and slides his much longer frame in beside me.

"Look." I point to the marks above us.

"Are you wearing your *headlamp*?"

"Dram. Look at the marks. What do you see?"

He stares hard, a line creasing between his brows. "Give me a hint?"

"Tunnel seven."

He looks at me then, concern in his eyes. That's where our mothers died. It's been a closed tunnel since.

"They brought up the least cirium of any team," I muse aloud. Even if we haven't seen the ore weights in the Cavers' Log, we've heard the stories.

"That's because seven was tapped out."

"No." I shake my head and the light from my headlamp flashes over the markings. "It's because they weren't even looking for it." I trace my finger over a line of Xs. *Danger.* Beside them, a row of hashmarks. *Impassable.*

"What is this, Rye?"

"It's a map. Our mothers weren't mining seven. They were searching for a way out."

———

The flash storm sweeps in the next day, giving us a stay of execution. At least, that's how Cranny puts it. Apparently, the Congress won't send a hover through radiation winds—not even to discipline a rebellious teenage caver.

Clearly, Cranny feels more threatened by me than by an imminent storm with winds that will bring the radiation of the flash curtain to our doors. I vent my anger tearing rags to bandages in the infirmary.

"You're muttering under your breath, Orion," Dad calls. He looks up from a mixture bubbling over a burner.

"Some of the words I'm saying aren't appropriate for impressionable young ears," I murmur, nodding toward Winn.

"Ah." Dad looks out the door. Despite the weather, he's propped it open.

"Looking for something?"

"A shift in the wind," he says, going back to his notes. "There's an experiment I mean to do."

A chill runs down my spine. "Must be important."

"Life and death," he replies softly, tapping a vial of fluid. Glowing blue particles swirl inside it.

"Not your death, right?" I ask, and Winn glances at me sharply.

Dad gives her a reassuring smile. "Of course not. I'm sixty percent certain it won't kill me."

Winn's face pales. She doesn't know about our morbid humor. But my smile freezes on my face as I lift the vial. "Is this the orbie cirium?"

"The altered cirium, yes. I distilled it into a compound."

"The poison theory again."

"Congress is sending my daughter to a cordon—I'm willing to try anything to save her."

My heart trips. "So it's like . . ." I study the radioactive particles. "A sort of vaccine?"

"More like an extra layer of protection. It should strengthen your natural resistance. It won't prevent radiation sickness entirely."

Every night he's stayed up long after I've gone to sleep, working by the light of a candle so guards won't see a light on. His voice is tired, strained, a match for the shadows under his eyes. But past the exhaustion—and worry for me—is a spark of something powerful. Hope.

"How long will this last?" I ask, holding up the vial.

"It's only temporary."

"But if it works . . ."

"Then it might be the foundation for a cure. Combined with other elements, it could be used to create permanent immunity to the effects of the flashfall."

I glance outside. The wind has shifted. My scout's senses are telling me to get deep underground. Fast.

"I'll test it."

Dad shakes his head. "It could kill you. I haven't tried it yet."

"You are the only physic at Outpost Five. Let me do this. If something goes wrong, you can help me."

"I'm testing a theory, Orion—that's all."

"You're never wrong." I set my lips to the vial. Dad grasps my arm, but I pour the liquid down my throat.

"*Glenting hell!* It's radioactive!"

I can't speak. My throat aches like I've swallowed a rock.

Dad watches me as if he's waiting for me to explode. I force a smile. It feels more like a grimace. "What now?"

"Now?" He spits the word. I've rarely seen him this upset. "You get belowground like everyone else."

"Dad—"

"It wasn't your risk to take." He's not angry, but terrified. "You're too *impulsive*, Orion! You need to learn to *think* before you—" He breaks off and shakes his head. Wind spits flaming dust beyond the doorway. "The storm's picking up. You have to get down nine with Winn."

"What about you?"

"Cranny's convinced people that the lodge is safe. I'm going over to talk sense into them. Then I'm going to find you so I can monitor you." He folds me into his arms. I know he's thinking of Wes, probably wishing he'd held him tighter before the last flash storm. "You don't have to convince me you're brave. You are the bravest person I know. Sometimes foolishly so."

"You're the one going to the lodge."

I feel his smile. "True enough."

"How do you know that word?" I ask. "*Glenting.*"

I feel his soft laugh, a puff of breath against my ear. "Your mom," he says. "She used to say that sometimes." And it's as if he's given me another page to add to the Book of Mom, another side to her that I never had the chance to know. Somehow knowing that she occasionally cursed with the Really Bad Conjie Word makes her seem closer. More real. My throat tightens again, and I'm not sure if it's from the cirium compound or my mother the caver, who was maybe more like me than I realized.

He grasps my arm as I pull away. "If . . . if anything should happen to me—I need you to destroy my research. I'm afraid to think what Cranny would do if he discovered it."

Fear slips along my spine. I glance at his assortment of beakers and burners.

"Not here," he says. "Main room of the house—you'll find a loose floorboard. Beneath it there is a hidden space."

My emotions are as turbulent as the storm outside. A secret room? My throat tightens. "Don't talk like you're not coming back."

He cups my head. "And you will that compound to make you strong, not sick. Don't let it be poison."

We push through the door, and I tell myself this is not the last time I'll see my dad. There won't be a need to destroy whatever he's hidden.

And I didn't just drink something that will kill me.

I wrap Winn in a flash blanket and we run for nine. I can practically feel the radiation increasing. It's the hint of sulfur on the wind, like a flameless breath from a dragon.

Dram and Lenore are waiting a few meters inside the tunnel.

"Where's Roran?" Lenore asks, looking past me for the boy.

"Not with us," I gasp.

Lenore stares at me in panic. "He was headed to your house."

"We were at the infirmary!"

Lenore covers her mouth with her hand. We have enough memories of past storms to paint horrific images in our minds.

Dram drags his hand through his hair. "Fire." He kicks the cave wall, and kicks it again. There is nothing we can do. Going back out now is too risky.

My heart feels like a bird trying to escape a cage. I can go back for him—Dad's experiment is coursing through my body.

"We should get deeper," I say. I can't tell them what I intend to do. Dram will never let me leave.

Lenore nods and draws Winn farther along the path.

"What about Roran?" Winn cries.

Lenore murmurs something I can't hear.

"I'm going to stay here a moment in case he comes," I tell Dram. I can't look him in the eye, or he'll know I'm lying.

He hesitates. "All right. We'll meet you down there, just before the neck." He turns toward the path.

I count to twenty, then run, not even slowing as I near the tunnel entrance. Heat and dust blow in from the outside.

My father has never been wrong.

I take a breath and wade into the storm, fiery dust swirling around me. My brother ran from this, and I've seen it melt people from the inside out.

I tuck my chin to my chest, still holding my breath. Pulling my neck cloth over my nose and mouth, I take a cautious sip of air. It's impossibly hot, like I'm sucking on a flare. Tears stream from my eyes and moisture fogs my goggles as I wrap my flash blanket around me. I imagine this is how Dram's father felt— how anyone ever sent to mine the burnt sands feels just before dying. Only, I have an antidote. Possibly.

Clinging to that belief, I lift my face to the sky. It glows red and orange, like it's on fire. I am still alive. I hold my hand out in front of me and watch in wonder as flaming ash swirls over it.

The scent of rain teases my nostrils, and suddenly I freeze— it's like I'm twelve years old again, smelling the promise of the flash storm, the promise of death. Just past the reaches of Outpost Five, lines of virga appear, stretching from orange clouds to the ground, a hissing mix of rain and steam.

The ends of my hair break off. Still, I stand transfixed. I've never seen a storm approach. No one has seen this and lived. Part of me wants to stand here, testing the limits of Dad's compound. The other parts of me remember the sound of Wes's screams. I tug my flash blanket over my head. Acid rain spatters down, burning patterns into the dust. Burning everything it touches.

I run. The shape of my house shimmers beyond the waves of radiation. I pray that Roran is there, because I doubt I'll survive another minute without shelter. I burst through the front door.

"Roran!"

"Here!" He ducks his head out from beneath my father's bed.

"You're not safe," I shout. "Help me pry up these floorboards!"

He races to my side and we drop to our knees, running our hands over the cracks in the wood.

"We need to get belowground. My father says there's a loose board concealing a hole." I find the board and drag my glove off with my teeth so I can wedge my fingernails in the seam. "Here. Help me!" Together we pry it up. There's just enough room for us to squeeze through. I crack a light stick and drop it down. "Jump!"

He lands easily. The space is large enough for him to stand with arms raised, and as wide as five people. I find iron hand-holds mounted to the side and climb down, sliding the panel back into place above us. It's not deep enough to save some-one from radiation. I shine my palm light at the underside of the floorboards. Wood. I was hoping they might be lined with cirium.

"What is this place?" Roran asks. He has his rock in his hand, and he rolls it in his palm as he looks around.

"I have no idea." I let my gaze wander past the microscope and rudimentary lab equipment, recognizing vials of the altered cirium I drank earlier. "Roran . . ." I search his face for the burn and swelling of radiation sickness, and realize I'm waiting for him to vomit or complain of a headache that won't go away.

"What is it?"

"We're not deep enough to keep you safe."

"What about you?"

"Subpars can endure exposure better than Naturals." Part of that's true. It's why we mine the tunnels and the Naturals do not. But I would have already died without my father's cirium mixture.

His eyes linger on my face, and I wonder what he's hoping to see in my expression. "Can you keep a secret?" he asks.

I think of the Sky, and the map Dram stole. I think of Dad's compound streaking through my veins. "Yes," I whisper.

He lifts his rock. The shape has changed. Just moments ago, it fit his palm, flat and rounded. "My father told me to try. So I've been practicing."

The things he's saying make no sense . . . unless—

"You're a Conjuror."

He nods. "I can handle flash storms better than Naturals, too."

The rock isn't the only thing that's changed. He speaks differently, his words layered with an accent even stronger than Gabe's. No wonder he's usually so quiet—his words might've given him away.

My mind is spinning so many directions at once. A hundred questions jump to my lips, but for now there's only one that matters. "Can you conjure cirium?" He shakes his head, and my heart plummets. We're going to die down here.

Roran crouches and draws his palm over the ground. "What about rock? The other cavers went belowground, right?"

"Wouldn't you bury us alive?"

"I'll leave space over us."

I feel the power of the storm increasing, the same way I sense cirium. In the sparse glow of the light stick, my eyes find Roran's. They are a warm brown, and I wonder if they are like his mom's or dad's. His dad who told him to practice.

"Do it."

He tucks the stone in his pocket. It occurs to me that it's likely the last thing his father gave him, maybe some of the last words he spoke. *Practice, son.* But how do you practice the impossible? It's rare for Conjie ability to work so close to the flash curtain. But I saw what Roran did with that rock.

Roran closes his eyes and lays his hands on the earth. We wait—one moment, two. A fist squeezes my heart. I can't watch him die the way Wes did.

The ground trembles.

"Holy fire," I whisper. Dirt and rock twist up from the ground, arching over us, around us. Stone scrapes against stone, and I cry out. This isn't natural. People can't conform matter to their will. I've spent my life surviving the tunnels, only to end up crushed beneath rock, buried beneath my own home.

"It's all right," Roran says. He lifts his hands, and the rock stills.

Our breath fills the pocket of air between us. He's encased us in rock. I feel like I'm in the neck of nine with no exit. I try to clamp down the panic knotting my stomach, but I can't ignore the glaring certainty that if Roran dies, I am utterly trapped.

"Will this save us?" he asks.

He's not frightened by our tomb of rock. "Can you get us deeper?"

He places his palm beneath him and the ground dissolves and morphs, like he's building sandcastles instead of altering the crust. "Hold on."

I wedge my body onto a ledge of rock and watch the earth transform beneath me.

"Is this deep enough?" His voice doesn't express shock or surprise, and I wonder just how often he's seen his people perform these kinds of marvels.

I clutch a light stick and step down, tuning my senses to the curtain. It's a distant pulse now. "Deep enough. We need to conserve our air. We don't know how long the storm will last." I shine the light over the rock shelter he constructed. "Does Cranny know what you are?"

"No. My parents taught me to hide so I wouldn't be Tempered."

"Tempered . . ." I remember touching Gabe's metal hands.

"The Congress cuts off Conjies' hands and caps the stumps with cirium."

A chill runs up my spine. "Like Gabe?"

"He turned himself in, so they gave him hands." He presses his palm to the ground and green shoots thrust from the dirt, twining up the rock walls, bursting with fragrant white blossoms. He laughs, a breathless kid sound full of wonder. "I can't usually conjure this close to the flash curtain—too much cirium in the earth."

I pluck one of the blooms and press my fingers to the satin-smooth petals. "Then I'd say your practicing paid off."

His smile dims, and he stares into the middle distance, the rock turning over and over in his hand once more. I don't ask what happened to his father. I don't need to.

"You did something amazing," I say. "And your parents are a part of it, because they're a part of you." When I made lead ore scout, I wanted so badly to share it with Mom. I climbed the Range and told her all about it, a girl having a one-sided conversation with the wind. I like to think that somehow she heard, that part of her is still with me.

I tuck the flower in my pocket so I will have a reminder of this, the day a boy moved the earth to save me. "Why weren't you Tempered, Roran?"

"Because I'm really good at keeping secrets," he says. "So is my mom. Her name's Mere." His face is turned from me, but I don't need to see it to read the pain in his words. "They didn't give her hands."

"Where is she now?" I ask.

His gaze hardens. "Cordon Four."

The burnt sands. I try to imagine a woman mining flash dust with only cirium stumps for hands. "I'm sorry."

"She's alive," he says, as if my words suggested otherwise. "My people are survivors."

My gaze slips over the sanctuary he carved from the earth. "Yes, you are."

And so are mine. I cling to that hope as we measure out breaths beneath the stone and wait for the storm to pass.

———

The destruction is less than the cordon breach. Dad managed to get most people out of the lodge, which is fortunate, because it will need to be built a third time. His underground den of secrets will also need repair.

I find him in the infirmary, pulling a sheet over a woman's head. I recognize her from the Rig. Blood seeps through the sheet touching her nose and mouth.

"How many?" I ask.

"All of tunnel one's team," he says. "I couldn't get them to leave the lodge."

I look past him to the rows of beds, some with aides soothing the cavers still conscious.

"I lost two more to the ore mites sometime during the storm," he says. "The parasites got into their bloodstreams."

I try to imagine which death is worse.

His gaze focuses on me. "You're still standing. The cirium compound must not be entirely toxic." He's apparently not forgiven me for taking his experiment into my own hands.

"Dad." I lean close and whisper. "I walked through the storm to save Roran." I set his hand on the pulse in my wrist. "I'm not sick. Whatever you made protected me long enough to find shelter."

He clasps my head and studies me. Then he checks my Radband. Green. "This changes everything. I might be able to give you a chance out in the cordon." He steers me from the infirmary. "We need to get to my lab."

"About the lab . . ." My words trail off as I notice the crowd gathered in front of the lodge. Guards are hanging a new sign from the damaged eaves.

"A cordon list," Dad says, peering above the heads of other cavers. "Your name's at the top, with Dram's beside tunnel nine—" He breaks off.

"What?" Dread crawls through me.

"They added Lenore. Tunnel six."

No. This can't be. I push past the others and stare numbly at the sign, at Dram's sister added to the death list. Then I see the final name, just beneath it.

Tunnel one's team was decimated in the flash storm. Its two remaining cavers succumbed to the ore mites. That leaves only Winn.

They would send a child to the burnt sands. How could Congress require this of Outpost Five? Winn's not even a Subpar.

I stare at my name at the top of the list. I've led them to this.

I will find a way to lead them back out.

TWELVE

429.21 grams cirium

MOONLIGHT FILTERS PAST the flashfall and gilds tunnel nine in silver light, making it look less ominous than it is.

I've never gone down by myself. Life here presents many dangers, but none of them threaten disaster quite like caving alone. Nine is bad enough with Dram at my back. He will never forgive me for doing this.

If I don't do it, I will never forgive myself.

I slip inside and turn on my headlamp and palm lights. The risks I take now are all my own, and it makes me bold. I practically throw myself down the tunnel neck, pushing and pulling my body through the tight space, praying my pick doesn't catch.

"You're halfway through," I say aloud. "Get the ore, get it to Dad." I say the words over and over, imagining the path I'm going to take, mapping my steps in my head. I have to be faster than I've ever been before.

I crawl along on my hands and knees, pushing myself up as the headspace grows, so that I'm running before I can even stand fully. At the mouth of the passage I veer left instead of right. Red light bolts illuminate the ground as I jog past, my axe raised in front of me. I follow them like signposts:

Caution. Danger. Keep Out.

I listen for the drip of water that tells me this is the one I need. I break a light stick and toss it on the floor of a vast cavern. An orbie pool glows orange in the center. I open a tarred pouch and dip it into the pool, careful not to get any water on my gloves. When it's full, I seal the pouch and hang it from my belt, turning back to the tunnels.

Dram's bolts are activated by motion sensors, and they come to life one after another until I've reached the place where they intersect. It might as well be a locked door. These are marks we do not cross. But there is cirium here.

I step past, my heart racing, my senses on high alert for sounds or movement.

I'm inside a gulls' nest.

Mother flash gulls leave their nests to hunt, leaving the males and younglings behind to roost amongst the eggs. Females are larger than their male counterparts, with enormous hooked beaks. I have seen them crack open a person's head like a nut, but their real power is in their talons, which are nearly the size of my hand—another genetic anomaly courtesy of the flash curtain. The feathers on their wings are sharp too, each one edged like a blade.

I know they will come for me. In the glow of the red bolts, I take aim and swing my axe as hard as I can. The sharp ping of metal on stone reverberates around me as I swing again and again. Bits of rock and crude ore crumble at my feet. Half of me is absorbed in my task; the other is poised for attack, waiting.

I wear my hair tucked up inside my skullcap. It's what tunnel gulls go for first, before they make a meal of you. Human hair makes great gull nests.

I hammer at the rock as if I'm trapped and this is my only way out. Fear makes my palms sweat inside my gloves, and I grip the handle tighter, telling myself I am prepared for what's coming. Even now, I feel Dad's compound strengthening me, buffering me against the effects of exposure. I pull off my glove and study my blistered palm. Normally at this depth, cavern particles would sting my skin.

I have to tell him. If I live through this, I have to tell him how powerful his compound is.

At my back, the male gulls call to their mates. *Mew, mew, keow!* Others stretch wide their bills and fill the cavern with their warnings. *Ha-ha-ha-ha!*

A female responds from far off. Another calls, closer. Their shrill cries echo, so that I can't tell what direction they're coming from. I drop to my knees and sift through the rock, stuffing ore in my pouch with shaking hands. My knives and axe won't be enough against a nest of gulls. I wear Dram's light gun strapped to my side and both our bolt guns. Everything is loaded and ready. I stand and face the nest.

It stretches all the way to the tunnel wall. Dozens of eggs sit in rows, like crops awaiting harvest. I recognize the scalps and hair of my team. Even knowing this, I struggle with what I'm about to do. The roosting gulls watch me, their beady eyes following my every movement. They will not leave their perches. Their body warmth is the only thing preserving their young from the particle dust and cold of the cavern.

"I'm sorry," I whisper. They watch me unhook the pouch

of orbie water from my belt as they hunker over their eggs, cooing worried lullabies to their young. Tears sting my eyes as I unseal the pouch and aim it at the nesting gulls. I wish this could be a fast and painless death, but it won't be.

I squeeze the pouch. Water shoots out, and the gulls scream. Orbies cover their white and gray down. The gulls flap furiously, but the orbies hold fast. They do not fly. They will not leave their young. Eggs crack open as the orbies dig and devour. The gulls screech. I've never heard them make this terrible sound before. I put my hands over my ears, but their cries pierce me to the core until I drop to my knees, desperate for their suffering to end.

I know it's not over yet—I still have so far to go tonight. The hunting mothers return. One of them swoops at me, and I lurch away from her beak. The others fly to the dying fathers and young. Their screeching cries echo in pain. I can't bear it another moment.

I flatten my body to the ground as the gulls attack, holding back my scream as they hammer with their beaks and gouge me with talons. I kick and swing my axe, but I'm flailing, as desperate and helpless as those poor creatures covered in orbies.

I light a flare and yank the tube from my Oxinator. A sound explodes from my mouth, a yell of despair and triumph. The gulls are strong, but not as powerful as me. Holding the tube toward them, I crank the Oxinator all the way and hold the burning flare in front of it. Flames burst in a whoosh that blows me backward.

I realize I'm screaming along with the gulls. The scent of their scorched feathers and bodies fills the cavern. The flare burns down, and I drop it. It's so quiet, I hear the hiss of the air filtering through the Oxinator. I turn off the tank and fall to my knees. Soot streaks my face, running into my eyes with the sweat and tears.

I killed them all. I can't look, but I don't need to. I can hear the crackle of fires burning down, the hiss and pop of burning gulls' flesh, the high-pitched scream of orbies, the stench of death.

I lie in the burned-out nest until I find the strength to push myself to my feet and shoot a light bolt into the ground. Yellow light illuminates the wall. Breath saws from my lungs as I chisel the line of cirium from one end of the wall to the other. My hands slip inside my gloves, where blisters have formed and broken, and blood mixes with my sweat.

The first time I descended three, I had to hold Graham's hand because the dark was like a living, seething creature. It had swallowed Mom, it would surely come for me. Then I felt the pain of striking an axe against stone, and feeling that resistance travel up my skinny arms—but I had to keep swinging Mom's axe.

Graham said, "Don't think about how it hurts; just think about seeing the sky again soon. How the air's gonna feel on your face."

I let his words roll over me now, imagining him here beside me, holding back the darkness, reminding me to look up. I will not let Congress destroy me.

I am going to see the sky.

By the time I stumble from nine's entrance, I'm hunched over, barely able to walk. My gloves are ripped to shreds and

I feel like I've been in a battle, but the hidden pouches tucked against my skin are bursting with cirium. More than I've ever brought up at one time.

If Congress wants to murder us, I'm going to make them work for it.

———————

Dad treats my wounds by the light of a glow stick as I piece together the story of the gulls' nest and how I survived it.

He dabs my cuts with alcohol, not saying much. Then he transfers his attention to the ore I brought up, pounding it into dust and adding it to the mixture simmering on a burner.

"Did I get enough?" I ask.

"Yes," he murmurs, "but it takes time to extract the cirium from the ore and transfer the elements. I need time to get the compound right."

I can't think about everything I went through not being enough. I can't think about Dram and I not having a chance at surviving the burnt sands. So I take up a mortar and pestle in my bandaged hands and grind the cirium ore to powder. I have to believe we have a chance. Even if it is a small one.

———————

I wake disoriented and roll over in my bed. When did I fall asleep?

"Will it work?" a hushed voice asks.

I peer into the kitchen, where Lenore Berrends is hovering at Dad's shoulder.

"Orion survived exposure during the flash storm," Dad answers. "But there's not enough. I need more time."

Lenore lets out a shaky breath and twists her green memorial pendant around and around, staring at the cirium liquefying above a burner. "She didn't die right away . . ." Her voice is even softer than before.

"Who?" Dad asks.

"Ferrin." She says my mother's name on an exhale, like it was pulled from her chest.

I'm awake immediately, crawling off my bed and edging toward the end of the loft.

"They were all gone so fast," she murmurs. "The team . . . my mother. The rocks just . . . but Ferrin—she had her axe . . . w-wedged above me—" Her voice breaks, and her breath hitches. "She said, 'Take my axe to Orion.'"

I press my face into my hands. I never knew this—had no idea Mom was still breathing after the cave-in.

That her last word was my name.

Lenore takes a breath, then another. She stands up taller, like invisible hands are lifting her. "I crawled out of seven on my hands and knees, dragging her axe and mine," she whispers. "The entire time, I promised myself that I would grow up to be as brave as Orion's mom."

She watches the elements shift inside the beaker, but I think part of her is seeing the collapsed cavern down seven. "How much time do you need?"

"A day," Dad answers. "But we have only hours."

"We don't stand a chance in the cordon."

Dad sighs and drags his hand through his hair. "I'm doing everything I can."

"I know," she says. "Now I must do the same."

He studies her face. Even from where I'm watching, I can see the resolve in her expression. She's transforming before us, like the cirium; only something in her voice tells me she's even stronger.

"What can you possibly do?" Dad asks.

Lenore smiles, even as tears glimmer in her eyes. "Give you a day."

THIRTEEN

429.21 grams cirium

I'M NOT THE one to finally destroy the sign above the tunnels. Lenore took her axe to it sometime in the night. But her last act of defiance was going down six without her team, or any protective gear.

Lenore gave us a day. Her Burning Day.

Dram's door creaks when I push through, the way it has since I was a child. As I walk inside, I have this weird thought that Lenore will never hear that sound again. Dram sits hunched in the corner, weeping. I kneel and wrap my arms around him, trying to take some of his pain into myself. But I know I can't. Instead I press a vial into his hand.

He looks up with bleary red eyes. "Will it even work?"

"Dad says it'll either help us or kill us quick," I murmur.

He lifts the vial in a solemn toast and upends it in one toss of his head. I drink mine in two gulps, and it burns—like Lenore Berrends will burn this afternoon.

I weave my fingers with Dram's and lie down beside him. I squeeze my eyes shut, but it does nothing to hold in the tears. I find myself making more promises to Dram's dead family.

I won't let him burn.

––––––––––

As the only surviving member of his family, Dram is the one to set fire to Lenore's funeral pyre. He lowers the torch, and I clutch my mother's remembrance pendant. Mom always wanted to see the sky—the real one—so Dad had her ashes preserved in blue glass.

I've told Dad that I want mine saved in clear glass, so he can see my death unobscured, a clear reminder of what the Congress took from us. But I'm not going to a place where they preserve a person's memory.

I don't wear Wes's ashes. His small yellow pendant sits in my drawer, tucked inside one of Mom's old shirts. His death is too painful to bear remembering, so Dad and I don't speak of him. Not since Dad held a torch to that tiny pyre and blue flame took his round cheeks so, so fast.

My hand cramps, and I realize I'm gripping my knife. Graham slips his arm around my shoulders.

"Now's not the time, girlie," he whispers, helping me sheathe the blade.

"It's almost done," Dad murmurs, walking up beside me. "The other batch of liquid cirium." His gaze slides over the crowd. Everyone's watching the glassblower. "We may only have this moment. You and Dram need to drink the solution again before you enter the sands."

My eyes mist with tears, and I tell myself it is the smoke blowing into them. "Dad—" My throat constricts. I can't get the words out, and there is so much I want to say.

His eyes fill, and he stares into mine. "They always under-estimate your strength," he whispers. "Find a way to escape or survive. And when you do . . ." He looks over to where Dram stands watching the flames. "You bring that boy with you. He is part of what makes you strong." The tears slip down his cheeks.

I touch his face a last time. "So are you," I whisper.

———

When the hover comes for us, guards parade us from the Rig like a ritual sacrifice. We're wearing our cavers' suits, as if they will offer enough protection where we are going. Mine has a foreign lump that bumps my thigh when I walk. Dad sewed the remaining vials of liquid cirium into my suit.

I feel naked without my axe and knives. Where we're head-ing, neither is necessary. Tunnel nine is a playground com-pared to the burnt sands of Cordon Four.

The caving roster hangs beside the lodge, but for the first time in years, my name is not on it. It's at the top of the new list marked CORDON FOUR, and there are six others beneath it: Dram, Ennis, Graham, Reeves, Gabe, and Winn. Lenore's name has been crossed out.

We're going to die, but our names will live on as caution-ary tales to future Subpars. I was right about Winn's age. She's eight. It's posted beside her name. Mine says sixteen; beside Dram's, eighteen. Graham is seventy-one. For some reason, the ages unnerve me even more than the names. Like the Congress is making a point that no one—child or elder—is beyond the reach of corrective action.

Dram walks beside me, a shadow of his former self. His hol-lowed cheeks show that he's not been eating even our meager rations.

"I've dreamed of leaving this place my entire life," I murmur. "This was never how I imagined feeling."

He takes my hand in his. Without the barrier of gloves, I feel the warmth of his skin, the gentle scrape of his calluses against mine. I steal a glance at Reeves and see the warrior he's kept concealed, the one who ate tunnel gulls and strung the skulls from his belt. He wears his caver's suit knotted around his waist. His chest is bare, showing all of Outpost Five the scars of being forfeit, along with Foss's black memorial pendant, and one other beside it. Lenore's.

"Duck your head," a guard says as we climb into the craft. I slip onto a narrow bench beside Dram, holding tight to his hand.

The engine rumbles, and the door seals shut. The hover lifts, but there are no windows, no last glimpses of Outpost Five.

"I'm scared," I whisper.

"We have nothing left to lose," Dram says. It's the most I've heard him say in two days.

But as his arms steal around me, and I press my cheek above his heart, I know that he is wrong.

There is still so much to lose.

FOURTEEN

0 grams flash dust

THE AIR GROWS increasingly turbulent, and we bounce around on our seats pretending we're not feeling the heat seeping through the cirium-reinforced walls. The running lights flicker, and the hold plunges into darkness as the craft drops like a stone.

"Dram?"

"Right here." He finds my hand in the dark and squeezes.

"The flash curtain affects navigation systems," Gabe says. "We must be descending into the cordon."

The lights return just as we slam into a cushion of air. Winn bounces off the bench, and I catch her arm. She's crying.

"It's going to be okay," I say.

Dram gives me a look. We are unlikely to survive the day.

The loading door opens with a hiss. Needles of fear prick my heart. Humid air blows into the cabin, carrying with it a stench like charred wood.

A beautiful woman steps aboard. "You are at Cordon Four," she says, her eyes skimming over us. "I am GM487. Follow me, please."

GM487. A genetically modified human. We call them Gems, though I've never seen one before today. I stagger across the hold, craning my neck for another glimpse of her. They come from Ordinance, the only city-state we share an alliance with. Alara focuses its efforts on building physical shields against the curtain, while Ordinance works to develop genetic ones. I try to remember what Dad told me about them. Altered postconception, during the embryonic stage, in ways that mimic the genetic coding of Subpars and Conjurors. But it's risky; the manipulations destroy more embryos than they alter.

The woman—her insignia says COMPLIANCE REGULATOR—examines our Radbands as we line up beside the door. The inside of her forearm is illuminated beneath the skin with glowing blue symbols I don't recognize. I suppose it's the designation Ordinance assigned her. A Codev, I think they call it.

"Orion," she says, glancing at my sleeve, at the lead ore scout patch I wear with less pride than I used to. "Your director warned me about you. Can I expect your compliance?"

I hesitate long enough that Dram kicks my foot. "Yes," I say. She doesn't know about the vials of Dad's compound hidden inside my suit. Whatever else Cranny warned her about, it wasn't that. She looks past me at Dram, and something in her composed expression distorts, like the wood around a screw turned too far. He carries his father's features—the eyes, the jaw, even his hair is like Arrun's was when he was sent here. It's possible she knew him. It's possible she said the same thing to him that she said to me.

Your director warned me about you. Can I expect your compliance? If we comply, do we quietly sicken and die, or are things here better than we've been told?

I have my arms around Winn, so I notice when the Gem skips her without checking for a Radband. I suppose she's been warned about her, too. *The Natural girl who doesn't stand a chance.*

"Follow me," the Gem says. "You must be properly equipped before you mine the sands." Her condition gives me hope. She is more healthy looking than anyone in Outpost Five.

I step off the hover, and my heart plummets.

"We're in hell," Dram mutters.

This is worse—so much worse than I imagined. Black smoke billows from burning heaps of rubble. It's impossible to tell the time of day—the daylight's blocked by low-hanging clouds that drift in a listless red haze. Bits of ash and cinder float through the air like flaming butterflies. A glowing orange piece lands on Winn's head, and I pinch it out with my fingers.

We wind past rows of small tents, their canvas A-frames flapping like warning flags. Our guide shows us a collection of sparse buildings: privies, a bathhouse with a collapsed wall and rusty water spigots, a ration station, guardhouse, and infirmary.

I try to decide what Dad would call these living conditions. His term "archaic" is too charming for this bleak existence. I look over the space and settle on "barely habitable."

Beside the guardhouse three massive flags beat the air: one with the seal of Alara, a black flag with a red stripe signifying the cordon, and an indicator flag. Yellow with two orange stripes. Congress and its love for indicators—as if the flashfall doesn't already shout, *Danger! Keep Away!*

Our Gem leader doesn't take note of the flags. Her eyes follow the swirling dance of tiny insects as they whirl above us in the thick red haze. Their bodies glimmer.

She turns toward the nearest guard. "Emberflies! Raise the alert!" The guard, a male Gem with a glowing blue Codev on his arm, hauls on the ropes of a fourth flagpole. Within seconds, a solid red flag rises above the others.

"Cover your noses and mouths," the Gem commands. "The haze has brought them low, and they fill the air—like spores from a plant."

I whirl to yank Winn's neck cloth over her face, my gaze darting to the creatures I had mistaken for sparks of ember.

Emberflies.

On our Radbands, a red indicator is the final warning, the step before death. I tighten my neck cloth and watch the red flag, thinking that the flashfall is different here, more than air and elements. It is *alive.*

Ahead of us, Ennis stumbles. He hunches forward, trying to drag in a breath, and coughs, his eyes wide and tearing.

"Ennis?" Dram takes his arm. "What happened?"

Ennis flails his arms, gasping.

GM487 strides toward him. "Your comrade inhaled an emberfly."

"How do you *inhale* an insect?" Graham says.

"They attach to particles in the air. I warned you—"

"How do we help him?" Dram demands. He struggles to support Ennis as he thrashes, his eyes wild and bulging.

I slip his other arm over my shoulders. "He needs an Oxinator!"

The Gem shakes her head. "I'm afraid there's nothing to be done. I suggest you don't watch."

I stare at the Gem, openmouthed. I had forgotten to fear the beautiful things. I've barely processed the thought before I've got GM487 up against a wall, my fists clenched in her pristine gray and red uniform. "Help him!"

"Orion!" Dram hisses.

The woman's gaze lowers to where Ennis kicks and sputters on the ground, white foam dribbling down his chin. "There is no help for him." She pulls free from my grasp and straightens her jacket. "You will learn this quickly." She turns and strides toward a massive fence. "Leave the body."

I don't recognize the sounds coming out of my mouth—like a sob that twists into the snarls of a wounded animal. Dram catches me, and my feet come off the ground as he locks his arms around me.

"Ennis!" I cry.

"He's already gone," Graham murmurs.

He is worse than gone. As we watch, Ennis's body swells as if he's being pumped with a bellows. Blood seeps from his unseeing eyes. Embers continue to swirl past us.

"Protect yourselves," Reeves says, pulling his neck cloth up over his nose and mouth.

I cover my face as we head toward the glowing bit of horizon that is brighter than all the rest.

The flash curtain.

———

It's the most beautiful thing I've ever seen. I can't compare it to the real sky, or a sunrise or sunset, but the flash curtain drapes across the horizon with all the colors I've been told about. It shimmers in waves of luminescent brilliance, a terrifying, radioactive rainbow. It's endlessly shifting and changing, as if it's trying to contain its own energy. The particles shift on wind currents like luminous clouds that hug the burnt sands and stretch upward for kilometers in a massive wall.

We stand behind the fence of the cordon encampment, far away from it, but it has never been so loud inside me. I feel the shift of its vaporous, auroral bands, like a hand moving a bow across the strings of an instrument. It called to me before. Now it demands I answer back.

Winn gasps and turns her head. Even with our new eye-shields and the clear hoods of our cirium suits, it's hard to look at the curtain.

I'm not sure why they gave us earpieces. Maybe they want us to feel like we actually stand a chance out here. Or maybe they want us to experience the horror of hearing each other burn up. But it's Winn I hear in my ears, her breathing a step beyond panicked. I grasp her arms and force her head to mine.

"I'm right here," I tell her. The best comfort I can offer is that she won't die alone. And she won't die until I've done everything possible to get us out of this hell. At least the ember-flies are gone; the red flag is nowhere in sight.

Graham takes Winn's hands and crouches in front of her. A hiss of pain escapes his lips as he puts weight on his injured leg. He picks up her dust bucket and wraps her gloved hand around the handle.

"We've got a job to do, girlie," he says in his gruff voice. "We're a team—just like in the tunnels. You just step where I step, all right?" She nods, and he hands her one of the metal sifters we've been given. Her hand, in its too-big glove, grips the sifter tightly.

GM487 herds us into a chute so narrow that we have to

stand single file. A blast from a horn cuts through the air, making me jolt. "When you hear that sound at the start of the day," she says, "you will gather here, at the corral."

So there's a name for this towering white monstrosity, I think, tipping my head back to take it all in. White paint peels from the sides of the wide wooden beams that divide the area into a series of pens. I wonder why anyone bothered to paint it in the first place. Maybe so we could find our way back to it through land that is a palette of ash and blood and coal and rust. Embers catch on my suit and slowly burn through. I brush them off before they reach my skin.

"This signal"—she pauses as an even louder buzzer drowns out her voice—"tells you to go through the turnstiles and proceed to your authorized mining sector. If you collect two grams of flash dust, you receive rations and rest."

Ahead of us, Gems push past the turnstiles. Some of them look at us, assessing, intelligent. They don't wear eyeshields, and most have their headpieces pushed back. Men and women, mostly young, but not one of them looks like the other. I have never seen such a variety of skin tones and coloring. They are exotic and alluring—unnaturally so—but what compels me to stare after them is the one characteristic they all share. Endurance. Whatever flags are raised here, these people will not succumb easily to the flashfall.

And now I know the feeling inside me isn't awe. It's resentment.

"Orion?" Winn asks in my earpiece. I realize I've stopped walking. The entire group has passed me. I squeeze her hand and lead her toward the turnstile.

My emotions tangle, fused with the same burn that drove

me to climb the sign in Outpost Five. I force myself to breathe, to think hard about everything that happened after I made that reckless move. Barely an hour here, and I'm already struggling to comply.

The director was right to warn them about me.

"Proceed to your sector, Subpars," the regulator says.

"What if we collect less than two grams?" Gabe asks.

"Then you receive neither rations nor rest." She points to a figure on the other side of the fence. "That Conjuror has been outside the fence for two nights now. She will not survive a third."

The woman sifts through the ashes on her knees. Instead of hands, crude metal sifters have been fitted to the ends of her stumps. They are pronged, like oversized, curved forks, with one tine bent away from the rest in a garish representation of a thumb. Her right hand has a screen of mesh exactly like the sifters they've supplied us with. It looks like it belongs to part of a machine, not a person.

"Appendages," Gabe says. "They vary depending upon the work Congress assigns a Tempered Conjuror."

"That's barbaric," Graham grumbles.

"They're considered a mercy. She wouldn't have survived out here with only stumps."

"You saw this in Alara?" I ask.

Gabe shakes his head, still watching the woman. "No. This sort of Tempering is . . . punishment. Reserved for resistant Conjurors."

I look back at the woman. The *resistant Conjuror.*

Sweat streaks the soot and blood on her face. Her pail lies on its side as she struggles to transfer the flash dust. She lifts her head as we pass, looking us over intently. The lower half of her face is covered with her neck cloth, but I'm struck with a sense of recognition. Brown eyes.

Roran has this woman's eyes. *She's alive. My people are survivors.*

I step closer, my heart galloping, wanting to be right—needing to be certain. Her skin is like his—a few shades darker than mine. She wears her dark hair pulled back, but it's a match for his. She focuses once more on her task, and it's then—the way her brows draw together—that I know it's her. Roran makes the same expression when he alters the rock in his hand.

My fingers twist around the fence. "Mere?" I shout. She doesn't look at me so I rattle the fence. "Mere!"

"What are you doing?" Dram asks. We've reached a metal turnstile, and he pushes through.

It's my turn. A line of people waits behind me. The Conjie woman's looking at me now, and I rip my hand from my pocket and press it to the fence. Roran's flower is tucked against my palm.

Her eyes widen. She pushes herself to her feet.

"Proceed through the turnstile, Subpar," calls GM487. I step through backward, my gaze riveted on the woman running toward me. The metal bars click around me as I press through.

"Return to your sector, Conjuror," a guard shouts.

Mere crashes against the fence just as I pass through the corral. I push my hands through the rusted wire and clasp her wrists just above her appendages.

"Roran?" she asks. Even her voice is a match for his, with the lyrical accent he works desperately to hide.

"He's safe." I slip the blossom inside her sleeve. A body shoves me from behind, and I stumble forward.

"Subpar, proceed!" GM487 commands again.

"I'll help you!" I shout, keeping Mere in my sights as I walk. She clasps Roran's flower to her chest.

"I'll help *you,* Subpar!" A smile breaks over her face. "What's your name?"

I feel myself smiling back. Something about this woman makes me feel invincible. "Orion!" I call. The throng of miners pushes me farther into the cordon, but she grabs her pail and runs to keep pace with me.

"A good name," she says. "A warrior's name."

For the first time, my name is not a joke. This woman has seen the stars. "A hunter's name," I say.

Dram threads his way past the people stepping around me. "Let's go, *hunter,*" he says. "You've got two grams of flash dust to find, plus extra for your new friend."

"She's Roran's mother," I say, following him into the swirling winds.

"So I gathered." He studies me through his eyeshields. "What did you give her?"

"Hope," I whisper.

I clutch my pail and wade into the flaming debris the curtain spits toward us. I found Roran's mother in a place filled with death and fear and fire.

Maybe I am the hunter my mother named me for. Perhaps I'll find the flash dust we need to survive the night.

Hope.

The word whirls through me, elusive, burning, and powerful.

We are going to die.

Beneath the cirium suit, my body shakes like I've climbed too high, too fast. I plunge my sifter into the sand again and again, but come up with nothing except scorched ground. I rake my hand through the burnt sands, and it feels like I'm holding my palm over flame.

"Let me sift," Gabe says. "Nothing can hurt these hands." He cups his cirium fingers around a handful of sand. "You just tell me where."

I wish I could. Flash dust is different from cirium. The conditions of Cordon Four don't help in sorting it out, either. All I want to do is burrow under the ground.

The winds kicked up an hour ago. I'm not sure what normal is around here, but this feels a lot like a flash storm. My Subpar senses are screaming at me.

"Never thought I'd miss nine," Dram says.

"Never thought I'd miss Outpost Five."

We stand like a couple of hands clasped in prayer, Winn tucked between us. Her skin is blistering beneath her suit.

"There's nothing here," Graham says. He lies on his side in the black and red sand, sifting sand into his pail. His left leg is swollen twice its normal size. Apparently, the parasites inside his knee have no more love for Cordon Four than we do. "You need to go farther," he says.

"We're not leaving you," I say for the third time.

"Shouting the words doesn't make them right, girlie," he says, cursing and tossing his pail aside. "Dram, I expect you to heed me, boyo. You know what's right."

Winn cries out. Her whimpering's been a constant sound,

like the wind, but this cry is new. I grip her headpiece and turn her so I can see her face. A blood vessel's broken in her eye.

I pull her doll from her pouch and tuck it in her hand. "She's scared, Winn. You need to tell her that everything's going to be okay." Before we left Outpost Five, I took Winn's yellow dress and cut it down to fit her doll. I'm not sure how long it will survive the flaming ash of the cordon.

"Don't be afraid. I'm here," she croons to the doll, smoothing gloved hands over it like it's got flowing curls instead of frayed climbing rope for hair.

"What's her name?" I ask.

"Len," she whispers.

Len. Lenore. Tears burn the back of my throat. "That's a good name." My eyes meet Dram's.

Reeves jogs toward us. "I found a shelter! It's about half a kilometer east."

Shelter! My gaze shifts to Graham. Half a kilometer might as well be ten kilometers. He can't even walk ten steps.

"Time for you kids to get going," he says.

Reeves hands me his pail, then stoops and lifts Graham, who hits him in the arm. "Put me down. Run with the others to safety."

"I can run and carry you," Reeves says.

"You're as stubborn as Scout," Graham mutters.

"I'll take that as a compliment," Reeves says.

Dram lifts Winn in his arms, and Gabe and I follow.

———

The cirium shelter is the size of an air cave. There is no chance we will all fit.

"Get inside!" Dram shoves me in behind Winn.

"Not without you!" I yank him inside, and we squeeze into a corner.

Wind howls past the entrance, and burning cinders pelt Graham and Reeves.

"Get them in!" Gabe shouts. He's hanging halfway out himself.

"Put Winn on my shoulders," Dram says, and he stoops as I boost Winn up. She clambers onto his shoulders, hunching her back to avoid the roof.

Graham pushes Reeves into the gap. "Away from the door, boyo," he says gruffly. He grunts as a gust of burning dust slams him so hard he stumbles from the entrance.

"Graham!" Gabe catches his arm, hauls him back.

"Put me on your shoulders, Reeves!" I cry.

"Ceiling's too low," Dram says softly. His gaze is fixed on Graham.

"What are you doing?" Gabe demands. Graham's pulling off his suit.

"Give this to the little mite," Graham gasps. "Another layer to keep her safe."

"Graham." My soft cry penetrates the eerie stillness of the shelter. Out in the cauldron, his eyes meet mine—the man who taught me to raise an axe and fight my way out of despair, out of fear. As I watch him drag his suit off and push it into Gabe's outstretched metal hands, I realize he's still teaching me.

"Don't cry for me, girlie," he says. "I'm going to see the sky today." He drags his mouthpiece off. Chunks of crystallized particles pelt him like hail.

"Close your eyes, Winn," I say. But I don't. I can give Graham this much. I will watch the sacrifice he makes for us.

"Let me go!" he shouts to Gabe. Wind gusts, taking his hair and eyebrows; his skin pits with holes.

Gabe releases him. Wind sucks Graham away from the entrance, turning him on one foot like a zealous dance partner.

"Graham!" I shout, as if I can heal him with my voice. He finds my eyes across the blowing cinders. His stream with blood.

"You've done your mom proud," he shouts. "Both of you." Then he hobbles backward into swirling debris.

The shelter is silent but for the radiation winds whining beyond the entrance and Winn's sobs.

"We're getting out of here." Dram pulls a metal tube from his pocket.

The weapon hasn't discharged, but as Dram holds up a flash wand, I feel a concussive blast rip through my shock.

"Holy fire," Reeves says. "How the hell did you steal one of those?"

"I didn't. Graham found it." He turns the cylinder in his palm. The metal's scraped, like it's already been used in battle.

"It's empty," Gabe says.

"Not for long."

Gabe shakes his head. "We can't get close enough to the curtain to collect enough dust."

"We don't need to." Dram's gaze slips outside the shelter, to where Graham stood just moments ago.

My gaze skips from Dram to Reeves to Gabe, trying to make sense of their hesitation. They seem to be seeing something I'm not.

"Orion . . ." Dram looks at me, his blue eyes haunted. "You don't know what the flash dust is, do you?"

"The flash curtain burns up the sand . . ."

"Not the sand, Rye." He looks pained, like he has to draw venom from my arm and he knows he's going to have to hurt me to save me.

I look out at the place where Graham stood. Now that the winds have died, I can see the sand more clearly. Flash dust sparkles where the storm swept over him.

The realization slams into me. "Oh, fire," I whisper. The dust. The flash dust.

It's what remains after the curtain consumes a person.

"I'm going to be sick," I murmur.

"Just breathe." He tries to give me space, but there is none. Gabe stares at the ground. Reeves's eyes bounce away from mine. They knew. How ironic that everyone knew but the ore scout. No wonder I couldn't find the element.

Another thought hits me, and it's so terrible I can barely breathe. "When did he give you that flash wand?"

"At Outpost Five," Dram says. "He found it the day they created nine. He's been holding on to it a long time."

Cranny thinks I have something of his. Graham's words the night the director withheld the treatment for his leg.

"He planned to die."

"He didn't know how or when," Dram says. "He just told me to be ready."

I take the wand. The metallic canister slides across my palm, lighter than a memorial pendant. I hand it to Gabe.

"Sift the sand beside the shelter. Pour the flash dust into this." My voice is shaky as a frayed rope. Gabe crouches and reaches his cirium hands outside.

The Congress forces Subpars to mine the dust that powers

their weapons—to *be* the ammunition in their weapons. They don't expect us to figure out how to turn it back on them.

But the caver who endured ore mites and cordon winds knew we'd find a way.

Ah, Graham. One last lesson.

FIFTEEN

14.6 grams flash dust

THE STORM LASTS less than an hour. We leave Winn in the shelter and press closer to the curtain. I've given up hope, so I let my anger fuel me instead. I'm determined Graham won't have died in vain. The shift in attitude affects my focus, and soon I'm picking up traces of flash dust like they're calling my name.

I'm lead ore scout once more.

Gabe's cirium hands strain the burnt sands faster and with more success than our thick gloves and sifters, but our pails slowly begin to fill. I lead us to a deposit and then we all drop down and mine the Congress's precious element.

"How long have you known?" I ask Dram. I can still hardly believe it. I never dreamed our government was this depraved. Or this desperate.

He doesn't answer right away, but taps his sifter into his pail. Finally, he meets my eyes, his own red-rimmed. I feel a punch of guilt. If possible, he loved Graham even more than I did. At least I still had Dad after Mom and Wes died. Dram has lost everyone close to him. Everyone but me.

"Graham told me," he says. "When he gave me the flash wand. I didn't know how to tell you."

"How is it even possible? They're just human bodies."

"They're not just human bodies," he counters. "Everything is altered by the flashfall—transformed by elements we still don't understand—and then the curtain alters them again when . . ." He trails off, and I have a vivid memory of Graham spinning on one foot before the flashfall swallowed him beside our shelter.

"Think of how the curtain affects living things," Gabe says. "It infuses everything with a bit of its substance. It doesn't incinerate its own elements, so it's left behind as flash dust.

"And in terms of it being ammunition?" He sifts the dust through his metal fingers. "We're talking about traces of the *flash curtain*—unexpended energy."

I still see Graham telling me my mother would be proud.

"Why don't they just have machines do this?" I grumble, my hands burning as I sift the particles into my pail.

"Machines malfunction this close to the curtain," Gabe answers.

"That's not the only reason," Reeves murmurs. "If we die out here, we're more dust in someone's pail." He slips his hand beneath his headpiece to swipe the blood trickling from his nose. His skin gleams, pale as bone.

I share a glance with Dram. Something's wrong with Reeves. He's sick—sick in a way that none of the rest of us are, which tells me it's something other than the cordon.

My stomach twists. I don't want to put a name to it. Not yet.

"What do you think is the other reason?" I say instead.

"It's a convenient way for the Congress to get rid of us."

"But we supply them with cirium."

"Which is probably why we're still breathing." He coughs, and I avert my eyes, half expecting him to vomit again. Dad's voice in my head catalogs all his symptoms, so I tune it out and listen for the elements in the sand instead.

"Wait," I command. I stand and face the curtain, closing my eyes. "Something's happening." I kneel and press my palms to the ground.

"Another storm?" Dram asks.

"Different," I murmur. "Hold this." I hand him my pail and pull my gloves off.

"Orion!"

"Just for a second." I set my hands on the sand and bite back a scream. Blistering welts form over my palms even as I shove them back into my gloves. But it was enough. Enough to read the elements pulsing across the cordon.

"We need to get back." I stand. "We have enough dust— enough for Mere and Winn, too. Let's go—quickly."

"What is it?" Dram hands me my bucket and jogs at my side.

I force my legs to go faster. "Sandstorm. Any moment now."

"Fire," Dram mutters.

"You guys head back," Reeves says. "I'll get Winn." He sprints past us toward the shelter, and I stare after him.

"He'll make it," Dram says. "He's still got time."

So he's drawn the same conclusion I have. And he's not putting a name to it yet, either.

———

Flash storms hint at their approach, streaking the sky with orange virga and sending ahead warning winds of sulfur and particle dust. Cordon sandstorms rise up like a snake striking. You barely register the fangs in your skin, and you've got venom coursing through your body.

We run for the corral, its white top the only indicator of sanctuary in the black sand swirling around us. It hasn't reached us yet—but I can feel that a massive wave of sand is about to break over the cordon. If it reaches us, it will swallow us down to the bowels of this hell.

"Almost there," Dram huffs beside me. Gabe ran on ahead of us. He's probably tucked safely behind the fence by now.

I'm slowing. Even with fear propelling me forward, I don't have the kind of stamina to maintain this speed—especially not through burning sand with the weight of a cirium suit slowing me down.

"There!" Dram points to a heap of rubble that looks like it might have once been a bridge. "Climb!" He leaps for a twisted projection of metal and hauls himself up.

This is like the Range. My hands slide into grooves, and my feet push off pitted cracks in the stone. Dram grasps my arm just as I reach the top.

"Lie down!" He yanks me over the side just as the wall of sand hits.

We flatten ourselves, facedown, our hands and feet anchored to bits of metal and concrete as the cloud of sand erupts over us. Sand fills the air, bites at us through our suits, until I feel like an ore mite's parasites are working their way in. The air clears of sand a moment later—the length of a few held breaths.

"Still with me, ore scout?" Dram asks, coughing like dust got through his headpiece.

"No," I murmur hoarsely.

The corral buzzer sounds. Congress, calling for its collection.

———

We empty our flash dust onto the scale one at a time, adding the dust slowly, until it shows 2.0 grams. We keep all extra hidden in our pockets.

"Deposit accepted," a voice says through a speaker. "Proceed through the turnstile."

We shuffle through, toward the small tents that await us beyond the corral fence.

"Fewer people," Dram murmurs. He pulls off his headpiece and eyeshields.

"Probably the sandstorm."

We search for Winn and Reeves, but the first few tents are filled with Gems.

"She's with the Conjie woman," Reeves calls, poking his head around a tent flap. "She met us beside the deposit with extra dust for Winn. The kid took to her like she took to Roran."

So Mere helped *us*, after all.

"I can't believe you have the strength to smile," Dram says.

"I can't believe you two have the strength to stand," Reeves adds, coughing into the dirt. Blood spatters the ash at his feet. He lifts his head and drags a hand through his hair. "Guess the sand got to me after all." His brow furrows, and he looks down at his hand. Long strands of blond hair fill his fist. "Fire," he whispers, meeting our eyes. "Don't say it. It doesn't matter anyway."

Dram and I don't say it. None of us want to acknowledge the horrible truth of Reeves's radiation sickness.

The sands didn't get to Reeves, but the cordon shards in Outpost Five did.

SIXTEEN

17.6 grams flash dust

I HAVE NEVER seen so many genetically modified humans in one place before. Well, actually, I'd never seen a single Gem before the sands, but they fill the tents here. According to Gabe, their service in the cordons is part of our alliance with Ordinance.

The way I can identify the non-Gems is that the rest of us wear our terror like it's part of a uniform. We all belong to the society of the soon-to-die.

But not the Gems.

"You resent them," Dram says, following my gaze.

I empty my nutri-pac into my mouth. Everyone gets purple foil here, even Winn. The Congress must want to fatten us up before we become the glittering dust beside the curtain. I crumple the packet in my fist.

"Rye?" Dram asks. "You know they're not here by choice, right?"

"Don't ask me to feel sympathy for them," I say.

"So they have a biological Radsuit and we don't," Dram

says. "You want to hate them for it? Should Winn hate us for being Subpars—because we can survive exposure that she can't?"

I give him a dirty look. "They can actually *live* here."

"This isn't living. Not for anyone." Dram steps into his suit. Together, we assist Winn into hers. She hasn't spoken since we watched Graham die yesterday. Her small body shakes as I draw her arms through the sleeves.

"I won't leave your side," I tell her. I have nothing to offer but inadequate words.

The first buzzer sounds.

"Quick, now," Dram says, guiding her foot into Graham's suit. We hurry to fit it around her. I tuck her doll safely inside. Winn stares at nothing.

Lenore would know what to do for her. The thought tears at my heart like a knife.

"You still with us, ore scout?" Dram asks.

I drag my thoughts to the pressing concerns of the moment—a corral and a mining sector and an impossible task in a furnace.

"Mere," Winn says, her face brightening.

Mere whisks into our tent and gathers the child in her arms. "Is there a little girl somewhere under all this?" Winn smiles. "How about I carry you on my back like a monkey?" She kneels, and Winn clambers on, holding tight.

"I'll look after her," Mere says to us. "Go as far as you need to."

My eyes lift to the little girl clinging to Mere. "Her doll's name is Len," I whisper.

Mere smiles. "She told me."

Something heavy lifts from my shoulders. I guess Winn found her words, after all.

Reeves waits for us with his back propped against the fence. He wears Lenore's tie in his hair and a smirk on his face. "We need to discuss our escape plan," he says. "I feel like I've experienced all that Cordon Four has to offer."

"Agreed," Gabe says beside him. "I'm not sure how many more sandstorms I can outrun."

"The flash wand is half full," I murmur. "We need more dust."

The second buzzer sounds.

"Let's go find some," Dram says.

I pull my headpiece on and push through the turnstile. I am back to weighing my freedom one gram at a time.

———

Our determination evaporates over the course of the day, until it's all we can do just to keep moving—keep breathing—out there beside the curtain. Especially Reeves. He's fading faster than all of us. From watching the scale at night, I've learned what 2 grams of flash dust looks and feels like. I made certain no one was looking when I dropped it into his bucket.

Freedom will have to wait. We're barely mining enough to survive.

We come back from our assigned sector covered in sand. It penetrates our suits so that the clothes beneath catch the crystalline shards. We leave them outside the tent and climb inside in our underwear. Radiation poisoning comes in many forms here, so we must avoid exposure however we can. Dram crouches to seal the tent flap. He's not wearing a shirt.

At Outpost Five, men and women dressed on opposite sides of a curtain inside the Rig. Here at Cordon Four, we just tear our suits off and stagger into our tent. No one has the energy to care about privacy. We have persevered through too much to die for modesty's sake.

"Here." Dram tosses me two foil packets. I'm too tired to ask who he swiped them from. I'm not sure the guards around here even care if Dram robs them blind. The curtain will take us soon enough. I tear into a packet with shaking hands. I've never been so hungry.

He drops a bolt gun on our mattress and turns to take his pants off.

"Where did you find a light bolt gun in a place with no tunnels?" I ask, ripping the second nutri-pac open.

"It's not a bolt gun." Dram tosses his pants outside our flimsy shelter. He turns back and my eyes stay too long on parts of him I never see. I study the words on the packet as if I care what vitamins and nutrients it's supplying me with.

"You stole a weapon?" I ask. "What if the guards find out?"

"Says the girl carrying a half-loaded flash wand."

I sigh and toss the empty packets on the ground.

My eyes stray back to Dram's chest. I long to touch him, to see if his skin feels as smooth and hard as it looks. He kneels beside me, and I make room for him on the floor pallet. He lies down, and I feel every part along his side where our bodies touch. We touched all the time in the tunnels, but this is different.

His memorial pendants hang down his chest, green and gold. He should have a third, for his father, but Arrun Berrends was given no Burning Day. His ashes are out there somewhere, beyond the thin walls of our tent, swept along with the burning sands.

Under the cover of our shared blanket, Dram and I examine the flash wand. Our Radbands glow, pale green and yellow.

"We need 9.2 grams more." He taps the indicator on the side of the reservoir. "We could go closer to the curtain—past the assigned sectors, where no one else has mined. There will be dust there."

"Only one of us needs to go that far," I reply.

I wait for him to protest. To say that I can't take the risk and to announce he'll be the one to fight through radiation to mine the sands we need. But he doesn't. He just holds my gaze steady with his. I am Outpost Five's lead ore scout. If anyone has a chance to find what we need, it's me.

I'll be the one to go.

The moment the thought settles in, a sense of peace envelops me. It's as if my whole life has been leading to this task—a final test that will lead to freedom, one way or another. But just in case our weapon doesn't work and we die out there, there is something I need to do at least once in this life.

I turn toward Dram, and he reaches for me. He kisses me, and my breath catches, like I've got a faulty Oxinator. He smiles, and I feel it against my mouth. I don't need breath—not for this. I throw my arms around his neck, and he makes a sound, a hum and a sigh mixed together. I lose myself to his touch, his taste. I'm floating, outside myself, like Serum 129, only I'm aware of every sensation, anchored to this moment by Dram's touch.

He pulls back, and I catch my breath. "I've been waiting a long time for this," he whispers.

My eyes widen. "But I thought—"

"How could you not know?"

"You and Marin . . ."

His smile fades. "She and I aren't . . . We don't have that kind of . . ." He sighs. "We were just a distraction for each other, Orion." He frames my face with his hands. "She isn't the one I crawled into the tunnels each day for."

His words unlock something inside me. I know the cost of the tunnels. Especially for Dram, squeezing himself through the neck of nine. Not just for cirium. For *me.*

This time, when we reach for each other, he angles his head. It brings us closer, closer than before. I've always been the one out front, leading him into the unknown—but this time I let Dram guide me.

He captures my mouth on a breathless sigh. I'm reminded of the first time I felt his lips, when we shared a breath outside the air cave. I saved his life—right before he turned around and saved mine. I've lost count of how many times we've done that over the years. Surely I can do it again come the morning.

He pulls away to press kisses along my neck. I close my eyes and thread my fingers through his hair. "I didn't know," I say.

"You were distracted by flash bats and orbies and tunnel gulls." A soft smile lifts his lips. "We were too busy saving each other's lives to figure out what it all meant."

"Then we should make up for lost time." I let my hands wander the hard planes of his chest, the way I've been wanting to, and he takes my hands in his.

"We have all the time in the world," he whispers.

His hands caress my back, slip down to my waist. My palms find the dip and swell of his muscles as he leans over me. We take our time learning each other like there's no hurry, like his words are true.

Like this moment isn't our last.

SEVENTEEN

19.2 grams flash dust

I TUG ON my cirium suit and decide that today is the last day I will contemplate my imminent death. By tonight, I will either already be through with it, or I'll be starting a brand-new life beyond the flashfall, far from the sands, far from Outpost Five.

This, I tell myself, is what I should focus on. But the places beyond the flash curtain are hazy, imaginary places in my mind, pieced together by the random bits of information I have about the protected city. I can't make sense of half the things Gabe tells me, and even then, I'm pretty sure he's only given me part of the picture.

I press my hand against the weapon hidden in my pocket, the flash wand I'm risking my life to fill.

"Just nine grams more," Dram murmurs. He checks my suit, as he's done nearly every day for the past five years. It hits me that this is the last time. I'm wearing pieces of cirium we ripped off the sides of a shelter, and he tightens the straps holding them secure beneath my suit.

"This is going to be heavy," he murmurs, lifting my cirium-lined arm.

I nod. Better exhausted than dead. We've done what we can to give me a fighting chance. When he's done, I check his suit, ignoring my shaking hands and the feeling that I need a pail to throw up in.

"Are you ready?" he asks.

I open my mouth, but words fail me. He slides aside my trembling fingers and pulls the final wrapped vial from my suit. He twists the stopper, and I drink down the last of my father's theory—the barrier that may or may not be enough to protect me from the full impact of the flash curtain. I drop the vial and crunch it under my boot, pulverizing the bits of glass. I don't want any part of this traced back to Dad.

"In case I didn't make it clear last night," Dram murmurs. "I love you, Orion Denman."

I can't get words past my tight throat. But Dram and I have never needed words to say the important things. His lips find mine in a way that feels familiar now, and I share a breath with him one last time.

———

The buzzer sounds. Dram and the others pass through the turnstiles and walk our ordered route. I sprint past them. I need to go much, much farther.

Gems throw me curious looks from the other side of the chute. No one is ever eager to head out—especially not Subpars. I force myself to slow. My mission is pointless if I draw too much attention to myself.

Wes's memorial pendant slides against my chest. I wear it

now, beside my mother's, and the cool yellow glass presses my skin, just above my heart.

"You with me today, Wes?" I murmur. I feel him somehow, a soft warmth like how I imagine sunlight feels. As I run, I shut out the glowing orange haze, the dark places of perpetual night, and let my mind go to the past, to the memories I've kept buried. There was a song I used to sing to Wes. At the end, I'd lift him up and tickle his tummy, and he would gasp, "Again, again!"And I would do it until my arms ached.

A flash vulture eyes me from a pile of rubble. Its dark wings extend, and it begins its dance of anticipation. I wish I had Dram's light gun. I'd shoot a red bolt straight through its head. Instead, I grip the shard of cirium that I formed into a knife and sprint forward. My breath seizes in my chest as I dart past it. The vulture screeches, and I see the shadow of movement out the corner of my eye. It circles above me, swooping through the flaming dust, its leathery wings adapted to the harsh environment like it was born for it. I suppose it was.

My steps slow as an idea forms in my mind. I stop and look up. The vulture cries above me, a hoarse shout of triumph. Its bones protrude, pushing against the black skin as if they might poke through. It's starving. The curtain takes everything for itself, not leaving enough for its children. It drops to the flaming dust three meters away. I need it to come closer.

"Hungry?" I call. It tilts its head, like conversation with its prey is unfamiliar. I push the layers of my left sleeve up, exposing the underside of my forearm. The top is plated with a narrow strip of cirium. I drag my makeshift knife along my skin, shallow, but enough to give the sight and scent of blood. I step toward the vulture, extending my arm.

"How hungry are you? Enough to come at me while I'm still standing?" It caws and flaps its massive wings. The wings I want.

This creature has armor of its own. Protection born of the burnt sands, and I intend to take it. It hops away and performs another dance, bobbing its massive torso and holding out its wings. It's waiting for me to die.

I collapse on the ground, grunting when the pieces of cirium dig into my back. My heart thunders in my chest, but I force myself to lie still. I let my mind slip back to Wes. To lying beside him, telling him stories until he fell asleep. The vulture flies closer. It takes everything in me to leave my bloody arm exposed, a vulnerable offering for a carnivore. I imagine I'm back in nine with Dram, that we're hugging the walls of a gulls' nest, waiting for the mothers to leave.

A beak pecks my arm, and I roll and seize the bird. One hand wraps around its leg, and the other drives my pointed shard of cirium through its body. It flaps wildly, screeching and pulling me along the dust. My hands slip over its protruding ribs as I wrestle it beneath me and shove the blade through its skull.

"Don't think about it, don't think about it," I mutter, wedging my blade into the cartilage between the creature's wings and body. I seize one of the tough, leathery wings, set my foot against the body, and pull. It tears free with a popping of bone and tendon. I carve the gristle off the large wing bone to make myself a handhold, grasping it like a shield. The fiery debris touches it and slides away. I waft it before me and the air clears. I will be able to see past the particles and ash as I run.

The humid winds carry the scent of blood, inviting more flash vultures. Four of them circle above me, drawn by the carnage. I wipe the blade and stash it in the arm holster I fashioned. A screech just above me draws my attention; at least a half dozen vultures circle. I hold the wings against my body and run.

Half the vultures drop and tear into the carcass. The others dive after me.

I no longer avoid the horrific beauty of the flash curtain. It stretches before me like a living, seething being. I run past broken road supports and hollowed-out buildings. The vehicles Gabe calls "cars" and "buses." The bones of Mother Nature's feast. My lungs burn, and I push myself harder, until everything passes in a blur of empty nothingness.

Just over my head, the vultures screech, spurred by the scent of blood. These creatures aren't waiting for my death; they are eager to make it happen. Talons tangle in my hair, knocking me off my feet. If I stay down, I'm dead—before I've even reached the curtain. I slash out with my shard of cirium and fight my way to my feet. Pushing past beaks and bodies, I run. One by one, they turn back. The hope of a meal is not enough to draw them past their boundaries.

I have reached the perimeter of the flash curtain. It is too bright, even with my eyeshields. I lift the vulture wing in front of my headpiece and peer between the feathers. Emberflies swirl around me, so many I can barely distinguish them from the flaming particles. I sweep the wing through them and run blindly forward, knowing that I will be either consumed or saved in what happens next.

The curtain pulls me. Its colors shoot like light from a

prism, around me—through me. I am fuchsia, emerald, a thousand shades of violet.

I am still alive.

I drop to my knees. No one tells you about the weight of the curtain. Its radioactive heat presses down on me like the rock walls of nine.

It emits a sound, thrumming with a rapid pulse that I feel down to my core. It tunes me like an instrument, tightening my strings until I am part of its discordant vibrations.

I force my watering eyes to search the ground and turn my scout's senses to the dirt and rock beneath my hands. Seven years of caving, of learning the heartbeat of the tunnels, comes to the surface of my awareness. I push my hands through the sand feeling for the pulse of matter that is unlike any other. It is alive. I am drawn to it, and it to me.

And I know I must go farther still.

I crawl, weeping, dragging myself closer to the curtain.

I feel it before I see it. Flash dust glitters before me, sparkling over an expanse of ten meters. I strain it through my sifter and pour it into my pail. Human lives made this—mothers and fathers and children whose lives were destroyed when the flash curtain fell.

The weight of the curtain presses, presses, and I breathe as if Cranny has assigned me another defective air tank. There's less than a handful of flash dust in the bucket. Not enough.

I force myself to my feet and stagger along the perimeter of the curtain. I am a dragon, breathing fire, only the fire is inside me. I am burning, my blood boiling—but no—it is just my cirium suit, breaking away in fragments of ash and dust.

I will be dust.

I collapse on the sand.

"Did you really think . . . let you . . . do this alone?" Dram says in my earpiece. His face appears above me, and he grasps my arm, pulling me over his shoulder. I cry out, but the sound is not a girl's. It is a dragon's. A dragon breathing flame into herself.

"Knew you'd . . . find it," Dram gasps.

I catch a glimpse of his bucket swaying from his belt. He has as much as I do.

Together, we have enough.

Sounds peal from my mouth. A keening wail that is relief and pain at the same time. It is a cry for the people whose lives were taken here, who will never in this life see the sky again.

But because of them, I will.

We will.

I am going to be free.

EIGHTEEN

28.4 grams flash dust

SOMETHING IS WRONG. We've stopped moving. Dram staggers. I grip his arms.

"Dram?"

He collapses, and we both hit the ground. I groan and push myself up.

My hands are painted with Dram's blood.

"Dram!" His suit is spotted with holes. He doesn't have my cirium armor.

"Sorry," he slurs. I smell his skin burning before I confirm it with my eyes. He groans when I examine his arms. "Wish we had Serum 129." He gives me a soft smile.

I search the perimeter, trying to get our bearings. The white bars of the corral rise in the distance, but we are far east of our sector—of any of the assigned sectors.

"We're close, Dram," I murmur, fastening the vulture feathers over his forearms. He studies the leathery skin.

"Was this thing dead when you found it?"

"No."

"You hunted a flash vulture?" A smile breaks over his face, bigger than the first. He catches my head and presses his forehead to mine. "Fire, I love you."

I love him too much to sit here a second longer. He's growing delirious—the flash fever Dad warned me about—and I'm not strong enough to carry him back.

"Come on," I say, pushing myself up. "Let's go."

He climbs to his feet. "Your friends are back."

I'd heard the flap of wings, a few caws and calls, but it does nothing to prepare me for when I finally look up and see just how many have gathered.

"Fire," I whisper. They swarm like a dark cloud, too numerous to count. "Where did they all come from?"

Dram stares at the swooping vultures as if they are of no more consequence than a cloud of shifting ash. Under his burns, his skin is white as bone.

"Hand me your bucket," I whisper, looking away from the birds only long enough to empty my dust into the weapon. I set aside just enough for us to get back inside the gate tonight.

"What are you doing?" Dram asks.

A dozen vultures drop to the ground. They hold out their wings and bob up and down, their beaks so wide I see their tongues. I step in front of Dram.

"See those black things?" I ask softly. "Tell me if they move closer." I force my hands to still as I carefully pour Dram's flash dust into the wand's reservoir, trying to remember everything Gabe told me. Once the canister is full, it's combustible. If I do this wrong, I'm going to blow us both up.

"They're closer," Dram says.

I look up. The vultures surround us in a half circle, less

than two meters away. I could take one, maybe two with my knife, before the others overwhelm us. Even if Dram is able to defend himself, we are outnumbered.

"They moved closer again," Dram says.

"Yes, I see that," I mutter. "Stop talking."

What else did Gabe say? I stare at the flash wand, at the silver cylinder we've pinned our hopes on. If I use this to save us now, I am only ensuring our deaths later. This is our only leverage to get free.

Dram tugs on my sleeve. I look at him and he points. Past the clouds of the flashfall, more vultures descend. If Gabe is right, the flash burst will only take care of what's in front of us. If I wait any longer, we're dead either way.

"Close your eyes and cover your head," I say. Dram eyes me curiously. "Do it!" He drops his head in his arms, and I hold the flash wand as far from my body as possible, gripping the tube like Gabe showed me. It was always our plan that I'd be the one to detonate it—just not yet.

I'm not sure I'm holding it right. What if I didn't seal the reservoir properly?

"Why are you breathing like that?" Dram asks.

I meet his eyes. The way the flash glow hits his face, I can see them clearly. As blue as the sky I've always told myself I'd see.

"Because we're going to see the sky," I tell him, then I press the trigger.

———

I lie on my back, spread-eagled, staring up at Cordon Four's nightmarish sky. The kick from the weapon thrust me back and sucked the air from my lungs. As soon as I regain the use of my body, I'm going to check on Dram. He lies in a heap a short distance away.

"Dram!" He's as still as the charred vulture corpses around us. Not even their special wings could protect them from the force of that blast.

"Dram!" I roll onto my stomach. I have no fresh burns or injuries. Dram must be suffering the effects of flash fever. I reach his side and roll him over.

"Rye." His eyes are glassy, his skin still white, but the blast seems to have roused him from his stupor. He looks past my shoulder. "What is that?"

I turn and look. The blast tore through a pile of debris. Beyond it, a metal structure protrudes from the ground.

"It must be a shelter," I murmur breathlessly. "It's cirium-plated."

The thing is cirium-plated in the way that I am—awkwardly, like it was an afterthought, the armor adapted from something else. We stagger toward it, searching for an opening.

"This is a helicopter," Dram says, his voice raw from particle dust. "Gabe told me about these."

By the look of it, helicopters were as effective against the flash curtain as cars and buses.

"I think this is a door," I say. "It's partly buried, but I think we can pry it open." I grip the lever, and together we tug the door up out of the ground. We clamber inside and force the door closed. Inside, all is dark and quiet. We push back our headpieces and drag in the musty, particle-free air.

Dram cracks a light stick.

"Where did you find that?"

"This craft is loaded with gear," he says, holding the light up.

My breath hitches. The things filling this structure are not from Outpost Five. They are not like the things at Cordon Four, either.

Weapons. Not flash wands, or the guns the guards use, but I'm sure that's what these black metal objects are. I study them, considering. Dram catches my eye and shakes his head.

"We need a flash weapon," he says, his voice hoarse. He's right. It's the only way we'd overpower the cordon guards.

"Rations," I murmur, smoothing the dust away from a box with pouches. I lift one out and tear it open. My spirits dive. Whatever it once contained is nothing but a film of dust. The water, too, has evaporated. I'm desperate for liquid on my parched, burning throat. We need to get back to camp. But first . . .

I crack another glow light and push toward the other side of the space.

"Where are you going?" Dram asks.

"Looking for serum." I dig through overturned crates and boxes. Cracked vials glint in the dim light, and I follow them to a container flipped on its side. "Found it!" I lift a vial. "What do you think Serum 456 does?" I put it back and search the box for a number that I know.

"Look." Dram points to a placard attached to the inside of the box. It lists the medical supply contents, along with a list of ailments and treatments. I scan the list.

Flash Fever = Serum 854

I paw through the box, but Dram stops me. He's already holding a syringe of 854.

"Who were these people?" he asks.

I snatch the syringe from his hand and prep it. "Right now, they're the people saving our lives." I tug his glove off and press the needle into his hand.

He sits against the fuselage, eyes closed. I watch him closely, listening as his breath evens out. Color returns to his face. I can't believe how quickly Serum 854 is restoring him.

"You should take it, too," he says. I inject myself, then tuck the remaining two vials in my undershirt, safely hidden beneath the layers of my clothes and suit.

We sit in the stillness of our shelter, clinging to life with climbers' grips. I can't help but think how similar this is to the air cave down nine. Only this time, help's not coming. We're on our own.

"Well," Dram murmurs, his voice a croak, "at least we haven't tried to drink our pee yet."

I laugh. Fire, I've missed his outpost humor. I smile at him, at the light in his bloodshot, flash-fevered eyes.

He holds the light up and looks around. "Look at this," he says, taking a placard off the wall. "I think it's a map." He turns it so I can see. "It shows all the cordons along the flash curtain."

This isn't like any map I've ever seen before. It has numbers—coordinates, I assume, that don't make sense to me. Some of them I recognize, and I point to the markings. "Depth coordinates, like we use in the tunnels."

"What do you think these Xs are?" Dram asks.

All at once, the diagram clicks in my mind, as if someone just handed me goggles and now I can see through the particle dust. "The Xs are outposts," I say. "There's Outpost Five, all the way south."

"Then what's this, beside Cordon One?" Dram points to a

mark I learned when I was nine and Graham taught me to read the markers that cavers draw. I know what this means, and so does Dram.

"It's a way out."

I wait for Dram to lift his eyes. His mind is muddled with fever, but he's making the mental leap right along with me.

He traces the twin slanted lines with a shaking finger. "So it's possible," he says. "Subpars have gotten free."

I study the map, committing it to memory. "We have no way of getting to Cordon One."

"We have hope." He grins, swaying slightly. "It's a start."

I stand and hang my glow stick from the topmost point of the tilted fuselage. It illuminates the packed hold of the flying machine. Dram and I reach for more light sticks at the same time.

"How's Serum 854 treating you?" I ask.

"Well enough," he says, cracking the lights. He's sounding more like himself again.

"Let's do some exploring."

Dram holds the light aloft. "Lead the way."

I turn toward the shadowed nose of the fuselage, my heart racing as it always does when I head down a path full of unknowns. Only this feels more dangerous somehow. It also feels right.

The buzzer sounds, distant, but distinct.

My wide eyes find Dram's. In all that's happened today, I completely forgot about Cordon Four's time limit, and everyone else waiting for us to complete our part of the escape plan. Everything has changed now.

"We have to go back," he says. "We won't survive the night without rations."

"We'll never make it in time. If we could run, maybe."

He sorts through the box of serum. "We can run," he says, tossing me Serum 61. Adrenaline.

I give the helicopter's shadowed hold one last glance. "We're coming back."

"Of course we're coming back," Dram shoves the needle into his thigh. "But not if we don't live past today."

I drop the light bars with a sigh and inject myself. I count down from ten and feel my heart kick into double time. Dram forces the door open, and the burnt sand and all its horrors intrude on the sanctuary of this half-buried tomb.

I look at the place where the nose of the craft hit the ground—where the pilot and crew probably lie buried.

"We're coming back," I say again, this time for the unknown people who died here, but who saved us from the fate of the curtain. I think they would want to know that their mission was not in vain.

That maybe their timing was perfect.

———

We collapse before the turnstile. The deposit box opens.

"Deposit your collection for processing," an automated voice says.

I laugh bleakly. We're half dead, and our only chance of escaping blew up with a bunch of birds. But we have just enough to get back inside our prison. I pour my flash dust onto the scale with aching arms. I feel every place a beak stabbed past the cirium.

"Proceed through the turnstile," the voice says.

A light beside the scale glows green, and the turnstile trembles with the sound of a bolt sliding open. I push through, and it locks behind me. I grasp the metal bars and wait as Dram repeats the process. We stagger past the fence a moment later, the last cordon miners to return for the night. The camp is oddly still and silent.

Dram and I lean against each other. His arms are the only things keeping me from hitting the ground. We collect our rations, drag our suits off, and collapse inside our tent.

"Tomorrow," Dram whispers. "We'll try again tomorrow." He tucks his arm beneath his head, but not before I catch sight of his Radband. I pretend I didn't see it. My throat is too tight to speak—and what could I possibly say?

Dram followed me to the curtain, and it cost him.

His Radband is amber.

NINETEEN

0 grams flash dust

THERE'S BEEN A shift in the air.

It's early yet, a dawn haze lifting over the burnt sands in shimmering pinks and corals. Before I even confirm it with a glance at the indicator flag, I feel the unexpected relief of low Radlevels. I step from the tent and let the air cool my face.

"Hell is taking a break," Dram says beside me. I touch his stubbled cheek, smiling. He smiles back, and I know we're both enjoying the newness of this. Touching each other and having it mean something more than survival.

We dress and suit up, neither of us mentioning his amber indicator light. Instead, we hold on to the only hope we have, whispering our plans to get back to the helicopter. Our flash wand is empty, but that wreckage might hold another means of escape.

The buzzer sounds, and we head toward the turnstiles.

"We have to find the others," I say.

Mere emerges from her tent, holding Winn's hand. As she walks toward us, Dram suddenly stops. His gaze narrows on the people moving behind the fence. Something in the tightening of his face makes me stiffen.

"What is it?"

"Cranny," he whispers.

Every warm place inside me dies. "It can't be." But of course it can. Outpost Five is just a hover ride away. The bigger question is—

"Why?"

"Seems you're still causing trouble, Scout," Cranny calls. "The commissary is occupied in Alara, so I've come on his behalf." He steps through the fence, and Gabe shifts into view beside him, wearing a look of remorse. My heart stops.

"One of your friends talked. One of them didn't." He signals and a pair of guards steps forward, hauling a large body between them. The man can barely stand, and he's bent over, his blond hair covering his face. Reeves.

"Show her," Cranny commands. A guard grasps Reeves by the hair and lifts his head. My hands clamp over my mouth, but my horrified moan escapes.

"I made sure he'll have bruises to match yours," Cranny says. Even with the space between us, I feel his dark gaze fixed on me. "Search her."

Two soldiers march toward us. These are not the guards of the outposts and cordons, but something altogether more menacing. As they near, I recognize the seal of Alara on their armbands, but their uniforms are made with fabric I've never seen before—a shimmery sort of material that takes on the hue of their surroundings, shifting as they move like adaptive camouflage.

"Striders," Mere says. She pulls Winn behind her. These must be the kind of soldiers who captured her.

The Striders haul me to my feet. Their suits emit an odd hum, as if they're alive with an energy all their own.

"Don't touch them," Mere whispers.

The empty flash wand lies deep in the hidden pocket of my suit. Dram leaps up and lurches for the Strider patting me down. When his hands connect with the soldier's suit, a current jolts through him, knocking him off his feet.

Winn screams. Dram moans and drags himself to his hands and knees. The Strider reaches for him.

"Stop!" I shout.

Cranny walks toward me with an air of anticipation. It reminds me of the flash vulture bobbing up and down. He's hungry for this moment.

"I know about the flash wand." His head tilts and his eyes slip over my body. "And I know where it's hidden." He reaches for my zipper.

Dram tackles him to the sand, managing one solid hit to Cranny's jaw before the Striders pull him off. One guard holds him while the other takes a swing at his face.

"Stop, please!" I shout. Dram grunts as the soldier punches him again, this time in the stomach. The Strider holding him moves; he's going to clasp his electrified arm around Dram's neck.

"No!" And then I realize something. Gabe told them our plan. They have no reason to believe we haven't succeeded in enabling the weapon. The only ones who know it's worthless are Dram and I. I reach for the hidden pocket.

"Keep your hands up!" the Strider commands.

I roll my eyes upward and pretend to faint. My knees hit the ground, and I tip forward. I fake unconsciousness, while my hand slips through a tear made by a beak. By the time a Strider drags me to my feet, I've got the flash wand in hand.

"Stand back!" I extend the cylinder. Everyone freezes. If it were full, I could blow them apart with this thing.

Dram's gaze collides with mine. He shoves the other Strider off him and moves to my side.

"Throw down your weapons," I say. "I want passage through the flash curtain."

Dram retrieves their guns, slinging one across his chest and aiming another at the guard who hit him. He wipes the blood from his nose and grins. It shouldn't be this easy.

"Where do you think you're going to go?" Cranny asks.

"To Alara," I say. Dram tucks a gun into my waistband. I'm not sure I'd even know how to use it.

Cranny gives me a pitying smile. "Are you sure?"

"You're going to take us there. Right now."

His smile widens. "No, I'm not."

My heart knocks against my ribs. This is it. He's calling my bluff. But now Dram and I are holding loaded weapons. Would I actually shoot these people to get free? I glance at Dram. Blood seeps from his nose, and one of his eyes is swelling. My gaze slips to the green and gold pendants around his neck.

Yes. I would.

"The place you're thinking of doesn't exist," Cranny says. "Not as you imagine it. The protected city is a myth told to Subpars to keep them doing what is needed."

His words burn into me like flash dust.

"And what is *needed* of Subpars?" I make myself vulnerable with the question, but I need to know.

"Test subjects," he says. "The cordons and outposts are controlled environments for series after series of radiation testing. But more than that, the Congress needs cirium and flash dust."

Dram catches my arm, wrapping his hand around mine on the trigger. I am falling. My world is crashing around me, sweeping me away like ash in a flash storm. I am nothing. I belong only to the barren sands of ash and flame, or buried beneath the earth. The sign was a lie. Subpars never leave the outposts. Only for the cordons. We are not the fortunate ones. We are monkeys in cages, like Dad said.

I was never meant to see the sky.

"The world on the other side of the shield won't offer you refuge," Cranny says.

Dram aims his pistol at Cranny. "Stop. Talking."

My fingers caress the trigger of the flash wand. I wish it was loaded. I want to unleash its fury on Cranny and all of Congress and obliterate their control. Maybe I am a revolutionary. Someone needs to be.

"You're lying," I say.

"Ask your friend Gabe. The people there want you here as much as the Congress."

"I don't believe you."

"The shield isn't just there to protect people from the flash curtain. It keeps everyone in their proper places."

Dram's finger squeezes the trigger. "Good-bye, Director."

All at once, red lights flicker over Dram and me. "What is that?"

"Marksmen," Cranny says. "With their guns trained on your heads."

I whirl, my gaze sweeping the top of the corral. A line of Striders hold rifles pointed at us.

"Your first mistake is thinking I brought only two Striders with me to confront a girl who single-handedly began a rebellion in Outpost Five," Cranny says. "Your second was thinking I don't know what an empty flash wand looks like." He clamps my wrist and pulls the wand from my hand.

Dram holds his gun trained on Cranny.

"Drop the weapon, Dram," Cranny commands. "You'll be dead before you hit the ground."

"But I'll take you with me," Dram says.

"And then they'll shoot her," Cranny says, sliding his gaze to me.

Dram swears beneath his breath and lowers his pistol. A Strider disarms him and twists his hands behind his back.

"Load them into the hover," Cranny says. "Deposit them in Cordon Two."

The Strider hesitates. "Sir, those weren't the commissary's orders."

"Director," GM487 says, striding forward, "Commissary Jameson ordered these Subpars returned to Outpost Five for questioning. He contacted me via com."

"That was before they attacked the Congress's soldiers and pointed weapons in my face," Cranny says. He crosses his arms, self-assured in a way I've never seen him. "I'm within my rights. You know the parameters for cordon law. Tell me I'm wrong."

She sighs, and I know we're in trouble. Gabe tipped them

off about the flash wand, but Cranny bided his time, worked over Reeves, and staged this perfectly. He knew we'd resist, that we'd fight back. He was counting on it.

"There are penalties for noncompliance," Cranny says. He slides a hard look at the Strider who questioned him. "I want these Subpars fitted with collars and prepped for Cordon Two."

Collars? My wide eyes find Dram's.

The Strider presses his lips together, stares hard at Cranny, then nods.

Cranny turns to us. "I'm afraid you'll find Cordon Two less hospitable than this place, but then, it is a prison cordon."

"Wait," I say. "I found something. Something you'll be interested in."

"What is it?"

I try to imagine how much I have to bargain with. "Let Winn and this woman go to Outpost Five." I know how he views them—a weak child and a crippled woman.

He points to Reeves. "Do you see that? I would *enjoy* doing that to you. It wouldn't take me five minutes to find out what you know."

"Maybe," I say. "But then you'd have to stay in Cordon Four long enough for it to burn holes in your uniform." My eyes flick to his dosimeter, which is spiking into the orange levels.

His mouth tightens, and he motions to a pair of Striders. "Take the child and the Conjuror to Outpost Five. Have them escorted to tunnel four."

Forfeit. My heart sinks. They won't survive, not without Lenore sneaking them supplies. Mere doesn't even have hands, and Winn is too young to defend herself. Dram nudges my foot, and I look up. Mere is working to hide her smile. I have given her what she's not dared to hope for—a chance to see her son again.

Roran. Of course. He will help them.

The Strider grips my arm and tows me aboard the hover. Another prods Dram on behind me.

Cranny sits across from us in the hold. "Tell me what you found."

"It's east of the corral, in an unassigned sector," I begin. A pang of regret lodges in my chest. I'm giving up my fellow rebels. Though they are long dead, they sheltered us, and they might've served as a beacon for future Subpars. "There's a downed helicopter filled with weapons and supplies . . ."

Cranny's gaze narrows as I describe the contents of the craft. A tech comes to take our blood. She pushes up my sleeve, her gloved hands moving my improvised cirium armor aside as if it might bite.

Her hands shake, and her dosimeter chirps a warning. She's probably thinking about the radiation seeping into her body. I wonder what would make a Natural choose to serve out here. Maybe she didn't choose. Perhaps she's more like me than I realize.

I watch my blood drain into her vial. Behind her, Dram eyes her med bag as if judging how much he can get away with stealing. Striders line the wall behind him. I stare at him, silently pleading for caution. These are not the guards of Outpost Five.

"Tell me again about the serums," Cranny says.

I bite my lip. I hate giving away our secrets, but this is the currency I traded.

"Serum 854," I murmur. "For treating flash fever."

Cranny smirks. "Now you're making things up. There's no such treatment."

"Yes, there is." My gaze shifts to the tech setting my blood carefully into a padded slot.

"I took it," Dram says, extending his arm. "I'm sure the techs will see it in whatever the hell it is you do with our blood."

"What else did you find?" Cranny asks.

"That's everything," I say. Not everything. But it's enough to convince him—more than enough to satisfy my half of our bargain. "The buzzer sounded, and we had to get back to the corral. There wasn't time to search it all." I bookend my lie with a bit of truth.

Dram meets my eyes over the top of the tech's head. I didn't tell Cranny about the map we saw. The one with Xs and coordinates, and the handwritten caver's mark over Cordon One.

The marker that shows a way out.

"Very well." Cranny stands and signals the soldiers. "Get them secured in a cell and deposit them in Cordon Two."

The Strider nods.

"Oh—and give him Serum 61." He nods toward Reeves. "I want him conscious when he sees the cordon." Cranny hesitates beside me. "It didn't have to end this way, you know. All your fighting. What did it gain you?" He shakes his head. "Such a waste." He strides from the hold. The door seals shut behind him.

A tear tracks down my cheek. I'm surprised I can muster the energy to feel regret. "I'm sorry, Dram." The engines roar to life, and the bench trembles beneath me.

"Roran's going to see his mother again, because of you." He stretches across the darkness and grasps my hand. "Winn is going to live, because of you. You just played Cranny like a fiddle. He has no idea of the trouble he's got headed his way. Mere is more than she seems."

His words wash over me like a benediction. I have not wasted my life.

I imagine Roran's face when he sees his mother emerge from the hover. She will smile at him, and in her eyes he will glimpse the steel and fire inside. The determination the Congress failed to temper.

Outpost Five will have its uprising, after all.

TWENTY

THEY'VE PUT US in a cage.

We are well and truly the monkeys Dad warned me about. Only, I don't think they're letting us out for a night of music and dancing.

Not if the collar around my neck is any indicator.

It's white, like the rest of my strange, skintight suit. The Strider who took my old clothes told me the Congress is testing these. They want to see how long they help us withstand the elements.

"This is a nice touch," Reeves says, holding up his wrist. Part of the fabric is cut away to reveal our Radbands. "Nice to have that visual confirmation that you're dying."

My heart twists. His band turns another shade closer to red each day. All our bands are shifting.

We dangle from a tow cable, six meters beneath the hover, exposed to everything the cordons have to offer. Even now, as we approach the prison cordon, I feel the winds intensify. Over the hum of the hover's engines, I sense the thrum of the flash curtain. We are getting close.

I reach toward the bars.

"Wait." Reeves sits up. "I don't think you should—"

My collar chimes loudly, and a jolt of energy shoots through me. I cry out, but the sound is muffled through my clenched lips.

"Rye!" Dram catches me as I collapse in his arms, shaking, my muscles pulsing.

"Don't. Touch. The bars," I gasp.

Reeves swears with words I've never heard before. He tears at his collar like it's a tunnel gull with talons clamped around his neck.

"How bad was the shock?" he asks me.

"Bad enough." It's still a struggle to form words.

He grabs hold of the bars.

"Reeves!" Dram shoves him, but it's the electric current of the cage that finally sends Reeves flying back.

"What the hell are you doing?" Dram shouts.

Reeves flops on the floor, his hair standing on end.

I'm still shaky, but I seem to have command of my muscles again. I crouch beside Reeves and hold his panicked, wide-eyed gaze. "Your breath will return—it just knocked the wind out of you."

"Holy fire," Dram murmurs. He stands at the bars, staring out over the sands.

I turn and look—and all the air leaves my body.

So this is Cordon Two.

Cages like ours move across the ground, held on giant cirium arms. They move forward and away from the flash curtain, as if guided by an unseen hand. It's a technological marvel, and

I have a vague memory of Dad telling me about places where Congress tests machines within the flashfall. I touch my collar and look down at my suit with new eyes. This cordon is more than prison and punishment. It's a site for some of our city-state's most important experiments.

The ground is a desolate wasteland, but it looks nothing like Cordon Four. The sands are white, as if the curtain has leeched all nutrients from the earth here. And no clouds block the curtain, so it is bright, with all its colors refracting over the cages and arms and sand.

There are no indicator flags, and we don't wear headpieces. Either they don't care what happens to us, or they're not concerned about the particles in the air here. The hover lowers, and as we dangle closer to the ground, I get a view of tall poles—four of them—each topped with a light that emits a crackling electronic pulse. Glimmering clouds shift around the lights, and I squint, trying to guess what these contraptions do.

"Emberflies," Dram murmurs. "They draw the emberflies."

I throw my hands up over my nose and mouth, reacting instinctively to the memory of Ennis and what just one of those things did to him. But none of the insects strays toward our cage. They swarm the tops of the poles, hungry for whatever the towers are transmitting. We lower farther.

I stand, bracing myself against Dram's side, and peer into the other cells as we pass. The people inside don't even look at us.

"Are those people sleeping?" I point to a cage where two bodies lie collapsed. One of them has his arms thrust through the bars. Even from here I can hear the man's collar beeping.

"Not sleeping," Reeves murmurs.

Dram's arm around me tightens.

"These people have been fighting," Reeves says. He stares into the cage across from us. A man paces the confines, his face a collage of bruises. His sleeve is cut away to reveal the Codev glowing beneath his skin. A Gem.

"There's no physic," I say, pointing to a woman who sits in her cell, bleeding from a gash on her head. I pat down the pockets of my white suit, checking every pouch, but there's no serum, just a few days' worth of nutri-pacs in orange foil. And a knife. I hold it up, my eyes wide.

"What exactly are they expecting us to mine with this?" Dram holds up his knife.

"Dusters," Reeves says softly. "A forfeit once told me about this, but I didn't believe him.

"What are you talking about?" Dram asks.

"He said the people of Cordon Two are so desperate to mine flash dust, they'll make it themselves if they have to."

"You're saying they kill people?" I feel like I just grabbed the bars again.

Reeves tucks his knife against his palm. "That's exactly what I'm saying."

We hover beside an empty metal arm. Our cell lowers toward the ground with a mechanical whine.

"It's dropping us! Dram—lift me up, we need to get to the hover."

A solid sheet of metal forms the roof of our cage. He lifts me, and I hammer at it, but it doesn't give. I wedge my knife around the edges—

———

I wake up in Dram's arms. My body aches as if I've fallen from a climb.

"She's back with us," Reeves says.

Dram smooths my hair away from my face. "I suppose you're not the first one to try escaping through the roof."

"The collar again?" My jaw is starting to unclench.

"I think you stuck your knife into a power conductor," he says. "Fire, Rye, I thought you'd—" He sighs. "No more escape attempts. Not without a plan."

"Okay." My lips feel numb, like I've been sucking on water posey. "How's our new home?"

"Cozy."

I shield my eyes from the glare of the flash curtain and take in our surroundings. No Gems greet us. No fences mark our boundaries. No tents wave in the wind offering a frail promise of shelter.

"They don't expect us to survive," I whisper.

"No," Reeves says. He sits in the middle of the cage, his arms wrapped around his knees. The look in his eyes tells me he's far away in his mind.

"Why would they do that?" My voice rises, shrill and desperate. "If they know we're likely to die, why wouldn't they intervene? They're wasting Subpars . . ."

Dram and Reeves both watch me, silently waiting for me to answer my own question.

Congress doesn't intend for us to survive. We are more useful to them as flash dust. My eyes scan the cordon, seeing it all from a new perspective. This isn't a prison camp. It's a factory. A flash-dust-making factory.

"What is that stone building with the smoke coming out of it?"

"Flash incinerator," Reeves says. "It captures the energy

and radiation of the curtain and funnels it into a chamber for . . . well . . ."

"How convenient," Dram mutters. "We don't even have to go all the way to the curtain to be turned into flash dust."

My eyes fill with tears. Every curse Graham ever taught me surges to my lips, but the only words I manage are—

"Not like this. After everything—" I have to swallow the lump in my throat.

Dram wraps me in his arms, but he doesn't say anything. There is no room in this cage for lies.

"Get ready," Reeves says softly. "It's time."

"How do you know?"

"Look at them."

I peer through the bars, at the rows of cages. People gather at the doors, as if responding to a silent summons.

"Come," Reeves says, walking to the cage door. "I will show you how a forfeit survives." His voice sounds different, like his mouth is speaking, but the words come from someplace far away.

Dram clasps my hand, and we stand.

Around us, the people—those still alive—begin to stir. I hear the rattle of the metal cages beneath their feet.

"Be sure to take their nutri-pacs before you flash them," Reeves says.

"I'm not killing anyone!"

"Shh," Dram says. "Think of the tunnels. Let's try not to attract too much attention."

"Fine," I hiss. "But I'm not going to kill someone just so I can live!"

"You will." Reeves stares out toward the curtain.

"Run for the perimeter," Dram says. "Let's see if we can cross into Cordon One. That's where the map showed a way out." He looks toward the door. "Reeves? You with us?"

Reeves nods, but he's got his fist clenched around his knife.

There's no buzzer or bell. No warning at all when the cage doors open. Just the bloodlust in the eyes of desperate, broken people—and all of it focused on us, replacement prisoners with fresh rations in their pockets and no experience fighting to the death.

"Go!" Reeves shoves me through the cage door, and I hit the sand, sprinting toward the cordon boundary for all I'm worth.

"They're coming for us!" Dram keeps pace at my side, even though I know he's faster. They're both faster than me. I'm small, which has served me well in the tunnels, but in a life-or-death sprint, those with long legs have the advantage.

I want to tell him to push on, but my breath already heaves from my chest, and it's everything I can do to keep my legs pumping faster than they ever have before. Besides, Dram would no more leave me than I would him. Whatever happens, we're in it together. I try to take comfort in the thought, and then I have no energy for any thought at all, save one.

Run.

A woman's scream pierces the air, followed by a thud and grunting, like several people are fighting over her. I think of the flash vultures scrabbling over the one I tore the wings off of in Cordon Four.

The Congress has turned these people into vultures.

We near the perimeter.

"There's no fence," Reeves calls, his breath sawing from his lungs. "No walls."

I squint, trying to identify the strange poles spaced apart along the edge of the cordon. My heart clenches. "Reeves! Stop!"

He's just a few meters from the poles and looks back over his shoulder.

"Collar!" It's the only word I can manage. He jogs toward the perimeter, but cautiously now. A man with a scraggly beard leaps for him. Reeves catches the man and uses the momentum to throw him toward the poles. Lights in the pole turn red just as the man's collar lets off a soft chime. His scream cuts off as his body jolts like an invisible beast is thrashing it in its jaw. He collapses to the ground, his eyes wide and unseeing.

I stagger to a stop. There is no escape here.

We have to go back.

I throw a glance over my shoulder. A man lunges for me, and I scream. His hand tangles in my hair, and we tumble to the ground.

"Rye!" Dram dives at the man, hauls him off me with one arm around his neck.

Men and women fall on us like flash bats, gripping any part of us they can get hold of.

"Get back!" I shout, lashing out with my knife. I force my way to my feet.

Dram's back presses against mine, and I realize we've taken the same stance we do in the tunnels. I search the faces of the people circling us, hoping to find hesitation, anything that shows a remnant of humanity.

"Please!" I cry. "I'll give you my rations—just leave us alone!" I rip my nutri-pacs from my pocket and hold them up.

"No, Rye!"

"I'd rather starve to death than be torn apart!"

Another man darts toward Reeves, and a moment later I hear a shout, a chime, and a strangled cry.

"Cease!" a man calls. The mob stills. They don't look at the man, but their eyes lower.

"I see you've met my crew," he says with a jovial smile. "You may call me King."

Reeves snorts. "How 'bout I call you the guy whose ass I'm about to throw against this fence?"

King's smile stays in place, but his eyes shift to one of his men. A second later, three men fall on Reeves.

He's stronger than his gaunt attackers, but one of them clenches a rock in his fist—not a rock, I realize, but some sort of bone. Dram tenses like a coil beside me, but a dozen maniacs with knives press in around us. If we intervene, we're dead. They have sheer numbers on their side.

"Enough." King's simple command works like a leash, reeling in the man with the bone. He wipes the bloody weapon on his suit and shoves Reeves to his knees before the leader.

"You will call me King," he demands softly.

Reeves lifts his head, and I cringe. He wears new wounds over the ones the Striders gave him. He spits blood onto the sand.

Metal flashes, and King presses the point of a knife to his throat. "Say it."

"Reeves," I murmur, tears filling my eyes. "Please." I understand his defiance. Part of me wants to spit on the ground too. But Lenore didn't die down six so we could throw our lives away like this.

His brown eyes find mine. "King," he says.

King smiles. "Wise choice." He sheathes his blade. "Two

strong men . . ." He walks around Reeves and Dram, sizing them up as if he's choosing a dog for a fight. "Yes, you'd be a nice addition to my crew." He turns to me. "And who do we have here?" He examines me like his eyes are hands. "Hmm," he murmurs. "Bruised, but still pretty. How badly do you want to live?" He reaches toward me, and I stiffen. "Not going to hurt you." He grins. "Not today, anyway." He catches a drop of my sweat with his finger.

"Now I'll show you why I'm king of the castle." He closes his hands around the bead of sweat and slowly opens them, revealing a handful of water.

"You can conjure?"

"Guilty," he says. He lifts his hands to me, and I turn my head. "Suit yourself." He drinks the water and sighs gustily. "It's only your first day. Soon enough, you'll be drinking out of my hands." He laughs and lifts his hand to the bone guy and his minions. "Let them keep their kills. It's good for them to get a taste of Sanctuary."

Bone Guy drops the body he was hauling. His face falls like he's just been denied a meal. Maybe he was.

"You'll find that Cordon Two has but one place of safety," King says. "Since there's no other authority here, it falls to me to point it out." He smiles again, like he's hosting a party and pointing us toward refreshments. "See the smoke? Dust the bodies there, and something quite wonderful happens. Sanctuary is a rare treat around here, but it comes at a price.

"I'll give you that time to consider. You're either with me or against me." His eyes slip down my body, revealing a hunger that has nothing to do with the nutri-pacs clutched in my fist. Dram shifts his weight as King's gaze lingers, until I sense he might actually take his chances with the mob.

King gives me a wolfish grin. "I do hope you choose 'with me.' " He strides away, and his crew falls into step behind him.

Breathe. Breathe. Breathe.

My hands shake as I stuff my packets back in my pockets.

"Rye—" Dram reaches for me.

"Don't—" I step back. "Don't touch me." I'm considering a run at the electric barrier. At least death would be on my own terms.

Dram's eyes narrow on my face. His gaze darts to the invisible fence and back, as if he's judging how fast he can stop me. He walks toward me, his blue gaze locking with mine.

"Not going to touch you." He holds his hands up. "Just this." He tucks his finger beneath my collar and pulls.

"What are you doing?"

"Reminding you," he whispers, pulling my pendants free. "We have survived worse than this. Worse than that bastard."

"I'm tired of just *surviving*." I choke the words out. My eyes fill. "What's the point?"

His gaze hardens. "The point? The point's the same as it's always been. One foot in front of the other, till we get to the other side of *that glenting thing*!" He thrusts his arm toward the curtain, his eyes glassing with tears.

"Dram," Reeves says, "help me with this body."

"Coming." His eyes hold mine a moment longer. Slowly, I nod. He turns toward Reeves. "Look away, Rye." His voice strains under the weight of his burden. "You don't need to see this."

I stare at the cages, reflecting in the light of the flash curtain. Then I turn and walk to Dram.

"Yes, I do." I don't meet his eyes. I don't say anything as I grasp the dead man's arm and haul it around my shoulders.

We walk toward the smoking chimney of the incinerator hauling our first kill.

———

Beside the incinerator stands a familiar, glass-enclosed scale. No automated voice asks for our deposit. There's just a dented button smeared with blood. We pour the dust from Reeves's attackers inside. A green light illuminates with a soft chime and then the weight registers.

209.86 grams.

Numbers turn above the door of a small red house. It seems the only colors here are white and red. Sand and blood. Above the door hangs a sign.

SANCTUARY

The numbers click to a stop: *48 Hours. 0 Minutes.*

Apparently, killing a person buys you one day of Sanctuary in Cordon Two.

We step inside the small enclosure, and the door seals shut behind us. A bolt clicks, and our collars chime. We are secure in our new cell.

Blood pounds in my head, like my heart won't let it pass. I have never seen such a place. We step into a large room with halls on either side. Dram grasps his knife and jogs down both. He returns a moment later.

"No one else here," he says. "Just bedrooms with bathrooms."

Reeves doesn't seem to notice his surroundings. He sinks

to the floor and puts his head in his hands. Blood streaks his arms, but it's not his.

I want to tell him we all have blood on our hands. I want to tell him that he was right.

"Leave him," Dram whispers. He takes my hand and leads me to one of the rooms.

I realize I'm crying. Not crying, exactly. Keening. And I just can't stop.

"What have we done, Dram?"

He guides me over to the shower and turns the water on. Steam lifts.

"Are you okay with me touching you, Rye?"

I nod, and my chin bumps the collar.

"Then let me help you." He unbuckles the white belt that shows I've missed far too many rations. It drops to the floor. There are buckles at my wrists, and he unfastens them one at a time, then peels off my leather gloves.

"Hold on to me," he says. He kneels and guides my hands to his shoulders, unbuckling my tight leather knee boots. There are so many buckles. It's like Congress wants even our clothing to feel like shackles.

Strange sounds puff from my lips between my shattered breaths. It's like I'm dying—or some part deep inside me is.

"That man is not going to lay a hand on you," Dram says. "Ever."

My hands tighten on his shoulders.

"Do you believe me?" he asks.

"Yes," I whisper.

"Right now we are safe. Tonight, we will sleep. Tomorrow, we will come up with a plan." He stands and turns me so my back is to him, then gently peels my suit down my shoulders. "Do you believe me?"

"Yes."

My glass pendants hang down my neck, a gentle weight against my skin. Dram takes my hand and guides me under the spray of water. It pours over me with comforting warmth. I let my tears fall down my skin and mix with the water.

"Dram?"

"Yes?"

"Will you hold me?"

"I'm right here." He holds my hand still. The water soaks through his sleeve.

"In here."

His eyes snap to mine. "I don't . . ."

"Please." My eyes hold his. "I know what I'm asking."

He sighs and lets go of my hand. Slowly, layer by layer, he drops his clothes beside mine. I don't look away. Water cascades over his shoulders as he steps under the spray and tucks me in his arms.

I cry against his chest, and he runs his hands over my hair. After a time, my breath finds a normal rhythm. The warmth reaches me, finally penetrating the frozen places where terror has taken root. I feel like maybe I can be clean again.

"Those men would have killed us," he says softly.

"I know."

"We may have to do it again."

"I know."

"I love you, Orion."

I smile through my tears. "I know." I catch his face between my hands and show him, the best way I know how.

We stay until the water turns cold, and then we wrap each other in towels and kisses and touches even softer than the blankets on the bed.

"Rye . . ." He catches my arms and gently pulls away. He doesn't say the words, but I read the concern in his soft blue gaze.

"You promised me sanctuary," I whisper.

It's like we're down nine and something's stolen his breath. I reach for him, ready to give him mine again.

He leans up, catching my mouth with his. I fall into his arms, where there is warmth and safety and love enough to chase away the dark. The scars, the loss, the imprisonment— it all melts away in the heat of Dram's touch. Our passion is a forge, and in its depths I am transformed into something beautiful.

His pendants brush my chest. I imagine I am like that glass—a bit of dust, altered by fire. But I am not fragile. If I were, the cordons would already have broken me.

Maybe I'm not like glass, after all. Maybe I'm the point of an axe, strong enough to shatter cirium.

TWENTY-ONE

0 grams flash dust

THERE'S A TIMER above the door. It counts down to the moment when the bolt will slide free and our collars will reactivate.

0 Hours. 21 Minutes.

Twenty-one minutes to finalize our plan.

Twenty-one minutes until we walk out of here and face King and his crew.

Twenty.

Nineteen.

"You're staring at the clock again, Rye," Dram says.

"Sorry," I murmur. "Tell me again about the hovers."

"Our best bet is to stay close," he says. "Wait for a hover to come for the flash dust deposit. Otherwise, we go after the ones lowering cages into the cordon. The cages are electrified, but not the hover's tow cable. If we can reach the cable without touching the cage, it might be a way out."

"Assuming we can ride it across the barrier to Cordon One."

"Yes."

"And assuming our electric collars only work at ground level."

"Yes."

"And assuming the dusters don't get us first."

Dram narrows his eyes.

"See? I was listening." My eyes dart to the clock. "Seventeen minutes."

He sighs and looks over at Reeves. We've lost him to whatever world he inhabits in his mind—the dark memories of tunnel four that draw him deep, even now.

"Do you want to shower, Reeves?" I ask. He's still wearing someone else's dried blood. It's the same color as his Radband.

He just looks at me. I wonder if the radiation is starting to take his mind.

"At least eat." I tear open a nutri-pac and wrap his fingers around it. He stares down at the orange foil.

"Len skipped meals for me," he says, so quiet I almost miss the words.

My eyes meet Dram's.

"She never told me," Reeves whispers, staring at the packet, "but I knew it was her. All those years."

The timer over the door clicks. Fifteen minutes.

"She's the only reason I came for that bell. I thought if I could . . ." He rakes a hand through his snarled hair. It comes away in clumps. "She made me want to—" His voice chokes off. He opens his hand, and the blond strands slip through his fingers.

I look at Dram. He's staring at the timer. Thirteen minutes. He turns and grasps Reeves's arm. "We're getting out of this cordon. We're getting free of all this."

Twelve minutes.

"Dram," I say. He nods.

We stand and check each other's suits, like we're going down the tunnels instead of into a battle with a maniac Conjuror. We've made a few adjustments to the suits Congress issued us. The buckles came in handy, after all. They make great places to store all our new knives and blades.

I meet Dram's eyes as he examines the long piece on the inside of my forearm.

"I hope you don't get close enough to use this," he says.

I hope I do. Somewhere between the shock and shower of the first day, and the remaining hours of planning, stripping Sanctuary of anything useful, and carving shivs from pieces of cirium, my fear of King hardened into rage.

I'm eager to see how well he conjures with my jagged pieces of cirium sticking out of his body.

Two minutes.

"Remember our deal," Dram says. His lips lift on one side.

"Step in my steps," I murmur.

"This time, ore scout, I'm going to be right at your side."

Our collars chime, and the bolt slides free.

0 Hours. 0 Minutes.

I grasp my knives and lunge through the door.

———

I stumble straight into the cage and nearly touch the bars in my confusion.

"Reeves, come on!" Dram shouts. He's apparently less disconcerted that we walked from Sanctuary directly into our cell.

Reeves's collar emits a chime, and he stares at us from the doorway of Sanctuary.

"You can't stay there," Dram says. "Time's up. Your collar's going to—"

Reeves jolts forward, his body a riot of twisted limbs.

"Reeves!" I grasp one of his arms and Dram the other, and we haul him into our cage. He stops kicking, but his muscles spasm as the door clicks shut.

Our cage skims above the ground, the metal arm guiding us closer to the curtain. I feel like the glassblower's pipe being moved toward the furnace. "How do we make it stop?"

Dram crawls to the edge of the cage and studies the other cells. "We mine. When it stops, we sift as much flash dust as we can and put it in that deposit." He points to a cylinder attached to the cage bars.

Our cage drops suddenly and the door opens.

The sands are hot on my feet, even through my boots. Everything burns this close to the curtain. Sulfur clouds suffocate the air in other cordons, but they're a barrier against the curtain. Out here, there is nothing to absorb its intensity.

My hands blister beneath my gloves. Someone should tell the Congress their newest suits need improvement. I try not to focus on the fact that they didn't provide us with sifters— as if successful mining isn't really the goal here. Maybe they are observing us, even now. Perhaps a tech is watching me on my knees beside Dram, lifting the sands, again and again, for every particle of dust.

Our collars chime.

I grip my pouch and lurch into our cage, a step behind Dram. We run for the cylinder, and he pours his flash dust in.

"Help me pour mine!" My hands hurt so badly I can barely get the pouch open. The deposit box glows red.

"No!" Dram punches the box.

Our collars chime, and the door seals shut. The cage jolts forward.

"We didn't get enough," I murmur. The winds blow my hair from my face. It feels like the start of a flash storm. "We're going too close to the curtain!"

Dram whirls toward Reeves, where he sits in a corner of the cage. "Snap out of it!" He grasps him by the front of his suit. "I loved Len, too. She's *dead*. And I'm sorry you're sick. It's not fair. *None of this is fair!*"

A scream rends the air—the woman from the cage on the arm beside us. She's a few cage lengths ahead, but her cries carry like we're standing beside her. I clasp my hands over my ears, but the sounds reverberate through me.

Silence descends, and her cage moves backward. Empty. It passes slowly enough that I catch the glowing indicator on the deposit box. Green. A full deposit.

The Congress gets its flash dust one way or another.

I fall to my knees and heave, gasping for breath.

"Reeves." Dram's tone holds a warning. "We have one more chance here."

"It doesn't matter," Reeves says.

Dram shakes him. "My life matters. Her life matters." He knocks him across the jaw. "Fight! We are going to be dust in this cage if you don't stand up and help us!"

Our cage clicks to a stop, and the door slides open. I crawl out on my hands and knees. My legs shake too hard to support me, but it doesn't matter. The closer I am to the ground, the faster I can sift the sand. At least there's more here, this close to the curtain. It's possible we'll mine enough.

It's possible.

Particle dust stings my throat, and I reach for a neck cloth that isn't there. The curtain is starting to sing its song inside my head again.

Reeves attacks the sand like a demon, throwing his bare hands into the cordon as if it's not searing his skin. He shouts, crying out from pain that I think is only partly from the sand.

My collar chimes, a soft warning.

"We're out of time." I pull myself into the cage and run to the deposit, sifting every last particle of dust into the box.

Red light.

Dram guides his in with shaking hands and stares at the light. It doesn't change.

Our collars chime, and the cage door begins to close. Sand streams from Reeves as he vaults inside and throws himself in front of the deposit. Blood trickles from his ears and nose, but his hands hold steady as he lifts his fistfuls of dust.

The box chimes just as the cage door latches shut.

Green light.

I collapse on the floor, telling myself to breathe, but my lungs aren't cooperating. I gasp like I'm at the bottom of nine without a tank.

The metal arm tows our cage backward over the cordon, until we hang suspended in the place we started from. Along the way, we see three more empty cages with green deposit lights.

The full horror of this place settles in. For the first time, I begin to feel some sympathy for the dusters. If not for Dram and Reeves, I would have been an empty cage with a green light.

Or, a darker place inside me admits, I'd have agreed to King's terms.

We take turns sleeping, so that one of us always has eyes glued on the cage door. The minute it opens, we're going to put our escape plan into action.

And do our best to avoid King's crew.

––––––––

"Dram. Orion." Reeves stands. "It's time."

With my heart pounding, I double-check the knife on the inside of my arm. The door opens, and we run toward Sanctuary. We're going to climb onto the roof, so we're on higher ground when they attack.

"Watch for hovers," Dram says. "If one lowers a cable, we get on it." We race past the other cages. No sign of King yet.

"Tell me how this saves us," Reeves says. "When the hover heads through the curtain, we're dust."

He was sick though the night, but the guy can still outrun me. I count the cages to Sanctuary. Ten more. My eyes scan for a pack of half-mad dusters.

"When it raises the tow cable," Dram answers, "we climb in through the bottom of the hover and stow away in the hold."

Three more cages, two more, almost there.

A niggling doubt breaks through my focus.

Last cage.

Something's wrong. If Sanctuary's walls could be breached, everyone with a collar would be hammering their way inside. That means . . .

"The walls are electrified!" I shout.

Reeves connects with the cirium walls. His collar screeches above the sound of the energy blast as it rips through his body.

"Reeves!"

He lies still, a crumpled heap beside Sanctuary.

Dram rolls him over, even while we scan for movement. No way King and his crew haven't seen us by now.

Reeves pulls in air like his body's resisting it. My hands hover above him. What would Dad do?

"I have to tell you . . . the forfeit," Reeves gasps. "They're not all dead. I lied to Cranny to protect them."

"What? What are you talking about?"

"We found a way out of four."

"Where are they?" I try to wrap my mind around the fact that Subpars could have left Outpost Five.

"Cordon Five."

"It's a closed cordon, nothing lives there."

"Exactly." And then I realize what he's telling me. They escaped through the prison tunnel where Cranny assumed they'd die.

"We can't stay here," Dram says. We haul Reeves to his feet, but his legs won't hold him. Dram props him up beside the wall of the incinerator.

"Well, this will be convenient for them," Reeves mutters.

"Fire," Dram curses, dragging a hand through his hair.

"We need to get inside again," I say. "We could break through the ceiling, climb our way up."

Dram nods. "Then we wait here. First one to attack us will be our ticket in."

"And if they all attack at once?" Reeves asks.

Neither of us answers.

"I'll watch the north and east sides," Dram says. "Rye, you keep an eye out south and west."

I turn my blade in my hand and stare toward the opening cages.

"When the other forfeit walked free, why didn't you go with them?" I glance at Reeves. "Why did you stay in four?"

"If you were forfeit," he whispers, "and Dram was on the other side of the bars, risking his life for you—wouldn't you stay?"

I open my mouth, but I have no words.

Reeves smiles in a way that reminds me of the boy he once was. "I don't think I'm the only one of us who's loved like that."

He pulls himself to the ledge of the incinerator.

"What are you doing?"

"I'm dead already. Let it count for something."

"No!"

He pulls Foss's memorial pendant from around his neck. "Dram, take this. I need you to help me keep a promise." He struggles to drag in breath. Blood seeps from his mouth and nose.

Dram grips the black glass.

"When you bury that in free soil," Reeves says, "you're doing it for me and Len, too."

Tears fill Dram's eyes. He nods.

"I'm glad I stayed in four," Reeves says, his eyes finding mine. "Glad I heard that bell." He grasps Lenore's gold glass and tips his body over the edge.

A wailing cry pierces the air. Dram catches me against his chest, and I realize the sound is coming from me. Smoke plumes from the incinerator, and the flash dust depository emits a soft chime. Dram holds me tighter, like he can pull me into himself—as if we're clinging to each other at the top of the air cave. It's so hard to breathe, and it hurts. It hurts too much.

But there's no help coming this time. We're on our own, and we have only this one chance Reeves has given us.

"He is free," I choke.

Dram knots his fist around the black glass. "Not yet."

We stare at the numbers scrolling above the red door. Dram's got his longest blade held at the ready. I'm holding my steel-lined boot like a club. We don't have to look to know that King's crew has almost reached us. Their snarls rend the air like wild beasts.

"You're mine, Subpars!" King shouts.

24 Hours. 0 Minutes.

The bolt clicks, and the door opens.

"Get inside!" Dram shoves me toward the door.

No way I'm leaving Dram to face them alone, so I wedge my other boot in the door. An alarm beeps as it tries to slide shut against my boot.

King grabs me. I whirl and slam my boot into the side of his head. He staggers back.

Bone Guy lunges for Dram, and I swing at his face. The open buckles rake across him and he roars. He turns on me.

"Marker!" I shout.

Dram slams his knife into my attacker's back, and it pushes out through the man's chest, impaling him like a flash bat. Two more convicts are on him before he can pull his blade free.

"Get into Sanctuary!" he shouts.

The door alarm beeps, and over its persistent chirp, I hear a new sound—the approach of a hover.

I look up. The distraction costs me.

King slams me to the ground and jams his knee into my stomach. "Let's carve up the rest of your pretty face." He leans over me, knife flashing.

I lunge up and wrap my arms around his neck, dragging him toward me, his head pinned to my chest. He struggles, and I wrap my legs around him, holding him immobilized.

"DRAM!"

Beside me, Dram grunts and there's a shuffling of feet. A man snarls; another gasps. King's knife shifts, the metal warms, and I know he's using his conjuring ability. The metal shoots up between us and clamps around my neck, pinning me to the dirt like a shackle. My hold on him loosens.

"MARKER!" I scream as the metal tightens around my throat.

"Mark!" Dram rips King off and drives his blade into his chest. He pulls another blade from his boot and slams it into King's arm. My metal shackle loosens, and I lurch toward Sanctuary.

"The door's closing!" It's finally forced my boot aside. I leap into the gap, wedging my body into the space. It feels like I'm holding up a cavern wall. "Hurry!"

Across the sands, the rest of the dusters see me and start running. I am the only thing barring their way to Sanctuary. "Shut the door!" Dram yells.

King slams his palms against Dram's legs. The metal buckles on his boots morph and encircle Dram's legs like twin snakes.

I pull a blade and throw it spinning, end over end, toward the nearest duster. It sinks into the man's chest.

Dram yanks King to his feet. "So you can conjure metal,"

he mutters. "How are you with fire?" He thrusts King's arm over the incinerator and slams his hand on the button.

King screams, and Dram dives through the door, which seals behind us.

"Hover," he gasps. "We need to get to the roof!"

"Lift me!" I scramble onto the table. Above the crazed shouting outside, I hear the metallic whirring of a tow cable. Dram leaps up and hauls me onto his shoulders, maneuvering me toward a vent in the ceiling.

"On three," he says. "One, two, three!" He thrusts me toward the ceiling, and I catch hold of the vent grate.

"Got it." I tear it free, grateful for all the times I climbed the Range—for the strength to hold myself suspended and pull myself up. I slide into the space and brace myself. Dram and I have done this hundreds of times down the tunnels. I reach down for him, and he climbs up beside me.

Congress electrified the walls of Sanctuary, but not the roof. They never imagined anyone would try to escape the only safe place in Cordon Two. We push through the vent and flatten ourselves onto the roof. We have no way of knowing if anyone's observing us—or if the hover pilot can see us.

"There," Dram says. "It's locked onto the flash dust deposit."

A few moments later, the hover begins its ascent. The deposit is half the size of our cage. Sand streams from the metal as it lifts from the cordon.

It's just close enough to reach—with a really good jump.

"We have to assume the deposit roof's electrified," Dram calls. "Jump for the cable."

We stand and edge our way to the side. I study the distance, once more cursing my short legs. I am strong, but it's a narrow, swaying target at least three meters from where I crouch.

Beneath us, the dusters yell. They've caught sight of us.

"Now, Rye!" Dram shouts.

I run for the edge and leap. The cable collides with my body, and I grasp it, my arms shaking. It sways as Dram catches hold beneath me.

"Hold on!" he calls.

The ground below drops away as the hover lifts. We sway with the cable, the flash dust collection sweeping above the ground like a pendulum.

"We're nearing the perimeter," he says.

I squeeze my eyes shut and press my forehead against the cable.

Please. Please. Please.

Dram grasps my leg, like his touch is enough to sustain me through an electric force field.

"We cleared it!" he shouts.

My blood races like it got tripped up on the way to my heart. "They're not raising the cable," I shout.

"I know. We're going to have to jump."

Jump. We are several meters above the sands of Cordon One. And rising.

"Now!"

"But—"

He grabs hold of my other leg and pulls. My hands slip, and we fall.

The hover's engines swallow the sound of my scream.

TWENTY-TWO

0 grams flash dust

WE DROP INTO a graveyard. I've never seen one, but Dad told me once of places where people used to bury their dead. Before the curtain fell. Before Burning Days.

A human skull rests beside my hand.

I lie on my back, waiting for my breath to return, taking stock of my injuries. I still have skin on my skull, so I suppose I'm doing better than I could be.

"Rye?" Dram gasps. He's half buried in sand an arm's length away.

"Still here," I croak. I have sand in my mouth. On my face. In my eyes. Maybe that's why I can't breathe. I slowly roll onto my stomach. "You?"

"Alive."

"Good. If you ever pull me from another hover cable, I'll kill you."

"Fair warning." He groans, struggling to his feet.

"So, Cordon One?" I ask, still hugging the ground. "What's it like?"

"Empty."

"Any cages?" I ask.

"Nope."

"Crazy Conjies?"

"Huh-uh."

"A big sign that says 'Welcome to the Protected City'?"

"See for yourself." I clasp his hand, and he drags me to my feet.

A massive, shining silver barrier rises up out of the sand in the distance, taking the place of the flash curtain. It towers more than a hundred meters high, curving like a protective arm. The ends of the flash curtain wave, in tendrils of light and particles, stretching like fingers from Cordon Two.

Maybe it's the cirium shield, but Cordon One doesn't consume its victims with fire and heat like the others. It leaves the bones to litter the ground like a monument to lost hope.

I search the white sky, expecting flash vultures, but there's nothing. No sound, barely any wind. This place is empty. A perfect place for a Subpar to finally let go.

I tip my face to the ash-soaked sky. I imagine it is blue.

"What are you doing?" Dram asks.

"The air is stable." I don't know this for sure. I just don't care anymore.

"Let's search the perimeter of the shield." He starts walking toward the massive wall of cirium. "They won't be looking for us that way."

"You still think there's a way out?" I ask. He stops and turns.

"You saw that map. Come on!"

"Look around, Dram," I call. "There's no camp, no turn-stiles." I lift my empty hands. "There aren't even collection deposits. The dead don't turn to flash dust here." He turns in a slow circle, his eyes scanning the distance. "It's because we're done. This is the last cordon."

"Then what is the point of bringing people here?" he asks, pointing to the remains of a former inhabitant.

"The same as the rest," I say. "To study us and see how long we last." And then, as if it's lending support to my words, a weathered sign, pitted with holes, catches my eye. I point at it and laugh. Dram walks toward it, but I can read the worn print from here.

DANGER: FLASHTIDE

Flashtide. The word sounds beautiful and horrifying at the same time. I glance at the bones studding the sand and settle upon *horrifying*.

"What's a flashtide?" Dram asks.

"I'm pretty sure it's what killed these people."

Dram hits the sign and curses. I hear the Really Bad Conjie Word and worse.

He stomps back toward me. "That settles it, then. We go for the shield. It's our only option."

The shield. Like we can just walk up and ask nicely for them to let a couple of rebel Subpars into the jewel. It seems all my strength drained away the moment I touched this sand. I'm as brittle as the bones at my feet.

"I think I'll just rest here with my new friends for a bit." I gesture toward the skulls. Dram squints at me, and I know part of him is trying to gauge if I hit my head when we dropped here. "Have you *looked* at your Radband? At mine?"

He stiffens. "So you're just giving up? After everything we've gone through—"

I press my hand over my mouth and turn away. I can't stand for him to see me break apart. But my Radband is yellow as a caver's suit, and his is like the tip of a flame. Dark amber. I don't have magic, like Mom once told me. I'm just a girl who was reckless and naive, and now people I loved are dead.

Dram turns back to the cirium shield. I watch him run toward the barrier, like it's got the answers he needs.

I drop down onto the smooth white ash. It snowed once at Outpost Five, when I was little and Mom was still alive. We took Wes outside so he could feel it—before Dad told us it wasn't safe.

I spread my arms wide and push them through the ash of Cordon One, the way I wanted to that day at Outpost Five. The snow that day seemed like a promise from the sky. *I am here, just past what you can see. Reach for me.*

My life has been one long empty promise.

Dram shouts, and my eyes shoot open. Flash vultures circle above me—two of them.

"Flash me," I curse. Cordon One will not take me this way. I lunge to my feet. Dram sprints toward me, shouting at the vultures, waving his arms.

A dark shape dives for me. My hand flies to my arm sheath, but I used all my blades escaping the dusters, and I stand defenseless. It slams into me, knocking me to the ground, talons raking the front of my suit. I lurch away from its beak.

Dram shouts my name. He sounds terrified. Two more vultures land beside me. Someone in Alara is probably observing this moment, and I wonder if they feel sympathetic to our plight. Or ashamed. If they feel anything at all.

We're Subpars, after all.

Rage wells inside me.

I drive my hands toward the creature's face. Its snapping beak opens, and I shove my gloved hands straight in, grasping either end of it and tugging it wide—wider than it should go. The bird struggles; its leathery wings slap my face as it tries to free itself.

It's making strange, desperate cries, which echo mine. I roar, rising up and snapping my arms wide. The creature's jaw cracks apart. It flops and flutters, and I shove it off me. Another vulture seizes it, tearing into it. I roll to my feet and run.

Toward Dram.

He stands a few meters away. Somehow he drew the other vultures away from me, and two of them circle above his head. One bobs up and down just in front of him. Blood drips from Dram's arm where he cut himself open.

"No!" I search the ground for a weapon, anything that might help. I grab a leg bone. It's splintered on one end.

I hold it like a spear and run toward the hopping, dancing vulture that's got the scent of Dram's blood. It doesn't seem to notice my approach, or maybe it just doesn't consider me a threat. I jam the bone straight through its body. It caws and writhes, and I lift it high, waving it toward the other vultures, whose beady eyes fasten on new prey. They're hungry for flesh. Any flesh. I toss the skewered vulture to the ground, and they descend. Dram and I back away and run. I shut out the sounds of their zealous feasting, the delighted caws of the living vultures and the violent death of the other.

We stop to catch our breath. Dram pulls me into his arms, so tight I can barely breathe. He draws his sleeve back down over his arm without letting go of me. He is courageous, my Dram, but never reckless. Not unless it concerns me.

We stand beside the cirium shield, so close I imagine I feel the hum of its metallic pulse. It's made of the ore I was taught to chase. I know its call like it knows mine. If this wall of cirium has secrets to tell, I will hear them.

I pull off my glove and set my hand on the smooth barrier. It is warm, not cool like other metal. I close my eyes.

"What are you doing?" Dram asks.

"Listening."

"There's no sound."

But there is. The cirium shield emits a low hum, an echo of its mother, the flash curtain.

I helped put this barrier here—me and Dram and Graham and Mom and countless Subpars before us. I look down. If Subpars had ever tried to get past it, they would never have gone over. They would have gone under. That is what we do best.

"There's a tunnel," I whisper. I drop to my knees and feel under the layers of fine white sand and ash. I can feel it inside myself—a break in the cirium's song.

Dram kneels beside me. He grabs a piece of bone and starts digging. I grab his wrist. "Wait." I squint at the silver wall. It reflects the white light of the sky so brightly it's hard to look at. My eyes start to water. "I thought I saw something."

"A door?" Dram asks dryly.

I smile. "No. I thought I saw something etched into the cirium. Like writing."

"Fire," Dram whispers. We both see it at the same time. A short distance to our left, scratches mar the smooth surface of the metal.

I crawl toward the line of words painstakingly carved at the base of the shield. We kneel side by side, reading the message. The sign. One that only Subpars would truly understand.

WE ARE THE FORTUNATE ONES.

Tears blur my vision, but they don't keep me from seeing the symbol carved beneath the words: a caver's mark of parallel lines. The way out.

Dram scoops away layers of sand. "Too bad whoever did this couldn't leave us a light bolt to mark the entrance."

"Maybe he did," I say, lifting an object in my hand. It's tethered to the ground with a shard of bone. Before I wipe the dust away, I know what it is. A caver's memorial pendant.

"Holy fire." Dram smooths his fingers along the green glass that matches the one he wears. And the one Lenore wore.

We know who carved the words.

Dram's father.

TWENTY-THREE

0 grams flash dust

ARRUN BERRENDS DID not die at Cordon Four. He survived the burnt sands and whatever else the Congress put him through. He made it at least this far, maybe farther.

Dram and I work our pieces of bone into the earth, neither of us speaking. Sweat drips from our foreheads, spattering the white ash like tears.

Someone used everything the Congress turned us into to mine the most important thing of all. A way out.

I look at the bleached skeletons beside the shield with growing respect. If there's a tunnel to the other side, it would have taken more than one person to dig it—more than one life given so that future Subpars could be free. Us.

We are so close.

I dig into the ground with renewed vigor.

"What if someone's watching?" Dram asks.

"They would already have stopped us." I've struck something hard. I drop my bone and push my hands into the dirt. "Something's here."

"A cover," Dram says. "Like the one used over tunnel one." He crouches and blows the dust away, revealing a mat of woven cloth and bone.

I wedge my shard of bone beneath and pry it up. We peer down the dark hole.

"Well, ore scout," Dram says, "you ready to lead us down one last tunnel?"

I can't speak past the emotion clogging my throat, but Dram reads the answer in my eyes. I flip onto my stomach and stretch my legs down the hole, finding bits of bone wedged into the earth for hand- and footholds.

"I'll be right behind you," Dram says.

"No." I look up at him. "I need to see what's at the bottom first."

Concern knits his brow, but he nods.

I grip the shards of bone, descending slowly, and darkness closes around me. After a few minutes, I can see only a pinprick of light at the tunnel's mouth. When I hit bottom, I blow out a breath and push my hands along the space, hoping for a widening, another stretch carved into the earth beneath the cirium shield.

"Found it!" I shout. Dram immediately starts descending.

I stretch my hands into the tube of space and push forward, thankful for once for my glowing yellow Radband indicator. "Here we go, bone tunnel."

"Is that what we're calling this one?" Dram says behind me. He must have dropped halfway down.

"Seems right." I stretch my senses, inhaling the musty air.

"How about, the tunnel to end all tunnels?"

My breath grows shallow as the tunnel evens out. The walls

close tighter around us than they did on the descent. "You will be pleased to know that this is just like the neck of nine," I say. "Except a little less wide."

"Excellent," Dram mutters.

"And I have almost no light, so I have no idea how far this goes, or what's ahead of us."

"Perfect. I'll let you know if anything comes up behind us."

"A sound plan," I murmur. Even without my earpiece, I hear the panic tightening his throat. We can't be sure anyone actually finished digging this tunnel. The only thing I'm sure of is that Subpars died in the effort. A tunnel this long—dug with only hands and bone—would have taken years. I reach out before me, half expecting to touch a decomposing body at any moment.

I imagine that Dram is having similar thoughts. I can hear each one of his staccato breaths. If we hit a wall or even an obstacle like a body, we are stuck. It would be nearly impossible to work our way back out of this tube of earth.

"I have flash dust in my pocket," I say. "Not much, but enough to flame up. Do you have anything we could use for flint?" My breath gasps from my lungs as I propel myself forward, stretching my hands into utter darkness, praying, praying they don't hit a wall.

"Um . . ." Dram follows so close, I feel his hands brush my feet. "Bone—would that work? Wait—the zipper on my suit. Maybe if we wrap the dust in a bit of cloth and . . ."

He continues, but I'm only half listening. I've given him something else to focus on, a problem he can actually try to solve. Meanwhile, my scout's senses are picking up a change in the air.

"We've cleared the cirium barrier," I say. The tunnel is so close to my face I taste the dirt when I talk.

Dirt.

"Dram, there's soil. Actual real dirt with nutrients in it." I can't hide my excitement—and my relief. This earth is something *other* than what we mined at Outpost Five, and nothing like the radioactive sands of the cordons.

My hand hits a wall of dirt. At first, I don't understand. My emotions swing wildly from hope to despair.

"Why did you stop?" Dram's voice is small, like he's preparing himself for my answer.

I push both hands in front of me. My nails gouge the earth, searching for a turn or crevice I can't see with my eyes.

"Rye?" The panic rises in Dram's tone.

"Breathe with me, okay?" I drag in a shaky breath, and Dram follows. We exhale slowly. I hear Graham's voice in my head. *You've got a job to do, girlie.*

Inhale.

I'm so scared we're trapped I can't move I can't move!

Step in my steps.

Exhale.

"Dram, push backward. I'm going to feel around and see if I missed a turn." I know I didn't miss a turn.

He's still frozen in place. "Dram?"

"Can't breathe," he bites out. "Can't. Do this."

"Here we go," I say, as if I'm Jameson and there's no arguing with my orders. "Together. Pushing back." I lever myself on my arms and slide backward, my feet pushing into Dram's face. "Go, caver. Right now."

He eases backward.

I try to remember what Dad said about Dram's condition. His fear of tight spaces is fed by the terror of having no control. I need to give him a sense of control.

"Dram?"

"Yes?"

"You're leading us out of here. I can't see when you move, so every time you push back, I want you to say 'marker.'"

"Marker." He shoves his body back.

"Mark." I push mine into the space he freed up.

"Marker," he says, sliding farther.

"Mark."

We're going to make it. I shut out every thought but the call of his voice and my response.

"Wait." I sense something. A subtle shift in the air. A thought hits me, and I reach up. The space is wider above our heads. Not enough to sit up, or even crawl, but high enough that I didn't notice the extra space initially. With my heart in my throat, I kneel and then slowly stand. A tunnel of earth surrounds me, the width of a man's body.

"Dram." I reach up, digging my hands into the walls of the tunnel, searching for handholds. This is not rock, like the walls of nine. I can't wedge my fingers in cracks of stone. "Dram!" There is nothing to climb, but he can lift me.

"You found an opening?" He slides into my legs. "Oh, fire, you're standing!"

"There's only room for one at a time," I answer. "I'm going to wedge myself up here until you can stand beneath me."

"Like the air cave in nine," he says.

"Yes." I tuck my knees to my chest and hold myself in the tube above him. He raises his hands and slowly stands.

He forms a ledge with his hands, and I place my feet on them.

"Ready?" he asks. And I know he's not just talking about lifting me, but everything that comes after. If the tunnel ends now, we'll have to face whatever life we have left digging with bones in the dark to escape the flashtide. And if it doesn't end . . .

Am I ready for the world that lies beyond Cordon One? For all I know, there are guards with guns waiting to apprehend us.

For all I know, there's nobody, and we are going to stare up at the sky and see what freedom looks like.

"Ready." I stand, and he pushes me up, as hard as he can. My head hits something. I cry out, and instinctively catch myself, my feet splaying wide to hold myself aloft.

"Rye!"

"I'm all right." I reach up, feeling the surface I whacked with my head. "It's some kind of cover. Wait . . . there's something wedged against it." I try to make sense of what I'm feeling with my hands. "It's a light stick!" I call, cracking the tube. Green light glows to life in my hands. My breath catches.

"Is it a way out?" Dram calls.

"I think so. Come up here. You need to see this."

I hold the light toward him, and it illuminates a pattern of hand- and footholds, carved by whoever made this last climb. They are just the right size for Dram.

Step in my steps.

I wonder if they are his father's. Arrun Berrends may be alive somewhere on the other side of this cover. Alive, because he carved a path to freedom in the dark, with his bare hands and the bones of rebels before him.

Dram holds himself below me. "What did you find?"

I shine the light on the items attached to the cover. Reaching up, I pull down a bottle of water and pass it to Dram, then open a narrow pouch of foil with some kind of writing on it. "I think this is food." I take a cautious bite, but I'm not used to chewing my food. My tongue explodes with foreign flavors and sensations. "Here—" I pass the rest to Dram.

He makes a face as he chews. "What's that other thing?"

I tug down the folded card and open it up. "A map." My eyes scan the words and then fly back to the diagram. I have to read the words twice more before I believe what it says. "Holy fire."

"Rye?" Dram shifts closer to me.

"This tunnel doesn't lead into the city. Alara's thirty kilometers south."

"Then what's on the other side of that cover?"

I hand him the map. "Striders."

TWENTY-FOUR

O grams flash dust

DRAM STARES AT me like he's looking for signs of flash fever.

"Look at it." I point to the diagram that shows a hoverfield surrounded by Strider barracks. "We've escaped to the Congress's military compound." We study the words on the page, as if they'll make better sense the longer we look at them.

"What do you think an 'Inquiry Module' is?"

I shake my head. There's no picture on the map, just dire warnings to avoid them.

"So we may have to fight our way to the city?" he asks.

"Or we go back and find out what the flashtide is." Even now, my muscles shake from holding this cramped position. If we don't go now, I won't have any strength left for whatever's on the surface.

Dram looks down at the darkness beneath our narrow tube of dirt. There is nothing in that direction but death.

When he meets my eyes, I'm wearing my resolve like armor. He nods.

We set our hands to the tunnel cover and push.

Using Dram's hand for leverage, I slide up through the narrow passage. A tangle of weeds and underbrush covers our exit. A hand seizes hold of me.

"Don't speak," a young man commands softly. Kohl lines his eyes, and his shaggy brown hair hangs past his ears. He draws me from the tunnel and guides me behind a wall before lifting Dram free and tamping the cover into place with his boot. I watch the man throw his back against the wall alongside us. Silver rings span his fingers, and he wears more pendants than I do. The knotted green sash at his waist jingles with tiny charms when he leans to peer around the corner.

"Who are you?" I whisper.

"Bade Imber," he says. "And you, Subpar?"

"Orion," I breathe.

"You're charmed Congress didn't pick up your movement," he says in his thick Conjie accent.

I stare at him, trying to make sense of his words.

"Get down!" he whispers.

A hovering metal machine whirs by. It hangs above the place we emerged, and a light, like a caver's headlamp, radiates from beneath it.

Bade draws his hand from his pocket, cradling a bit of dirt. He opens his fingers and a flame flares to life. My breath stops. I watched Roran conjure stone, but I can hardly believe what I'm seeing.

"We're slayed if it finds you." He angles his hand, like he's preparing to throw the fireball.

The machine pivots slowly, and I realize it's a miniature hover with a glass viewing shield in front. It glows from within, illuminating an empty containment capsule lined with metal clamps and arms.

Fear penetrates my haze of shock. I thought nothing could be worse than the cordons. Perhaps this side of the shield offers no refuge, after all. The machine's light clicks off, and it skims by, silent as a breath.

"I think that's an 'Inquiry Module,'" I whisper to Dram.

"Forget the machine," he says. "What the hell is he?"

Bade stretches his hand, and the flame dissolves. "Free Conjie."

"You can *make fire*?"

A cocky grin lifts Bade's lips. "It's a rare talent."

"I thought you couldn't conjure anything this close to the curtain."

"Not in this dirt," he says. "Too much cirium. But my pockets are filled with the earth of the provinces, and it's very much alive."

"How did you know we were coming?" I ask.

"You set off a beacon when you entered that tunnel. One of ours."

"Bade!" A woman runs from the shadows. "They caught Vale and Asher—" Her words break off when she sees us. "You got them in time. Good."

Her beauty is startling, her green eyes so intense they seem unreal. *Gem,* my mind shouts, but she's dressed like Bade and speaks with his accent. And her arm doesn't bear a Codev, but a woven metal cuff that matches his.

The woman studies Dram with equal intensity. "Bade," she murmurs, "look at his face."

Bade narrows his eyes on Dram. "Who are you?"

"Dram Berrends."

"Fire, he's Arrun's son!" she says.

"My father," Dram says, "he's alive?"

"He was before the Striders found us."

Arrun's alive. I glance at Dram.

"How do you know my father?" he asks, his voice hoarse.

"He leads the resistance," she says. "We were on a scouting mission, tracking the—"

"Enough, Aisla. This could be a trick," Bade says. "Congress could be using them—"

"It's not a trick." Aisla lifts Dram's green memorial pendant in her hand.

Bade's eyes widen. "You two are the first Subpars to find your way here in years. There's a lot to explain, but there isn't time now—we've got to get you out of here."

"Striders coming," Aisla says.

Soldiers march past, herding two Conjurors toward a small craft. I stare at the Conjies' hands. They're covered in mesh gloves that look like woven links of cirium.

"Binders," Bade whispers, following my gaze. "Keeps them from conjuring until Congress can Temper them." He glances at Aisla. "Can you fly the Skimmer?"

"Yes," she answers.

"I'll provide cover and get Vale and Asher. You lead the Subpars on." They share a conversation in a glance. I feel like I'm watching Reeves and Lenore outside tunnel nine. He reaches into his pockets, and his hands come away streaming dirt.

Aisla draws a gun. "Follow me." She springs forward, clearing a path as we sprint for the craft.

Fireballs blast past us, taking down Striders one by one. All at once, the ground erupts and thick vines burst up through the dirt, weaving a tight screen that shields us as we run.

Dram leaps into the winged craft, and I follow, clambering into the cargo space.

"Where are we going, exactly?" Dram asks.

"To the mountain provinces, but I'm gonna try to lose them in the curtain first." Aisla dives into the cockpit and flips switches above her head. The sound of turbines whines through the air, and the engines rumble to life. "Clear the door. I'm sealing her up."

Bullets spray the side of the craft, and I drop down, pressing my body flat. Vale and Asher leap inside, and Bade slips through just before the hatch closes.

"Get moving, Aisla!" he shouts.

Sirens erupt from the compound.

The hover lifts, and Bade grasps Dram's arm. "Your sister— is she still in Outpost Five?"

"You could say that," Dram replies, an edge to his voice.

"Lenore died," I say.

Bade drags a hand over his face. The sounds of the engines roar around us. "You should know," he says, loud enough to be heard, "your father never stopped trying to get you out—to free everyone trapped in the flashfall. That beacon you set off was his design."

"My dad was just a caver. A marker," Dram says.

"He's more than that, Subpar. Strap these on." Bade tosses us each a harness and pack and ducks into the cockpit. "Follow their lead." He nods to the other Conjies pulling on gear.

"What are these?" I call.

An older man grins. "Parachutes." He hands me a large wrist monitor. "Altimeter. Pull the cord at six hundred meters."

The craft streaks into the air. Cirium shields slide over the windows.

"Hold tight," Bade calls through the ship's intercom. "This won't be smooth."

I think of the hover rides I've had and tighten my grip. The Skimmer climbs, and I catch myself against the side of the hold.

"I'm taking us up," Aisla says. "We need as much altitude as possible before we stall out in the curtain."

"Hang on tight," Bade says. "Curtain's gonna rob our power for a sec—"

His voice cuts off, and we plunge into darkness. Emergency lights come to life, bathing us in blue light. The ship wobbles, like it's not sure which side it wants to drop toward.

"Pull yourselves to the hatch," the Conjie beside me says. "Hurry!"

We move toward the back of the ship, our hands wrapped in the net along the sides. The Skimmer plunges and dives, and we make our way, hand over hand, to the hatch.

"Prep your chutes," Bade says. "I'm going to fire a pulse blast to shake them off our tail."

Vibration rumbles up through the floor of the craft, so loud that I feel it rattling my bones. Dram hauls me to my feet and checks my harness. My hands shake too hard to fasten the altimeter.

"I've got it," he says, securing the band around my wrist. A thundering boom shakes the Skimmer. He guides me to the floor, and we weave our arms through the net.

The lights flicker back on.

"Still on us," Aisla says. "I'm gonna try to lose them. Hold tight!"

I can't possibly hold tighter than I already am. The ship climbs so fast, the force presses me to the floor with the weight of a cordon shard. Beside me, Dram groans. I feel like someone's stepping on my stomach—then suddenly the pressure eases and we plummet.

Dram and I grip the net as our bodies fly upward. I use every ounce of strength I have to hang on; the force of the pull wants to rip me free and plaster me against the ceiling. My eyes tear, and the pressure builds until I can't take a breath without effort.

"Lost them!" Aisla announces breathlessly. The ship levels out, and I gasp for breath on the floor of the hold, arms shaking.

"Flash. Me." Dram mutters.

The hatch grinds behind us, opening slowly.

"Don't get too close," Bade says. "Don't want you falling out till it's time."

I squint my eyes at the widening space. It's . . .

"Sky." I scramble across the hold and clutch the net by the hatch. It opens fully, like a window over a world I'm seeing for the first time.

"Flash. Me." I whisper.

TWENTY-FIVE

0 grams flash dust

WE MADE IT past the curtain. I can still hardly believe this one unequivocal truth. But the sky—big and blue and cloudless—fills my line of sight all the way past the mountains in the distance. The land stretches out in shades of green I never knew existed—grass and trees more vibrant than I ever imagined.

In an instant, my life's divided between what was before and what comes after. I lived in oppression on one side of the curtain, and now . . . I live.

"We made it," I whisper. Wind blows tendrils of hair against my cheek. My eyes water from staring so hard at the view.

Without taking his eyes from the sight, Dram weaves his fingers through mine.

"One last step." My hand tightens on the strap of my parachute.

Dram squeezes my hand. "Nothing we can't handle."

We watch the ground shrink beneath us as the Skimmer climbs. My heart hammers against my rib cage. Can people really survive such a fall?

"We're almost there," Bade says over the ship's intercom. "Do you remember what I told you?"

"Jump away from the hatch," I call over the wind blowing into my face. "Arms and legs out."

"Pull altitude?" he asks.

"Six hundred meters," Dram says.

"Good. And after you land?"

"Ditch the chutes and head up the north face of the tallest mountain peak," Dram shouts. "Use our names."

"Or your face," Bade says. "They'll take one look at you and know who you are. That works both ways, though—if Striders see you, you're slayed."

I stare down at the valley hugging the mountain pass, trying to imagine myself gliding to the ground.

"It's time," Aisla calls. "I'm emitting an exhaust burst to cover your jump."

My fingers dig into the metal door frame. "Dram!"

He catches my face between his hands. The gauge on his wrist glows orange, ready to count down every meter that we drop. His eyes shine, lit with excitement. We've traded places. It's like the neck of nine, only I'm the one frozen in fear. "I can't—"

"This is like the cliff before the second orbie pool," he shouts over the wind. "How many times have we scaled it?"

"Hundreds." I shake so hard, my teeth chatter.

"This is easier. Nothing out there wants to eat us!"

"Dram . . ." How can he smile right now?

"We're doing this now. Together. I'll be right behind you."

"You need to go!" Bade shouts. "I'll count it down for you. Ten, nine, eight . . ."

"I'll be right behind you, ore scout."

". . . six, five . . ."

I grip the sides and stare down at the ground. I will be brave. I will honor my mother and Wes—and Reeves and Lenore. I will finish what I started when I climbed the post above the tunnels and cut down the sign.

". . . four, three . . ."

The Congress says we are nothing beyond the tunnels. They are wrong.

I step to the edge.

We are the fortunate ones.

———

I let go and jump.

My stomach plummets. Air hits my body, pushing against me so hard I can't breathe. I may never breathe again. My eyes shut tight, but I can't remove myself from the horror of this fall that won't end.

That's not right. I need to see. My wrist gauge. I'm supposed to check . . .

Panic seizes me. Numbers scroll through my mind—429.21 grams; 3.7 milliliters; 22 hours, 19 minutes—but they're not the ones I need.

I free-fall, staring wildly at the numbers spinning on my altimeter. I try to find Dram, but he must be above me—I can't see him. Has he already pulled his chute? Am I late?

Fire oh fire oh fire!

Coordinates spin through my mind, but I force myself to recall the only number that matters now.

The ground rushes up at me. My arms and legs stretch out from my sides, and I drop through a layer of cloud.

Six hundred meters.

I glance at my altimeter: 552 meters. I pull the cord.

My chute plumes, yanking my body. I finally take a full breath. Finally take my first good look at my landing area.

That's when I see the hover.

TWENTY-SIX

0 grams flash dust

THERE IS SOMETHING about gliding to certain death. It's serene and catastrophic at the same time. I run a list of possible escape options through my mind, but in the end, I'm powerless to do anything but float from the sky like a broken bird, right into the waiting circle of Striders.

My legs buckle when I touch ground. I don't even try to get up when the soldiers cut my pack loose. I press my hands into the grass, feeling it, sun-warmed and verdant, before they—

I'm yanked to my feet with grumbles of "let's go, Subpar," and steered aboard the craft. I tip my head back, watching the sky as long as I can, for a last glimpse—

The hatch shuts, sealing me inside.

"Welcome back," Cranny says.

I make a sound of shock. *How?* my mind screams.

"You're running out of cordons to send me to," I say, working to hide my despair. I collapse onto a seat.

"The commissary sent me to collect you," he says.

A week ago, Cranny's inflated self-importance would've

annoyed me. Now I just feel empty. *Where's Dram? Did he make it?*

"You have a talent for survival, Scout," Cranny says.

I don't trust myself to speak. Right now I'm wishing I had Bade's talent for fireballs.

"Alara has further need of your service."

"I would rather run toward the flash curtain." I don't recognize my voice. Steel laced with venom. Dram would tell me to tread lightly. He'd remind me that Cranny holds the power here.

"Ah, defiant to the end," Cranny says. "You're not the one heading toward the curtain, though. We picked up Dram not far from here."

I thought I was beyond feeling. I was wrong. Anguish grips me. "What do you want?"

"First, let me tell you what I'm willing to offer. Dram will be spared the flash curtain. He will be taken to Alara."

I'm glad I'm sitting. I feel like I'm dropping from the Skimmer again.

"You told us there are no Subpars in the city."

"I'll have his Radband carefully removed. The Congress will find a place for him."

Dram will be safe. Free.

"And me?"

"You will return to Outpost Five." My head spins as his statement crashes down on me. "You are the best ore scout we've ever had. Your team brought up more cirium in one day than any outpost ever."

"People's lives were at stake."

Cranny smirks. "They will be this time, too. Dram is safe as long as you continue to impress Jameson."

"But we've already mined nine."

"We've expanded it."

Something in my expression makes him smile. "Yes, there have been a few changes at Outpost Five while you've been sifting sand in the cordons. Seems the last batch of cirium was different. It's something Jameson wants—enough to find you and bring you back."

"Will I . . ." I have to clear my throat. "Will I be able to earn my four hundred grams again?"

"Of course. The Congress is nothing if not fair."

"Fair," I whisper. The word hesitates on my tongue, like a flavor I'm tasting for the first time. I try to process the turn my future has taken. Tunnel nine. Outpost Five.

"You're only seventeen, Orion. You might actually stand a chance at earning four Rays again."

I had turned seventeen. In all my efforts to survive the cordons, I didn't even think about my birthday. I let my mind mull this thought because the rest is . . . inconceivable. It makes me want to tell him no, and then Dram will die.

"I'll do it," I murmur. My voice sounds like it's coming from a long way off. I force myself to hold Cranny's dark gaze. "Under one condition."

———

Dram is standing in a ring of Striders when the Skimmer comes for him. He cranes his neck, searching for me. Cranny grasps my arm, and it's that motion that draws Dram's attention. His eyes widen, and I can tell the exact curse words he's using.

I wish I could explain, but it's not part of Cranny's arrangement—neither is saying good-bye. There's no point, anyway. Dram can't know what I've done to buy his freedom.

It would destroy him. I soak in the sight of him, knowing this is the last time I will ever see him.

I made an addendum to Cranny's agreement. If I die down the tunnels, he cannot revoke the protection he's extended to Dram. What he and Jameson don't realize is that, without Dram, I won't survive nine. As Dad said, he is part of what makes me strong.

Pain knifes through my heart at the thought of Dad. He was the condition. By the time the hover lands at Outpost Five, Dad will already be gone, taken to the protected city. Free.

As much as I'd like to see him again, to spend my remaining days with him, I will not force him to watch the charade I'm playing with Cranny. Nor will he have to light my pyre when I'm taken by nine. The other cavers will honor my Burning Day. Dad will never wear my ashes.

The Striders force Dram into the Skimmer.

"Orion!" he shouts. I can't breathe past the weight in my chest. He fights against the soldiers, and they knock him to the floor. He's still shouting my name as the doors close.

"Time to go home," Cranny says, steering me toward the hover.

I watch Dram's craft disappear into the sky.

I'll never be home again.

TWENTY-SEVEN

0 grams cirium

OUTPOST FIVE RECEIVES me like a long-lost daughter. The cavers greet me warmly—as if I were away taking a break instead of being punished for inciting rebellion. They don't ask about the others. Perhaps the cavers have made their own arrangements with Cranny, and this is all part of the charade.

Marin hovers on the perimeter, hugging the light of a fire pit. Her eyes flick over me head to foot, like she can't quite believe I'm the same person. I can hardly believe it myself.

"So you're back," she says.

"Yes."

She nods as if it makes sense, but her eyes are full of questions. "And Dram?"

Pain knifes through my chest. "He earned passage through the flash curtain."

Her expression wars between surprise and confusion. "I'm happy he's free."

"Me too."

Something shifts in her eyes, and I can tell she's seeing past my walls. "You want to get a pint?"

"Flash me, yes," I say. She smiles and leads the way to the lodge.

Perhaps I won't be alone at Outpost Five, after all.

———

The fire pits have burned down to embers by the time I finally push through the door of my house. The home I shared with Dad, now an empty shell. It smells like him, the cream he rubbed into his hands, the chemicals he worked with in the infirmary. But even in the dark, I see that the shelves are bare, his books and microscope gone.

A sudden thought has me kneeling, prying up the floorboards.

Come and find me, Orion. This time it's Dad's voice I hear. His underground lab is dark, so I grab my headlamp and drop in. A piece of metal sheeting covers the chasm Roran conjured the day of the storm. I step carefully across it, the metal creaking beneath me as I explore the space.

He cleared it out. Just a few boxes of supplies and some vials remain. It looks like infirmary storage. I climb out, fighting the urge to cry. I don't know what I hoped he might've left me. A final message, maybe, or some clue as to what I should do next.

It feels strange lying in my loft bed in this empty house. Dad's bed doesn't feel right either, so I end up wrapping myself in his blanket and sliding under the bed. I wear my headlamp on dim and fall asleep staring up at Mom's map.

———

I walk toward nine with a sense of inevitability, like my destiny has always been tied to this tunnel, its fate interwoven with mine. Even from this distance, I sense the changes within its depths.

Like me, it has been reshaped by the Congress.

Cranny stands beside the Rig next to Jameson. His eyes narrow when he catches sight of me, and I hold back my smile. I'm not wearing a uniform. Nothing marks me as the Congress's ore scout but the remembrance pendants hanging down my shirt. I lift an Oxinator off a cart and sling it over my shoulder. I found a pair of my old gloves at the house, and Dad's satchel is strung across my chest. Mom's axe swings from my hand.

I stopped at Dram's house and got the knife he kept hidden under his mattress. I allowed myself a few moments, wrapped in his blanket, breathing his scent, before I slipped the blade into my boot and headed here.

"Cavers up!" Owen calls. Cavers pour through the doors of the Rig, but I notice they don't tap the sign supports as they head toward the tunnels.

Instead, they look at me.

"Scout," they murmur, as they walk past.

"Hunter," a man says.

Hunter?

Owen meets me at the mouth of nine, wearing a depth gauge and a light gun strapped to his hip. He's dyed his suit black. "I'm going with you."

Marin walks up beside me. "So am I." She hands me a skull-cap and a headlamp.

"Have you done this before?" I ask.

"No."

"I have no idea what's down there," I say.

"Maybe a way out." Her brow lifts, and she grins. I wonder what happened to the girl who ran when she saw my orbie-infected hand. She seems to read my thoughts. "You got past the curtain."

"I came back."

She studies my face. "I'm sure you have your reasons."

"Dram." I want her to know. "Dram is my reason."

Her eyes widen. "I figured Cranny had some hold over you."

My eyes slip down her suit. The ore scout in me leaps into action. "Keep your axe on the left, so you can reach it with your right hand," I say. "Your harness needs to be tighter." I pull the strap at her hip. "You don't want to keep your flare in your belt like that—it can ignite if you scrape the rocks." My hands move over her suit as I continue to adjust her gear, speaking softly. I realize I'm checking her the same way I did Dram. A fist squeezes my heart.

"I know how much you care for him," she says. "I think I knew before you did."

"He's easy to love," I murmur.

"No." She watches me solemnly. "You've traded your life for his. I wouldn't call that easy at all." She swings her axe to her left side and walks into nine.

———

"Do you understand your task today?" Cranny asks.

"Perfectly."

"You can't afford any mistakes. Jameson has high expectations."

"I know."

"Do you have everything you need?" Jameson asks, striding forward.

"No. Dram is gone. I need a new marker."

"Take your pick," he says, nodding toward a group of cavers.

"They're too big," I lie. "I need someone who can follow me through tight spaces." He raises a brow. As my marker, Dram towered over me. "I need that kid. What's his name?" I adjust my Oxinator on my back, like I don't really care what Cranny says. Like it makes no difference to me if he assigns Roran as my marker. But Mere's son is essential to my plan. I need a Conjuror for what I intend to do.

"The Natural?" Cranny asks. He shakes his head. "He's not commissioned as a marker—"

"I'll commission him myself," Jameson says. "Give her what she needs."

My hearts pounds, and I tell myself to breathe normally, look normal.

"Fine." Cranny mutters. He waves down a guard. "Get the boy. He's in the Rig." There's a palpable tension between him and Jameson, something volatile in the spaces between their words, like the wrong phrase could set fire to their fragile civility. I can't help feeling that it has everything to do with me.

"Scout!" Roran shouts, streaking toward me.

I want to shout back and throw my arms around him. Instead, I narrow my eyes. "Don't raise your voice like that down there, or you'll get us killed." His brow furrows. "You're with me now." I hand him a bolt gun. "Secure this to your belt. Step in my steps. Let's go."

He eyes me curiously, like he expected to touch a blanket and instead put his hand in an orbie pool. Good. Hopefully Cranny bought my act, too.

The new passage is a world unto itself. I'm starting to think that the Congress sent Conjurors down here to carve these paths and ledges—which is an interesting thought, since I'm going to try the same thing myself.

A few meters in, I pull my mouthpiece away. "I'm sorry for the act, Roran. Cranny can't know we're friends. No one can."

His scowl lifts.

"Did you see your mom?" I ask.

"Yes. I've been sneaking her stuff."

"I knew you would. Did she tell you how I found her in Cordon Four?"

"She said you gave her my flower."

I smile at the memory, that tangible bit of hope Mere and I exchanged through the fence.

"Where are Dram and Reeves?" he asks.

"Not coming back." I squeeze his shoulder.

Owen walks toward us. He's the only one I trust to guide Roran across. He understands structure and stability, and I'm trusting it will be enough to keep them from bringing the tunnels down on our heads. I turn to Roran, hoping I'm right about his ability, that he adapted to the elements.

"Roran, you're not going to be my marker. Each day down here, I want you to go with Owen."

"To where?"

"Four."

His eyes widen as the meaning of what I'm saying sinks in. "You want me to make a path across the tunnels?"

"Yes."

"But I can't conjure this close to the flash curtain—"

"Remember what happened the day of the flash storm?" He nods, wide-eyed. "I need you to be the Conjuror you are."

His eyes light up, and I can practically feel the energy pulsing from him. I take his hand and lay it on the cavern wall. It shudders at his touch.

"Are we going to get my mom and Winn free?"

My eyes meet his, and I know they're just as bright. "We're going to get everyone free."

―――――――

We make it four hundred meters the first day. A fair distance scouting a new passage, but I want to press deeper even more than Jameson does. I have never been separated from Dram before, but this is more than just missing him. Something is wrong, and I feel it the way I feel the presence of cirium. It's a song in my veins, and this time it's discordant.

When we emerge from the tunnel, we're greeted by a sight I hoped to never see again—the long wooden struts of a cordon corral. My breath seizes in my chest. Only someone who's shuffled through the turnstiles of Cordon Four understands what this means.

I don't have all the pieces of the puzzle, but I feel like there's an invisible clock hanging over us—like the one above Sanctuary, counting down the minutes until the illusion of safety is shattered.

I need to find out what the Congress is planning. My gaze narrows on Central's stone walls, and it occurs to me that there's just one place here I've never climbed.

―――――――

The mansion is like an island of civility, complete with artificial lawns and trees, a façade that distracts the eye from the patrolling guards and cirium shields that protect it as a command center. It's stood here for generations, a symbol of Alara's strength.

But there's a chink in its armor.

"You're sure the security sensors are down?" I ask Owen.

"They shorted out during the flash storm. That's why they've posted extra guards." We watch the guards milling around the front in Radsuits. Suits that give them limited visibility.

"Whenever the Radlevels rise, the interior sensors malfunction. That's why Jameson had Barro make a lock and key for his quarters." Owen grins and hands me the key Barro made. An exact copy of the commissary's. "Just look for the door with the sturdy iron lock."

I smile. If any Subpar was ever on the side of cavers, it's the man who forges our axes and makes our memorial pendants.

"I'll let you know what I find," I murmur.

The stone is pitted from the elements and uneven in places, which makes climbing it possible for a girl used to the Range. Doing it quickly without being seen is the hard part. My foot slips, and my cheek scrapes the wall. I'm nine meters up, on a backside wall that's obscured in shadow. My worn Subpar clothes nearly blend with the stone as I scale one of the only places around here not patrolled by guards. They cover the entrances, not realizing that the exterior walls need defense from an ore scout with nothing left to lose.

I wish Dram could see me now. And Reeves. They would have loved seeing the mountain goat climb right past the Protocol-protected sanctity of Central. I cling to a pipe and break open a window, then drop inside.

As scared as I am, I can't help but notice the obscene grandeur of the place. Paintings hang in ornate frames, and dainty furniture sits in alcoves next to shelves of books. Books. I'd never imagined so many existed at Outpost Five.

My steps echo over the polished floor as I keep to the shadows. Tech rooms line this wing, filled with monitors and men and women in gray uniforms scurrying from station to station. A door seals shut as a tech walks past, and I duck around the corner.

I slip down to the second floor and scan the corridor. The door at the end is secured with a metal lock. I run toward it, hoping Jameson's not inside. Surely, the fact that his guards aren't present must mean he's away. The key slides smoothly into place, and the door opens with a click. I take a breath and step inside.

Maps cover the walls and electronic screens. The scout in me wants to examine each one, but I force myself to focus. I ignore the table and chairs, the bed and wardrobe, and head straight to his desk.

There's a weather report and supplies log. I imagine he keeps his communications on the kind of screencom I've seen his guards use. I sigh with frustration and look back to the maps. There's a smaller one tucked behind the others that catches my eye. It's labeled TUNNEL NINE.

My blood quickens. This is no map for nine. I trace the depth readings written over it in sparse black writing. They're wrong. For tunnel nine, anyway. Too shallow, and the winding stair-step patterns he's indicated are more like . . . seven.

I've stopped breathing. Seven was Mom's tunnel, closed since the collapse. Congress declared it unstable, not worth the sparse amounts of cirium the team had been bringing out of it.

Now all the blood is rushing through my body like it can shake me from my shock and get me moving away from here. I check under the bed, then the wardrobe, searching through uniforms, even running my hands along the wood, feeling for hidden panels. If Jameson's recording those measurements, he needs a depth gauge.

I run to his desk and drag the chair out. I drop to my knees and feel beneath his desk. Wood, wood . . . tech—wedged in a corner.

A depth gauge, glinting with fresh particle dust.

The commissary is not what he seems.

Still, this doesn't explain the corral going up beside the lodge. I shove the gauge back and rifle through his papers, looking for something with the word *cordon*. A flat, silver tech device sits in the middle of the desk. I slide my finger along the side, and words and numbers illuminate above it. The word *cordon* is here more times than I care to read, and beside it—a timetable.

Voices drift up from the stairwell. I turn off the projection, dash through the door, and twist the key in the lock.

I turn and crash into a guard. A guard wearing a chain of office.

"Flash me," I whisper, and look up into Jameson's startled eyes.

"What's going on?" Cranny calls. He strides toward us from the end of the hall. "What have you done, Orion?"

"I had questions for her," Jameson replies smoothly. I look at him, trying to mask my surprise.

"Subpars are not permitted inside Central," Cranny bristles.

"I don't require your authorization, Director," Jameson says, a note of warning to his voice.

"You've breached Protocol," Cranny says, his face flushing. "Be assured that I will inform the council."

Jameson stiffens. "The *council* is currently occupied with the threats of two hostile city-states and a shortage of flash dust, which makes Alara's only military advantage—flash weapons— ineffective. They are therefore having to negotiate an alliance with Ordinance that will give that government *unprecedented* access to our resources. At the same time, we are dealing with a Conjuror uprising in the outlier regions." He steps toe-to-toe with Cranny. "But do please interrupt the council to inform them that a Subpar was allowed to walk inside your outpost building."

Cranny's mouth gapes. Jameson is back to wearing every insignia on his uniform like it was created just for him. Even the way he stands in the mansion gives the impression that it's *his* and he's simply allowing Cranny to use the space.

If I didn't despise the Congress, I might actually like the man.

"I'll see this Subpar out," Jameson says, "and restore the Protocol." He steers me down the stairs, and my heart hammers against my ribs.

He could have—*should have*—exposed me.

He leads me out. "Don't ever risk that again," he says. "I won't be able to cover for you a second time."

Words trip on my tongue. I'm not sure what to say.

"I assume you found what you were looking for?" he asks.

I can't think straight, not with his piercing stare boring into me. "You're scouting seven," I murmur. His brows creep toward his hairline. "I found your depth gauge. And the map."

His face doesn't change, but for the barest tightening of his jaw. "You must not speak of it. To anyone."

"Are you a Subpar?"

"Orion—"

"A Natural wouldn't risk it." My eyes drift to his dosimeter, pulsing green. "What is your interest in a closed tunnel?"

"Trust me when I tell you to leave it at that."

"Why did you help me?"

"I couldn't risk you being punished again."

"You sent me to a prison cordon!"

"No. Cranston was operating under temporary authority, and he crossed a line. I'm sorry you endured that."

"You're *sorry* for it?" Suddenly, I've found my words, and there are too many, and none of them right for a commissary. "You're *sorry* that there are cages where people are *turned into flash dust*?"

His face changes, as if he's struggling to hold on to a proper commissary expression. "Yes, I'm sorry for it," he says, his voice raw.

"What about the new cordons I saw on your screencom? Are you *sorry* about those, too?"

His expression hardens. "The tunnels are tapped out, Orion! Flash dust is everything to the Congress now."

"What will happen to the people here?" I ask.

"Congress will evacuate Central and send Gems to serve as Compliance Regulators."

His words leave me cold. "When?"

"It depends on the Radlevels. Three days at most."

"And you won't stop it."

A look crosses Jameson's face, and it's not the commissary kind. "I've done what I can to stall the inevitable, but I'm one voice of *five*. If I protest too loudly, they will see in me things I can't afford for them to see."

There is so much I need to tell the others. And we have so little time. I leave, my mind a riot. I try to figure out what all the secrets mean . . . and why a commissary of Alara trusts me with his.

———

I meet Marin beside the tunnels. She takes one look at my face and curses long and low.

"My house," I whisper. "It's not safe to talk here."

We run through the outpost, keeping to the less-used path beside the mill, my blood racing to keep pace with my feet. I push through the door and wedge a chair under the knob. I've never feared the Congress more.

"I saw Jameson's screencom. They're going to blow the Barrier Range and extend the cordons," I announce.

"What about the outposts?" Marin asks.

"There won't be any more outposts. Congress is clearing everyone from Central."

"The Subpars," Marin breathes. "What happens to all of us when the Range falls?"

I don't want to be the one to tell her. I've witnessed it firsthand—the hell and horror of mining the burnt sands. We die. That is the real answer to her question.

"We're not going to be here when they blow the Range," I say instead. "I'm leading everyone out through nine."

"Leading us where?"

"A place they'll never look for us."

———

We wake to the sound of a buzzer. It echoes through the outpost, jolting me back to a place of fire and ash.

"Orion!" Marin cries. She stayed the night in my old loft room.

"It's all right." I slip from bed as she clambers down the stairs. It's really not all right.

"What is that?" She has to shout over the sound. "Is it a cordon breach?"

"We need to get down nine." I pull on clothes with shaking hands.

She watches me, her face paling. "Orion?"

"Hurry!"

She tugs on boots just as the sound cuts off. "How do you know what that thing was?"

"It's what they use in Cordon Four." I grab her arm. "Let's go."

I've never seen a single Gem at Outpost Five before, but now ten of them stride from the hover, wearing identical gray and red uniforms. A mix of men and women of various ages, but they all have the same severe posture, unnatural beauty, and a restrained strength that gives the impression of a spring wound too tight.

Compliance Regulators.

We are out of time.

My gaze stretches across the path. Owen watches me through the line of Gems. He nods. We must finish today.

———

I sit atop the Barrier Range. It's dying. I feel it in the shifting stone beneath me, and I see its lifeblood poured out in the distance, like a beast with part of its spine carved out. Sometime during the night, Congress began blowing apart the mountains to the north of us. There is no longer any barrier shielding Outpost Four from its cordon. I hope that Dram is right and the other outposts are empty—that we are the only Subpars left. If not, we will be soon as the rest of the Range is brought down. And then we will be nothing at all.

The Congress must have its flash dust.

Roran sits at my side. I don't have to explain what I see. He knows enough to put the pieces together—maybe even more than me.

"Alara's at war," I tell him. "Flash weapons are the only thing giving us the advantage."

"You think that makes it right?"

"No. It just makes them desperate." I look out over Cordon Five. It's the day's end, and the flashfall reflects off the glass cordon in shades of pink and gold.

Trepidation tingles along my nerves. It's a closed cordon for a reason. What if there are creatures there I've never encountered? What if there are emberflies? I remind myself that I've survived emberflies. And worse. Cordon Five's our best option.

Our only option.

"Have you been practicing?" I ask. It's why we're up here. A final test.

"Yes." He twirls an object in his palm and tosses it to me.

I catch it—round and red, it's some sort of fruit. My eyes fly to his, and he shrugs like it's no big deal that he can make food from outpost dirt.

He laughs at my expression. "It's called an apple, Subpar."

"It's *magic,* Roran."

He rolls his eyes. "It's the curtain in my blood, is what it is." His expression darkens. "I can't manage the water, though— not this close to the curtain."

My nerves tighten. Water is crucial to my plan. Unless he can conjure water, we won't survive in Cordon Five. I have a sudden memory of King in Cordon Two, making water from a bead of my sweat. I tell Roran about it.

"Scammer's tricks." He waves his hand in dismissal. "He just multiplied the matter. What you saw was him drinking a lot of sweat." He scoops up a handful of rocks. Maybe because I'm focused on his hands, I feel the shift of energy, the elements in the stone pulsing. Then, abruptly, it stops, like a snuffed flame. He curses and flings them to the ground.

"Wait," I say, placing the apple in his palm. "Use this. Make water from this."

"I can't—"

"You *can,*" I say urgently. The light is fading. Guards will begin making rounds soon. My pulse feels like a clock, ticking down the minutes. "You made this. It is yours to alter." Because the alternative is that we all survive off of apple juice, and I'm not enough like Dad to know if that will actually work.

He exhales, holding the fruit with just the tips of his fingers. I feel a charge in the air, like I'm standing beside an electric fence. Roran's breath stutters, and he closes his eyes. I stare at the apple, willing it to change, wondering if he can *feel* its elemental makeup alter. All at once, the apple collapses in on itself with a soft crunch and burst of juice. Then it dissolves into water, clear and filling his hands to overflowing. He laughs, a pure sound of shock and delight.

"Not sweat," he says, grinning.

I throw my arms around him. "Magic," I whisper fiercely. A hundred things could still go wrong, but this one crucial part of our escape is going to work. We can survive in Cordon Five.

If I can just get us there.

TWENTY-EIGHT

0 grams cirium

THEY WATCH ME. Guards follow at a distance as I duck into Dram's house. I set a chair to the door just as two shadows pass the window. I take Dram's spare shirt from its peg and pull it on, then snatch his blanket off the bed.

The door bangs against the chair.

"Scout," a man calls through the door, "come with us, please."

I slide the chair aside and open the door. "I haven't done anything wrong."

His gaze skips over me, and I see that these are the commissary's guards, the ones who carry flash weapons. "The commissary wants to speak with you," he says.

"Fine." I ignore the fear racing through my veins.

His gaze slips to the blanket. "You cannot appropriate provisions from other houses."

"But—"

"There are penalties."

"I'll switch it with mine," I say. "Please."

He nods, and I wrap it around me as we walk, hoping he doesn't notice the extra shirt I appropriated too.

"It's past curfew," the guard says.

The reply that jumps to mind will only get me in deeper trouble, so I press my lips together. The guards lead me toward Central. I must have done something worse than break curfew.

They lead me through the back gate. I have never seen guards slip behind the mansion like this. We push through the tangles of ivy, and I watch them exchange a furtive glance.

"What's happening?" I ask.

"Shhh!" The guard ushers me up the stairwell. The other darts ahead and checks the hallway.

"You're breaking Protocol," I murmur. The guard scowls at me. I open my mouth to say more, but he shoots me a warning look.

"We're on your side," he hisses.

The idea renders me speechless. I let him tow me down the hall and into a room, where Jameson stands leaning against his desk.

"Commissary," I say.

"Hello, Orion."

I can't make sense of the transformation in him. Gone is the austere representative of the Congress. He wears the same uniform and his chain of office, but his face is the one that told me he was sorry there are cages in Cordon Two.

"Things are not as they seem," he says.

My hands fist in Dram's blanket. I've got my knife in my boot, but I feel defenseless in this place.

"When you collected four hundred grams of cirium, you presented the Congress with a situation it's never had before."

"The sign says—"

"The sign," he says ruefully. He looks at me like I'm a child asking if the moon is made of cheese. "Have you ever heard the saying 'To get a horse to move, use a carrot and a stick'?"

I shake my head.

"At Outpost Five, they didn't even use a carrot—just the promise of one." A ghost of a smile crosses his lips. "And then you actually mined four hundred grams."

"But we can earn passage—"

He shakes his head. "Congress needs you here. Their tech can't do what you can do. Subpars are still the only ones who can find and mine cirium, and the ore you mine has a greater purpose than insulating a single city against a flash curtain."

"The Tempered Conjurors—"

"Yes." His face darkens. Shifting, changing, too quick for me to follow. "It's also the commodity we trade to other city-states, the means through which we maintain alliances that are the only thing keeping our enemies from overtaking us. But the tunnels are depleted, and Congress needs flash dust to power its weapons even more than it needs cirium."

Questions riot in my mind, but there's one thought that rises to the forefront. "If there are no Subpars in Alara, then where is Dram? Cranny said—"

"Cranny lied." A pitying look shutters his gaze. "Dram's in Cordon Three."

A guard clamps his hand over my mouth. I'm yelling, thrashing. I'm going to tear Cranny apart like the vulture he is.

"Calm down and listen to me," Jameson says. "Cordon Three isn't like the others. It's an agricultural test site. Or was—the things they were able to sustain are poisonous and uncontained. The project was abandoned years ago, but there's an underground compound there supplied with rations. It's where I had your father taken also. I had planned to keep him and Dram there until I could get them into Alara."

"So they're safe—"

"They're missing, Orion. Two days ago, Congress began blowing the Range. When the charges detonated, it cut power to a portion of the fence between Cordon Two and Cordon Three. Prisoners escaped. I haven't had contact with your father or Dram since."

Prisoners. All I can think of is King and his crew. My blood is suddenly ice, and if I move, I might shatter.

Jameson opens a panel in the wall and lifts out a case with four vials of distilled cirium. Dad's compound. "Your father trusted me with this. It's all he was able to make, apart from the vial he took to Cordon Three." He hands it to me. "You'll need every one of them to help you survive out there."

My hand tightens around the case. *Out there.* Surely he doesn't mean . . .

"I need you to find them," Jameson says. "You're the best scout I know."

"Me? You're a *commissary*—"

"Congress follows every transmission I make, every hover flight. If I do anything more to assist your father and Dram, I will be caught. If they discover who I really am, more lives than mine will be affected." He glances at his guards, then back to me. "You won't be alone. I have friends working out their own plans to get into Cordon Three."

I try to make sense of what he's telling me. "Friends?"

"You aren't the only one who resists—not everyone agrees with the Congress of Natural Humanity."

"Why are you helping us?"

"Because I need your father. If he can develop an antidote to radiation sickness, we can free all the Subpars."

"You have Serum 854."

"It's considered a danger to Alara." He taps his fingers on his desk, like he's debating how many of his cards to lay on the table. "Only the Prime Commissary has access to it now."

"She should give it to everyone in the flashfall! It could help people!"

"It would make them a threat to the Congress," Jameson says. "If Subpars and Conjies have a treatment for flash fever, what stops them from revolting in the cordons?" He shakes his head. "What we need is a *cure*, Orion. Serum 854 treats only the symptoms of flash fever. It doesn't shield a person from radiation sickness. Your father believes it could be one component of a cure."

I take a shaky breath. It's like my lungs are already rationing my air, preparing me for the cordons. I pull Dram's blanket tighter around me, a shield over my secret. I have two vials of Serum 854, taken from the helicopter in Cordon Four. When Dram and I recovered from flash fever, I knew the potential of the treatment. So I hid them in my bra, one of the only articles of clothing the Striders didn't take when they clothed me for Cordon Two.

I should probably come up with a better hiding place.

"You represent the Congress," I say, my gaze shifting to Jameson's chain of office.

"Only so much as it allows me to aid a greater cause."

"You're not working with Cranny?"

"I'm no more with Cranny than you are."

I try to select a single thought from the jumble tangling through my mind.

"Your questions will have to wait," Jameson says. "We've risked too much time as it is."

"What do I do?"

"I'm afraid I have to leave that up to you. They're watching me. The actions I've taken to protect you in the cordons and bring you back have made me suspect. These guards are with me." He points to the men who brought me here. "Don't trust anyone else. I cannot be seen speaking to you again. If you must relay a message, do it through one of these men."

"I'm just a girl—"

"Orion." He smiles, a full-bodied, genuine twist of his lips that lights his eyes. "You are the only person who's crossed the cordons and lived to tell about it. Orion. The Hunter. The Scout who can find anything."

Chills tingle along my spine. I tuck the vials inside my pocket, feeling the weight of too much responsibility. "But I—"

"You'll find a way," Jameson says.

My eyes stray to the maps on his wall. The one marked TUNNEL NINE is gone. A question forms on my lips, but he stares at me—hard—like he's saying things with just his eyes. I glance at the guards he trusts. But doesn't trust enough.

I walk to the door, drawing my own maps in my head. I will find Dram. And my father.

Even if I must cross the cordons again to do it.

TWENTY-NINE

0 grams cirium

I **LIE IN** bed, going over my half-formed plan to cross the cordons. I'd found Owen and given him the list of things I'll need. I'd told him everything Jameson said, and he's getting word to the others—we leave tomorrow.

Someone taps on my door. I stare at the ceiling a moment, trying to make sense of what's happening.

Tap.

Tap. Tap. Tap. Tap.

I slip my knife from my mattress and jog to the door. "Who is it?"

"Jameson sent me."

I slide the chair aside, and one of his guards ducks in.

"They're bringing the last of the Range down tonight," he says in a rush. "We're to begin evacuating now—guards and techs only."

And just like that, the clock over our sanctuary reads *0 Hours. 0 Minutes.*

"It's worse," he murmurs. "Cranny's coming for you."

My stomach knots. "What do you mean, 'coming for me'?"

"An order came through from the Prime Commissary. She wants you in Alara. Jameson says, whatever you're going to do—do it now." His gaze flies to the window, to the dark night outside.

I push him out the door. "Fine. Go." I whirl from the door just as Marin vaults down from the loft, dressed and ready.

"Tell Roran to raise the signal," I say. "Get everyone down nine."

"But Cranny—"

"I'll meet you there. Go!"

She darts through the door, and I scan the path. We are out of time, and it's up to me to stall the evacuation as long as possible. I drop to my knees and pry up the floorboard, a plan forming in my mind.

Cranny doesn't knock. Minutes after the guard leaves, he pushes through the door. Any sooner, and I wouldn't have finished. I slide beneath the bed, wincing as a knife handle digs into my back. I wear Dram's shirt, and beneath it, I'm sheathed in weapons. Just in case Cranny goes after me instead of the trap I laid.

"You've been summoned . . . ," he says, sweeping into the house. He hesitates at the loosened floorboard in the kitchen. "Pry it up," he orders a pair of Striders. The hum of their electrified suits fills the space. Cranny wasn't taking any chances when he came here. He obviously wasn't expecting my compliance.

They drag the boards away and peer down into the dark space.

"I knew he was hiding something," Cranny says. I imagine

he's thinking of all the times he stood over this spot scolding my father for using a light. He and a Strider climb down into the space.

I wait for the other to follow, but instead he steps away from the hole. Toward me.

The electric hum grows louder. I take silent breaths and watch his boots approach. My hands sweat beneath my gloves as I clasp a glass vial. My most dangerous weapon. Tiny pronged feet scratch the glass, but all I hear is the thrum of electric current.

I have one shot to get this right.

I lurch from beneath the bed, and the Strider catches hold of my arm.

"Director!" he shouts.

I search his eyes, but there's not even a flicker of remorse. It makes what I'm about to do easier.

"I learned something in Cordon Four," I say. "Your gloves aren't electrified." I slip the vial beneath his glove and slam my boot against his wrist. Glass crunches under the suit at the same time a shock rips through my body. But it's nothing compared to my shock collar in Cordon Two. I force myself to breathe, to focus my rioting nerves. The soldier pulls his gun and then an agonized cry rips from his mouth. His weapon clatters to the floor.

"What's happened?" Cranny shouts from belowground.

The Strider tears at his clothes, stumbling around and flailing even more than Winn did when ore mites covered her. The glass cut the mite open, and all its parasites are digging into the man's skin. I grab a chair and knock him off balance. He drops through the hole, just as the other Strider is climbing up.

I tip my ore pouch, filled with writhing ore mites, over the side. The second Strider fires off a couple shots, and I hug the ground.

"Don't shoot! They're combustible!" I shout, but I'm not sure he can hear me over his screams. I slam the floorboards into place, ripping my bolt gun from the belt I'd hidden under Dram's shirt. I think of all the times I called "marker" and Dram answered.

I fire a bolt into the panel. It glows red. Danger. Do not cross. I load another and aim it over the other board. A bolt slams through the wood, anchoring it to the floor.

Now Cranny is screaming like the Striders. My breath saws from my chest. This is like the gulls' nest. I am the source of their suffering.

But all I have to do is think of the cordons and what they are preparing to unleash over all of us. Someone fires off a shot.

They won't suffer long.

I grab my satchel and run for the door. I'm ten meters out when I hear the explosion. The ground shudders, but I hang on to my balance and look back. A bullet struck an ore mite. My house sits silent and unimposing, like nothing's changed. The underground lab must have contained the blast.

A hover lands beside the lodge. Striders pour out of it, and Jameson stands in the midst of them.

"Find the director!" he orders. He catches sight of me and looks away. He knows Cranny was heading to my house. "Check the mill first."

The mill. I almost laugh. Cranny would never have gone there, but the troops jog away obediently—to the building farthest from the tunnels.

They won't leave without him, and they're not going to find him anytime soon. I've bought us a little more time before they bring down the final stretch of the Barrier Range. Before they destroy our only hope of breaking free.

Jameson grabs hold of a passing guard. "Call it off!"

"Sir, the flash charges are activated remotely by techs in the city—"

"Tell them I'm ordering them to cease. The director is missing. We cannot evacuate without him."

Another tech runs up, one hand over his earpiece. "Communications are down. We're getting too much interference from the flashfall."

Jameson curses. Striders run past me, and I hug the shadows, grateful for once that this is a place without stars and moonlight. I sprint for the Rig, where my mother's axe hangs beside Dram's. I'm bringing them both.

As I pass Central, I catch a glimpse of white flowers dotting a sprawling vine. Roran's signal.

It's time to head down the tunnels one last time.

THIRTY

0 grams cirium

I SLIP INSIDE nine. Twenty headlamps turn and pierce me with their glare. I squint against the light.

"They're bringing down the Range," I call. We don't have earpieces or transmitters—nothing that techs could use to track us. "If we don't go now, it'll be too late."

"Here." Owen hands me a metal spring clamp the size of my hand. "I swiped it from the supplies building. Is that what you needed?"

I open the metal jaws and clamp it to my belt. "Perfect. Guard the entrance." I jog to the front of the group, searching faces, counting heads. "We're missing tunnel five's team."

"Changed their minds," a man says. I don't know his name, but I recognize him as one of the replacement people Congress sent us. A Natural. "Said nine's a death trap—they'll take their chances in the outpost."

Five's team is about to redefine its understanding of *death trap.*

I peer past the headlamps, looking for wiry red hair. The lodge mistress is missing. "Where's Anna?" I find Marin's face. Her eyes tear.

"She wants to stay," she says.

"And Barro?" I search the group again, hoping to see the glassblower's knowing brown eyes.

"He said to give you this," Roland says. He lifts a narrow rod of metal as long as my body, a piece of rubble I found in the Range. "He attached the copper wire at the top like you asked. And he got you the water, too." Roland reveals the bottle strapped in his belt. "I'll carry them for you."

"He's not coming?"

Roland shakes his head. "He said he's needed here."

"Fine." I switch on my lights, pretending my heart doesn't ache for the people we're leaving behind.

"What if they tell Cranny?" he asks.

"No one's telling Cranny anything," I murmur.

"But they'll know we're down nine—"

"We're not going down nine." I take Roran by the shoulders and steer him in front of me. "You're lead scout now. Time to show us what you've been working on."

"This way." He flashes his palm lights, illuminating a hidden tunnel of rock and sparkling crystal that looks like something from a fairy tale.

"What is this?" Marin asks.

"A path across the tunnels," I answer. "There's a way out through four."

Owen beams like a proud father. "Show 'em what you did with the sulfates, kid."

Roran sets a flame to the rock. Patches of sulfate ignite like the flaming shard of a cordon breach, the metal ions illuminating the tunnel.

"It'll burn and light up—just long enough for us to pass by," he says.

"He made this with . . . an axe?" Roland asks.

"I've got movement," Owen calls from his post beside the entrance.

"Everyone in!" I call. The cavers file past me into Roran's tunnel.

"They're coming—two squads of Striders!" Owen runs toward us.

"Seal it off, Roran," I say.

Roran grips the cavern walls, eyes wide. "They'll know my secret—"

"Do it!"

The Striders lift their guns. Rock scrapes over stone with a sound like screaming. The bullets ricochet.

"Conjuror!" a Strider shouts.

Roran shuts his eyes, and the entrance to nine pushes together, weaving the earth like the strands of a rope.

Our team stares at him with wide eyes. Most of them have never seen a Conjie in action.

"He's conjured a path across the tunnels," I say. "A way to escape through four." Further explanations will have to wait.

"Get inside!" The muffled shout reaches us from the other side.

It makes me smile. Good luck breaking through this rock without any cavers. I glance at the two ore carts full of provisions I've been stowing.

"Grab as many nutri-pacs and serums as you can. Put them in your pouches, your suit—every space you've got."

They dive into the supplies while a huge blast rocks the entrance. Bits of rock and dirt pelt us.

"Helmets on. Let's go!" I guide Roran to the front of our group. "We're going to have to run it."

Roran sets a flare to the wall. Color bursts across the stone, spreading like a contained fire. The tunnel glows in muted shades of red and blue and gold.

"Step in my steps," he says. Then he turns and runs, the last lead scout of Outpost Five.

———

We're crossing tunnel six when the first explosion hits. I trip and slam against the ground.

"Everyone okay?" I call. I'm at the back of our group, rounding up stragglers, pushing anyone not going fast enough.

"We're not going to make it!" Rita Calder cries. She's the one I've been pushing most.

I tug her to her feet. "Come on, we have to keep going."

"It's too late," she says, sobbing. "They're just going to blow us up."

"Don't say that." I pull harder, but the woman won't budge. She digs her hands into my suit. I look past the others and meet Owen's eyes. "Go on," I mouth.

His brows lower, and he strides through the group to where I strain against Rita's bulk.

"Look here, woman," he says. "You can stay right here and whine all you want. You want to quit? Fine." He pulls her hands off me. "But you're not taking Scout with you."

He guides me to the front. "Your place is up here," he says

gruffly. "The rest of you—keep up or let the tunnel have you."

I press forward with Roran, but keep looking over my shoulder. The stragglers are getting farther and farther behind.

"You can't do their running for them," Owen says, huffing at my side. This pace is strenuous, even for a veteran caver like him.

There's a shift in the cirium. I feel it, like a tap on the shoulder. The Range is crumbling.

"Axes up!" I shout. The cavers lift their axes above the heads of the people in front of them. They watch me, wide-eyed, waiting.

Rita's not at the back. Neither is the Natural whose name I don't know.

"Stay with Owen." I lower my axe and tuck Roran in front of the other caver.

"Scout," Owen says, his tone conveying more than his words.

"I'm going after—" Five steps forward, the explosion rocks me back. Axes arch above my head, the cavers protecting me. Stone rains down, but the tunnel holds. Roran and Owen have done their work well.

A woman screams.

"Rita!" I push past the line of cavers. The Natural shouts, his voice too distant to hear clearly. "I'm coming!"

"Scout!" Owen shouts. "We have to keep moving!"

"You go!" I call. I can just make out the Natural. He shouts again. What is he saying?

"Scout!" Roran's voice. He must sense the change in the earth, too.

A deep rumble lifts from beneath us. I close my eyes, waiting for the tunnel to collapse around me, to enfold me in a tomb of rock.

You've got a job to do, girlie.

It's like Graham's with me, reminding me that I promised these people a way out.

I turn my back on Rita and the Natural. I slam my bolt gun in my belt and run toward the others. Dust and debris roar toward us, shooting through the tunnel like water bursting down a pipe.

"Oxinators!" I shout. "Get your masks on!"

Roran stands in the path.

A woman shouts from behind me, her voice distant, followed by another.

"Seal it off!" I tell Roran. "Now. Before it hits us."

I brace myself behind him, strapping his Oxinator over his nose and mouth as he faces down the rage of the tunnels with his hands pressed to the earth.

"But those people—"

"No time. Do it!"

Crystals shoot from the walls of the tunnel, splintering the rock in massive bursts. Gnarled roots buffet our bodies as they erupt from the earth in tangles of limbs and leaves.

Roran's efforts are extraordinary. But this is not shield enough.

"Roran!" Mineral dust explodes over us like the winds preceding a storm. I cough, choking on dust as I drag on my Oxinator.

A cascade of rock pours down the tunnel, illuminated in the still-burning glow of metal ions. Our deaths will be beautiful and swift.

"AUGH!" Roran yells. Rock slams together an arm's reach away. The tunnel shudders, and I shelter him with my axe and my body. His wall holds. White blossoms float down like snow.

"We're going to make it." I will myself to believe it, so he will too. "We're almost there."

"That woman—" A sob tears from his chest. "She's dead. And those others—"

"We have to keep going." The stone beneath us trembles.

"I killed them!"

"No." I force him to meet my eyes. "*The Congress* killed them. You are giving the rest of us a chance to live."

I catch one of the blossoms clouding the air and tuck it into his fist. "Your mother is waiting for us, Roran. Winn is waiting for us." I turn him toward his path. "Run!"

Cordon Five. The east end of the flash curtain. An unpredictable, shifting tail of radiation that emits flash bursts, which turn the sands to glass. No one mines here, not even the Gems. It is a closed cordon, and the Congress has no use for such a place.

It is a perfect place to hide.

Glass crunches beneath my boot.

"Careful, Orion," Mere says.

The curtain shimmers in the distance, beyond clouds of flashfall. I feel it pulsing—its energy erratic, like a moth trapped behind glass. I drag off my Oxinator and inhale. No particles scrape my lungs. It's as if the curtain is holding its breath—saving it for something worse.

"It's safe to breathe," I announce. I help Winn with her Oxinator, and she latches onto my hand as soon as I'm done.

She's been beside me like a shadow since we met them in four. She tugs her doll free.

"She's safe," I tell her. *You're safe.* I don't say the words, but I know she reads it in my eyes.

Marin runs her hand over a patch of crystallized sand. "This entire cordon is like a memorial pendant—ash and glass."

"Can they see us from Outpost Five?" Mere asks.

"No," I say. "It's nearly impossible to see past the sulfur clouds."

"They aren't looking," Marin says. "Nothing can survive out here."

"You might be surprised," I murmur.

"Do you think they'll come after us?"

"No. They think we died when they blew the Range."

"So we're free," Owen says.

"Free in a cordon made of glass," Marin says.

"Free in a closed cordon with an Untempered Conjuror," Mere says, her eyes glowing. "Roran will help us survive."

"Down here," he calls, waving us over. Exhausted as he is, he's managed to conjure steps into the side of a deep trench. I smile grimly. His instincts are as strong as mine. The only true refuge here is belowground.

A small hand squeezes mine. I crouch down in front of Winn. "It's just a place to stay safe when the curtain sends out flash bursts." I look at the Subpars. "When the Radlevels are high. You'll sense it before it happens." The day of the cordon breach seems like a lifetime ago, but I remember how I felt up on the Range with Dram just before it happened—like an instrument being tuned.

Marin looks away, but not before I see her swipe at tears. *At least you'll be alive,* I want to tell her. But this is no real life.

I've led my friends to a cordon that looks like a blend of all our memorial pendants. But I will leave them with more than ashes.

"Winn?" I ask. She looks at me, her dark eyes wide. I brush my hand over her straight black hair, fighting to keep my voice steady. "Have you seen the stars?"

"Yes," she says. Her fingers twist in her doll's rope hair. "I know how to find the North Star and the Big Dipper."

"That's good." I smile, even as my throat tightens. "Tell the Subpars what they look like," I say. "So they'll know them when they see them."

Owen watches me intently. "You making some kind of promise, Scout?"

"I hope so."

He nods, like he's not surprised the Scout is off to hunt another passage. One that might lead everyone to a true sky.

"I have to go," I announce.

"Aren't you staying with us?" Marin asks.

"No." I check my pendants, tucked safe inside my shirt. The only piece of Outpost Five I'm bringing with me.

"Why not? You're finally free."

I suddenly remember Reeves, before he made himself dust. *I don't think I'm the only one of us who loves like that.*

"I need to find Dram."

"But we need you," Roland says.

"No," I look at our little band of rebels with a small smile.

"You really don't. But Dram does. And I need him." Roran tows himself up out of the trench, and I stare at the hole in the ground. My fear shifts to conviction. "This isn't really freedom," I say. "I'm going after something more—for everyone."

"Where are you going?" This from Roran, who holds himself rigid, his rock clamped in his fist.

"Cordon Three." I touch his shoulder. "My dad's out there, too, and there's something I need to give him."

He nods, then looks away. Mere steps forward and puts an arm around his shoulder. There is so much I want to say, but my throat is tight and I'm out of time.

"You have the map I gave you?" She nods. "I'm not sure what my mother was scouting. Maybe an old passage to Alara. She ran into barriers that were impassable, but with Roran's abilities . . ." I shrug. "It's unstable, but it might be your best chance if you have to leave the cordon." I spent hours beneath the bed, copying the map Mom had died making.

Mere pulls me close, and I swallow hard.

"You have a warrior's name," she whispers fiercely.

"I have a hunter's name."

"You're *both*." Her arms tighten around me, and the vials I'm carrying press against my chest, where they're hidden above my heart. I'm hunting for more than Dram and my father.

I'm scouting a way out of the flashfall—for all of us.

I carry the elements close—possible makings for a cure too dangerous to tell anyone about. My father could do something with these. Maybe something that sets everyone free.

An antidote for radiation sickness would limit Congress's

power. Their so-called protection would be meaningless. How could they force compliance from Subpars and Conjies if we could survive without them? And without us, they have no way to acquire flash dust.

Dram and I didn't just mine cirium from that cavern.

We discovered the elements for a cure.

THIRTY-ONE

6.0 milliliters Cirium 2
4.0 milliliters Serum 854

I DON'T HAVE a name for the altered cirium. I will leave that to the techs to determine. For now, I've nicknamed the liquid I carry Cirium 2, and I've got three vials left in the case Jameson gave me, strapped carefully beneath my Oxinator. I wear full caving gear, down to the knives sheathed on my arms. I've never cared more about my safety.

Too much is at stake for me to succumb to something like mineral burn, so I've robbed the infirmary. In the chaos of the evacuation, not a single guard noticed. I wear enough serum strapped to my legs to get me through the cordons. Nutri-pacs line the inside of my suit, enough for five days. If it takes me any longer to find Dram and Dad, I'll be dead anyway.

Soot coats my boots as I wade through sand and ash toward the electrified fence that divides Cordon Five from Cordon Four. A buzzer sounds in the distance. My heart clenches, and I stare in the direction of Outpost Five. I can't see it from here, but I imagine freshly painted corral towers looming in place of the

Range, and my fellow Subpars forced into the burnt sands—Marin's mother, tunnel five's fearful team, and the millworkers who've never mined, ever. And Barro.

The metal girder he prepared for me cuts into my gloves as I thrust it into the ground beside the fence. I hammer the top of the stake with the flat of my axe, pouring my fear and frustration into every strike.

The metal spring clamp slips in my hands as I attach it to the end of the copper wire. Adrenaline roars through my body like I've already been shocked.

The second buzzer sounds. Soon, my friends and neighbors will wade into the horrors of Cordon Four.

If I'm going to help them, I must survive.

With shaking hands, I pour the bottle of water around the base of the stake and grip the spring clamp. Please, let this work. The fence hums in a way that reminds me of Strider suits and Sanctuary's walls. Deadly. Daring me to try.

I close my eyes and picture Dram's face and Dad pulling me into his arms. I picture myself handing him the secret I carry.

The pulsing cable third from the bottom. Eye level. I squeeze open the jaws of the clamp and release it onto the wire. An explosion of sparks showers over my arm. I gasp and jump back. The hum ceases.

With my heart hammering, I crawl between the dead wires of the fence, every muscle trembling.

Still with me, ore scout? I can practically hear Dram's voice.

"Still here," I murmur. A gust of burning cinders slams against me, and I draw my neck cloth up. My eyes water as I lope across the cordon, masking my approach behind sulfur clouds.

I focus on the tasks ahead. Crossing the sectors of Cordon Four without notice. Clearing the fenced boundary on the other side. Hunting down Dram and Dad in the unknown.

The place on my mental map that I can't fill in with a single detail.

Cordon Three.

But that's likely two days' journey. I need to stay present and alert in every moment before then if I'm to survive.

The ash-soaked wind pushes against me, as if warding me away from certain danger. Too late.

There's no turning back now.

———

Night falls, and I crouch behind a pile of rubble, watching people deposit their flash dust and push through the turnstiles of Cordon Four. Clouds of emberflies illuminate the cordon, swirling through the air like sparks from a fire. My body aches from holding this cramped position, but I force myself to wait. I'm desperate for shelter, but I can't afford to get caught.

An hour later, not even a Gem remains to guard the fence. The perimeter lights dim. They're not expecting anyone else.

I shake feeling into my legs and stand, Mere's sifter brushing my side.

"You need this more than I do," she'd said just before I left Cordon Five. She'd unfastened her metal appendage and thrust it at me while I'd stared at her in shock. "To sift the sands for flash dust. You'll need to mine as you go, and it'll be fastest this way."

I'd finally found my voice. "You can't give me *your hand!*"

"What if there's a dust storm? Or emberflies? Getting past that turnstile might save your life."

I'd backed away from her, horrified by the idea of taking her appendage—horrified by the truth of her words.

"I only give my hands away for important reasons," she'd said. My throat tightens now, remembering how she'd winked at me and hugged me close a final time, her right arm ending at the metal cap of her wrist.

I grip my pouch of flash dust and run toward the shadowed boundary of the camp. The rungs of the turnstiles gleam beneath the flashfall like exposed ribs. In my addled state, I feel as if I'm sneaking into the belly of the beast. I empty the pouch of dust onto the scale, my ears straining to hear a guard shout. Cordon sand swirls around me, stinging me with scorched grains. Wind whines through the slats of the corral towers so loudly I can barely hear the automated voice thank me for my deposit.

Something crunches the sand behind me—footsteps maybe—but I don't pause to look. The lock clicks open, and I shove past the turnstile.

It strikes me that I am willfully breaking into a place I couldn't escape from—a place that nearly stole my life multiple times each day.

And someone else is coming after me.

I duck into a tent and collapse. My chest heaves as I drag in lungfuls of toxic air. I'd forgotten how bad it is here. How the air can kill you even faster than the curtain.

The tent rustles. I crack a light stick and hold it high. A man stares at me.

I drop the stick and free a blade. He grips my wrist as I lunge.

"You're alive," he says.

"What?" I know that voice . . . "Jameson?"

It's Jameson . . . but not. This man wears a ragged cap pulled low over his brow, and plain clothes like those of Subpars. But Subpars don't wear rings and wrist cuffs, and they never wear beaded sashes belted around their waists.

"I knew about the boy, so I guessed your plan," he says quietly. "But when they blew the Range, I was afraid you wouldn't make it in time."

My eyes narrow. "Who *are* you?"

"My given name is Carris, but I haven't been him in a long time." He speaks the words like a confession—in an accent I've heard only one other place.

"You're a Conjuror."

"Free Conjie. From the mountain provinces. My people found you that day beyond the shield. It's how I knew where to send Cranny."

The full impact of what he's saying hits me like a fist to the gut. "You . . ." My words fail as a dozen implications whirl through my mind. I dropped from the sky into Cranny's waiting Striders because of him. "But you said you weren't working with him!"

Jameson's eyes soften. "Sometimes you have to sacrifice your bait to catch the bigger fish."

"Must you always speak in riddles? Is that a Conjie thing?"

He grins. "Actually, yes."

"So are you here to rat me out again?"

"I'm going to get you over the boundary fence. Though I admit I'm terribly impressed with how you managed the first one."

"So the commissary is going to escort me from Cordon Four?" I ask.

"No, Jameson can't be linked to you again. But Carris will gladly sneak you out."

Voices intrude, beyond our tent. I crouch and grip my blade. Jameson yanks a bead from his sash and grasps it in his fist. Seconds later, he opens his hand and releases a thick fog that blends with the heavy layers of flashfall. Not even Gems will walk past the low-hanging haze he's shrouded us with. Not in a place with emberflies.

"What kind of bead was that?" I ask.

"Wood. From a tree in the provinces." He lifts his ringed fingers. "More than adornment. Natural things made in dirt without cirium. That's the key to conjuring this close to the curtain—and even then, only some of us can manage it. The cirium in matter prohibits our ability within the flashfall. So we need a conduit."

"The dirt Bade carried . . ."

He nods. "Like flint to a spark." He drops onto a cot. "We've learned to hide our resources well." He swipes a finger along the lashes of one of his kohl-lined eyes, and it comes away darkened with pigment. He twists his fingers and presents me with a flower and a cocky grin. "I'm better than most."

"My mother told me Conjies have magic."

The grin slides off his face. He seems to consider this, hands tightening on the cloth of his sash. "What else did she say about Conjies?"

"Not enough. Instead she taught me about stars—things you can't even see living in the flashfall."

"Maybe she wanted you to understand that the world was bigger than Outpost Five."

"She knew the word *glenting*," I murmur.

He makes a choked sound, not quite a laugh. "Then she must've known a foul-mouthed Conjie." He lies back, exhaustion written over every line of his face. "Rest now. We have to leave before the morning patrols."

"How long did you know about Roran?" I ask. "You guessed my plan—but how did you know what he could do?"

"That boy and his rock . . ." Jameson muses. "If they're close enough, Conjurors can sense when elements are being altered." He tosses me a satchel. "Food and water. Don't use the nutri-pacs unless you have to."

"What's wrong with them?"

"Many things, but no time to get into that now. Sleep. Tomorrow I get you past the fence." He settles back and closes his eyes.

"Dram and my father . . . ?" I ask softly.

"If my people are doing what they do best, your father and Dram are still alive."

"What is it they do best?"

He smiles. "Revolution. Sleep now, Scout."

"Orion," I say. "We're not in Outpost Five anymore."

"Trust me, you're still Scout."

"To whom?"

"I imagine you'll meet them soon enough." He rolls onto his side, away from me.

"You said they're safe?"

"Today," he mumbles. "Tomorrow's another story. The Congress isn't taking any chances. They can't afford an uprising on this side of the curtain."

"So they'll send Striders."

"No. Not when they can just drop bombs."

I grab the satchel and leap to my feet.

"Sleep, crazy girl," Jameson says.

"But if—"

"I'm going back to Alara to stall the demolition. I'm a commissary. Go to sleep. You're no use to us dead."

I ease onto my cot, still clutching the satchel of food that apparently won't harm me like the nutri-pacs do. Curling on my side, I watch the tent canvas ripple as the cordon winds blow.

I'm coming for you, Dram. Wherever he is—I hope somehow he senses me. *Hold on,* I tell him.

I close my eyes and will my body to relax. In the space between waking and sleeping, I feel him answer.

Hurry.

———

We run the length of the cordon, north, toward Cordon Three. By the time the first buzzer sounds, we are well beyond the authorized sectors.

"You should eat something," Jameson huffs from my side.

I peer into the satchel he gave me with distaste. "I already tried the 'cheese.'" *Cheese.* Even the word sounds gross.

"You need nourishment," he says.

"I never needed that before," I mutter.

He laughs. I don't see the humor. Everything my body's ever needed the nutri-pacs supplied. Food seems like added effort.

"Finally," Jameson gasps. The barrier fence rises up beyond the swirling embers. It hums with electric current.

"Is this when you put your Conjie hat back on?"

"It wasn't a commissary who just ran the cordon with you." He pulls off his gloves and pushes his hands in his pockets. They come away grasping fistfuls of dirt.

"Do all free Conjies carry dirt around in their pockets?"

He grins and cradles his hands together. "Wouldn't you?"

I've seen Conjurors enough that I know what to expect, but I still gasp when plant roots thrust between his fingers. With the snapping of wood and branches, a sapling sprouts upward, its leaves consumed by the radiation winds before they've even unfurled. He drops it to the ground, and it arches over the fence.

"It won't last long here. Better get climbing," he says.

I can't shake the feeling that there's something I'm missing. I stare at him, so utterly non-commissary, and my suspicions click into place. "You knew my mother, didn't you?" His mouth drops open. "You taught her Conjie curse words."

"Orion—" He looks at the tree, where some of the leaves are starting to catch fire. "We can't—"

"She knew what the stars looked like, because *you* told her about them." He shakes his head, but the look on his face is screaming *yes.*

He sighs. Dying leaves drop from the tree and swirl past us.

"What's down seven?" I ask.

A line forms between his brows, and I wonder which version of the truth I'm going to get. "An old passage that leads under the curtain—all the way into Alara. But every route's collapsed." He scans the sky. "You need to go before we're seen."

"She was trying to get us free."

"Yes."

She died, not trying to earn four Rays to get herself behind the shield—but to get *everyone* there. She believed there was a way out beyond what Congress told us. I pull a folded paper from my pocket—a copy of the one I gave Mere—and hand it to Jameson. "Take this. Whatever you're after, it may help."

"What is it?"

"Mom was the only one at Outpost Five better at maps than me." I leap for a branch, and the wood cracks under my weight. Already, the curtain is stealing the life from it. I haul myself to a larger branch, and the tree lurches suddenly, dangling toward the electric fence.

"Hurry!" Jameson shouts.

I pull myself atop the next branch and climb across. The branch snaps and, as I clutch the trunk, hits the fence with a pop and sizzle.

"Jump!"

It's an echo of Dram's words to me when we rode the tow cable into Cordon One. The tree dissolves beneath me, and I leap once more into the unknown.

Only this time, I am alone.

———

Sometime during the third day of navigating Cordon Three's odd, jungle-like terrain, I determine that the voices I'm hearing aren't just in my head.

In fact, now that I've stopped, they're loud enough to recognize. Terror rakes along my nerves. King. The voice calling to me belongs to the King of Cordon Two.

"Fire," I gasp, and sprint north toward a corral tower, the

only thing taller than the bizarre canopy of trees. I have no idea what I'll be met with there, but it has to be better than the Conjie Dram stabbed twice.

Somewhere in the distance, King lets out a whoop. Other voices shout back in response, and I pound across the earth, throwing my arms out at the foliage that blocks my path. They chase me like a pack of wild dogs. I skirt the edge of a pond, where orbies gather in clusters. Losing precious seconds, I drag on extra gloves, dump my satchel out, and scoop it full of the glowing water. Orbies swarm over my gloves, and I quickly tear them off.

A crash in the leaves behind me signals their approach. I force myself to stay still, to wait, vulnerable, my back to my pursuers.

"Get her!" King shouts. He laughs, as if this is a game he's about to win.

My pursuers' hungry breaths fill the air. I don't have to see their faces to know they're smiling too. I hold tight to the bottom of the satchel and whirl around, flinging the water at the three men who reach for me.

Shock registers across their faces as water soaks their heads and shoulders. They look down, trying to make sense of why they're suddenly wet, then—

They scream. I turn and run, not waiting around to watch. The corral looms ahead, its white legs visible through the tangles of vegetation. My lungs are bursting, but I push myself toward it, faster, vines and leaves slapping my face.

King tackles me to the ground. I thrash, arms and legs aiming at every place Dram injured him. My Radband catches him in the face, and he reels back, clasping a hand over his eye. I scramble up, but he traps my legs.

"You're mine!" he snarls, knotting his fist in my hair. He says something else, but I can't hear over the sounds of his men.

Then his fist connects with my face, and I don't hear anything at all.

THIRTY-TWO

1.5 milliliters Cirium 2
2.0 milliliters Serum 854

I TRY TO sleep. To escape to the numb haze that blocks out the musty cold and my fear of dying at King's hand.

They have me belowground, in the Congress's old research facility. I'm not sure what these pitted iron bars once contained, but it works perfectly for a Subpar prison. I huddle in the corner, arms wrapped around my legs, imagining myself far, far from here.

Something rattles my cell. My eyes open, but I can't shake free of my stupor. I've gone too many days without light and air and food.

"Feed the little witch," King says. "She's useless to me dead." In the glow of a single lantern I watch him tear into one of the pouches of food he pulled from a box of rations. It oozes onto his plate in a gelatinous heap, and he stabs at the chunks with his knife. My stomach twists and I hunch over, waiting for the dizziness to pass. His men gave me a plate of it the first day, but my stomach rebelled at the unfamiliar solid food. They've only given me water in the two days since.

My bars rattle again. I peer up at the Conjie who made the noise. In the darkness, it's impossible to distinguish his features. He's dragging a metal plate beside the lock. I have just enough energy to glare at him. The least he could do is let me die in peace.

The Conjie kneels and slides the food beneath the bars. I reach for it, and he catches my hand. His rings slide against my fingers, and I struggle to pull away, but he holds my hand tighter.

"Let go," I snarl.

With the finger of his other hand, he marks something on my palm. His dark hair hangs in his eyes, but I see them flick toward King. He repeats the action, two parallel lines. A caver's mark.

My breath catches. The Conjie lifts his kohl-lined eyes, and I peer through the dim confines of my cell. His earring catches the light of a candle, and I try to see his face past the scruff of a beard. I realize I'm searching for the thin, long scars left by a flash bat. His eyes hold mine a second longer, but I can't tell if they're blue. It's darker than nine in here.

"Leave the girl," King orders around a mouthful of food. "She needs all her strength for what's coming."

The Conjie nods and slips through the door.

My heart races. Is it possible that Dram somehow found me?

"Eat," King commands.

I dip my fingers into the food. Dark chunks in some kind of liquid. My fingers brush something hard. I trace the teeth of a key.

A way out. The symbol the Conjie traced into my palm. Tears fill my eyes as I stare at the door.

Dram. Finding a way to rescue me from the depths once more.

———

I'm crouched against the wall with the key hidden in my fist, waiting for my chance, when an explosion rocks the compound. Dirt rains down over me as I hug the floor of my prison. King curses and grabs a vial off the table—the Serum 854 his groping hands discovered the day he knocked me unconscious. He storms from the room, shouting orders.

I leap for the cell door and thread my hands through the bars. I wedge the key into the rusty hole and twist. It's like I've got my double-bladed knife in a flash bat's skull, but the lock won't yield.

This is taking too long. King could return any moment.

I jam the key in farther and use every bit of leverage I can manage. It clicks. The door creaks open, hinges scraping loud enough to announce my escape.

I snatch a knife from King's plate, then duck through the door into chaos. People run up and down the corridors. King left his coat, and I pull it on, hiding my hair beneath the hood. No one seems to notice me as they scurry about, grabbing weapons and supplies.

I tuck the knife in my sleeve and search for the way out. It's like a cavern down here, darkened passages that lead so many directions, with no clear exit.

Cavers' marks. Remembering how Dram marked my hand, I press against the wall and wind my way back to the cell. My nerves riot against me, but I press on, determined to see if . . .

A V turned on its side, marked with chalk near the bottom of the wall. Dram couldn't tell me the way out, so he did the next best thing. I follow the direction of the arrow, jogging the corridor as I search for the next marker. Another V, this one at waist height. I continue east, my pace quickening. These aren't his bolt lights, illuminating my path in swaths of glowing yellow, but they're just as comforting.

"The girl's gone!" a man shouts.

Doors slam. Pounding feet echo along the corridor. I run.

A man grabs me. He grips a hand over my mouth, stifling my scream.

"It's Bade," he says, pulling me into an alcove just as three of King's men sprint past. I turn and recognize the Conjie who helped us in Cordon One.

"Where's Dram?" I whisper.

"Up top. I followed his marks down to you."

He lays his palms on the dirt wall and closes his eyes. The dirt shakes and pushes up, pressing around us like it's taking a breath. Roots twist up from the ground, stretching and extending their reach with branches and leaves. The air fills with a dust that I recognize as pollen, and the verdant scents of grass and blooming flowers.

"Hold on," he says.

I grab hold of a thick branch, and it tows me upward as he conjures a path. Dirt and rock rain down on us, but the branches weave a protective canopy over our heads. It reminds me of Roran, when we fled down his tunnel with the Range toppling down behind us.

We break through the earth. Hands reach for me before I've even cleared the dirt from my eyes.

Dram. He pulls me hard against his chest.

"Rye." He squeezes me so tight I can't breathe. I reach up and tug his shaggy Conjie hair. He eases his grip.

"You found me," I whisper.

He pulls away, his eyes roving over me like he can hardly believe it himself. "I wasn't sure I'd get to you in time."

His eyes look different ringed in the black liner the Conjies use. They stand out even more, blue pools, glowing like safe cavern water.

I grasp the sides of his head and pull him down to me. His lips find mine, and he sighs against my mouth as if he hasn't breathed until now—as if I am the only air he needs.

"I almost didn't recognize you," I say against his lips.

"It was the best way for me to get close." He's squeezing me again, and I let him hold me as tight as he wants. Sounds of muted gunfire lift, and he pulls away, taking in our surroundings before settling back on my face. His eyes linger on the place where King hit me.

"It's not as bad as the one I gave him," I say, hoping to erase the haunted look in his eyes.

"That black eye was your doing?" he asks, a smile tugging at his lips.

"Only because I'd already used my bag of orbies up on the other guys."

His smile widens, and he tucks me in his arms.

"You went with Cranny," he says, his voice rough.

"To save you. He told me he would send you to Alara."

He laughs, a harsh sound without humor.

"He's dead," I say. "And Congress blew the Range. Outpost Five is a cordon."

He looks at me through ghost eyes again, the blue dimmed with shadows. "I know."

"Out of time," Bade calls, tossing Dram a weapon.

"You know how to use that?" I ask.

Dram checks the chamber and slams the cartridge into place. "You'd be surprised the things I know now." He guides me past a team of armed men. "Your father's down there. We're going after him and the compound he's been working on."

"I'll come with—"

"You can barely stand, Rye." His concern marks his face. In the light of the flashfall, I can see the shadows under his eyes. "Reese!" he calls to another man. "How far out are the H-3s?"

"Bombers are less than ten," the man responds. He holds some sort of earpiece to one ear and calls out coordinates.

Dram leads me past him, and suddenly I see the source of the sound I couldn't place. Rotating blades cut the air above a flying machine. Not a hover—a cirium-plated helicopter like the one we discovered in the burnt sands.

"Stay with the chopper," Dram shouts over the noise. "I'll be back as soon as I can!"

My wide eyes search Dram's. "Who *are* you?"

"My father's son, apparently." He smiles, but it doesn't reach his eyes. He nods to a Conjie behind me, then runs back toward the compound—the smoking hole in the earth that contains my dad.

I grip King's dinner knife, preparing to run after him, but the Conjie grasps my arm.

"Dram asked me to make sure you got on," he says. "He was right—you don't like to be left out of a fight." He guides me into the helicopter, where I sit clutching the seat, staring toward the place Dram disappeared.

Smoke lifts, blending with the flashfall. It grows as the minutes pass, until I struggle to see beyond the opening of the craft. Suddenly, a figure emerges, his arm across the back of the soldier guiding him aboard.

"Dad!"

"Orion."

My arms close around him, and I feel his bones through the layers of his clothes.

At some point in that cell, I'd given up believing I'd see him again. The ache of loss slides away, leaving me adrift in raw emotion. There is so much to tell him—how I survived the cordons, that I traded my freedom for Dram's and returned to Outpost Five, that Congress blew the Range while we ran beneath it . . .

"I saw the sky," I choke out. He makes a sound—one that I feel rumble from his chest—like a sob and a laugh mixed together.

"Orion, you need to strap in," the Conjie says.

His soft command reels me back to the present moment. I pull away and settle into my seat. "Dad, I need to tell you what I found—"

"Serum 854?" he asks.

"How did you know?"

"The commissary told me what you and Dram found in that helicopter. You stumbled across something they'd given up on recovering."

My mind spins as I try to catch up to what he's saying.

He leans closer, lifting his voice above the sounds of the

blades beating the air. "Five years ago, Arrun Berrends sent a team to Outpost Five. They planned to liberate the Subpars there."

"They crashed in Cordon Four," I say softly. I picture the craft half buried in sand, the wreckage that housed our salvation that day beside the curtain.

"Arrun risked everything stealing that serum. His source inside Alara was exposed, and he's been on the run ever since."

"Didn't Arrun have more? Surely he didn't send it all with that helicopter."

"What little he had was used up in the process of trying to replicate it."

"H-3s are two minutes out!" the man with the earpiece shouts.

The remaining soldiers scramble aboard the crafts.

"Wait!" I grasp the edge of the door frame and lean out.

"Strap in, Orion," my escort calls. "We're lifting off."

"Dram's not back!"

"Time's up," the pilot calls from the cockpit. "Congress has hovers en route with flash bombs."

"We can't leave him!"

Shots fire, and Bade bursts from the compound. He leaps for the craft just as we lift off. Three pairs of hands grab hold of him and drag him inside.

"Got the serum," he says thrusting a vial into Dad's hands. I recognize the vial of Serum 854 King took from me.

"Where's Dram?" Bade asks, his gaze flicking around the seats.

"Down there!"

"I thought he was already in!" He stares out at the ground, a curse slipping past his lips.

"I see him!" I cry. "There—" Dram sprints toward the corral tower.

The soldier beside me sights down his rifle and fires, taking down one of the men chasing Dram, then another.

"We can't land," Bade says.

"That's not what he's going for," I say. "Lower a tow cable—"

"What cable? This isn't a prison hover."

"Then lower *me*!"

Dram grips the white intersecting beams of the corral and climbs.

"I'll do it," Bade says.

"It needs to be me." I don't have time to explain. My eyes beg him for understanding.

"Fire," Bade murmurs. He cuts the harness from his seat and fastens it around me. "Reese—get me that rope."

They knot the rope around my makeshift harness, and I crouch beside the open door, the wind buffeting my body and my legs dangling over the side.

"H-3s in sight," the pilot calls. "I'm taking us out—"

"No!" I step down, my feet braced on the leg of the craft. My hair whips around me, and my heart bashes my chest like a fist. I've never been so scared. I'm terrified that Dram will be ripped from this life by a flash bomb, right before my eyes.

"Orion, stop!" Dad shouts. "There isn't time—"

I pitch myself over the side, stretching my arms to make myself as long as possible, my hands open—ready to grasp any part of Dram I connect with.

The world tips upside down, and I twist on the end of the rope. I'm going to pass out before I reach him.

Some part of me registers the drone of approaching hovers. They're far above us. Only the foolish risk skimming along so close to the ground. Only the desperate—

Flash bomb.

They've dropped the first one. A concussive wave jolts the chopper, and I spin wildly, a puppet with too many loose strings.

"Dram!" I scream. The ground is on fire, and I feel myself lifting. They are pulling me back. "NO!"

Please, please, please.

We have a deal. I imagine I'm saying it to Dram. Screaming it to him.

My arms stretch, like I could touch the earth with the force of my will. Like I could make the earth shudder and shift and carry him to me with roots and branches.

I hit a wall. Not a wall.

Dram.

I slam into him, and he clutches me, clings to me. I am his lifeline.

They tow us up. I'm dying. I'm ripping apart. Dram's weight is too much for me and my harness of helicopter belts.

I scream from the tension. Dram echoes me.

"Almost there!" Bade's voice. Shouting from safety. "Hang on! They've dropped another—"

Blast of heat. I'm in the curtain. Her arms surround me, holding me. I am hers. I grip Dram with my arms and legs, but she grips me with luminescent death.

"Got you!" Bade's hands on me. I'm still burning, I cry out.

"Use the serum!" Dad's voice.

"It's the last one—you won't be able to replicate it!"

"She's dying!"

A needle pierces. Cool, liquid safety. Chases the curtain away. She runs, fast as my veins can carry her.

"Rye . . ." Dram's rusty voice, hoarse from yelling.

He's alive.

I'm alive.

The flash bombs did not claim us after all.

"Pull up her sleeve. We need to start a drip," Dad says. More hands on me. Another needle slides into my vein.

"They've both been burned. Get me Serum 60, and I'll need . . ." His voice fades to the background.

The helicopter bumps beneath me, and I imagine it's like riding a butterfly. High up and swirling, at the mercy of the wind.

"Lower the cirium shields," another voice commands. The door slams shut, cutting off the wind and the sounds of the rotors.

"Take us through the curtain," Bade says. "We're going home."

Home.

Past the curtain.

The words dance in my mind to a tune I don't recognize. They don't match—these two ideas. Home, past the curtain.

Cool spray mists my skin, and I feel less and less like I'm lying in the burnt sands of Cordon Four.

"Dra . . . Dra . . ." I can't push any more sound past my lips.

"He's right beside you, Orion," Bade says. "You got him."

I got him.

Lifeline.

I reached for him, and he reached back.

The tune in my head grows louder. I like this song, the one that mixes "past the curtain" and "home." They swirl and dance together in my mind until they are one and the same, and the tune is familiar now.

My fingers brush Dram.

He's right beside you, Orion.

Home. I'm going home.

I give myself over to the music.

———

Cool air brushes my cheek. I'm still riding the butterfly. My eyes open. Not a butterfly—a helicopter. My thoughts reorder themselves as I stare across at the boy watching me.

His eyes smile, even if his cracked lips can't quite manage it.

"You threw yourself . . . out of . . . helicopter for me," he says. "That's . . . a new one." His lips lift on one side.

"Well," I say, my voice as graveled as his, "you weren't keeping . . . your end of the deal."

The rest of the things we need to say, we do without words.

Dad hovers beside me, checking my vitals. "You don't have to keep proving to me how brave you are," he says.

"Maybe I'm just foolish."

"No." He grins down at me. "I've heard about all the things you've done. Only some of them were foolish."

"Dram." Bade crouches beside us. "Did you make it out with the cirium compound?"

"In my chest pouch," Dram says. He still can't move. He's

covered in a shock blanket and tubes stream from both his arms.

Bade slides the blanket aside and opens the pouch. He lifts out shards of shattered glass. No one speaks.

"I'm sorry," I whisper. I remember the moment my body crashed into Dram's. Like hitting a wall.

"I should've protected it better," Dram says. "There wasn't time—"

"And the serum?" Bade asks.

In my veins.

Dad hands him the empty vial. "I took a sample of her blood. I can try to replicate it—"

"They're both gone." Bade speaks the words like he can't quite believe them. Like he's wrapping his mind around the fact that all our efforts were in vain.

"Not all of them," I say softly. I lift my mother's memorial pendant from around my neck. With trembling, blood-streaked fingers, I caress the blob of wax at the top.

"Funny thing about tunnel gulls," I murmur. "Their talons are great for drilling tiny holes." I lift the blue glass. "Just the right size to shake out the ash and pour something else in." I drop it in my father's hand. "Like 1.5 milliliters of distilled Cirium 2 from tunnel nine."

His eyes slide shut. Bade murmurs something I can't hear. Dram just stares.

I slip Wes's memorial pendant from around my neck. I think of how I felt him with me, like sunlight, sustaining me when I ran toward the curtain in Cordon Four. And how I felt him again, close to me when I emptied his ashes on the Range the day before I fled Outpost Five.

I press the yellow glass into my father's hand. "Two milli-liters of Serum 854," I say softly. "The treatment for flash fever."

His eyes fill with tears as he takes it.

"Go test your theory, Dad."

THIRTY-THREE

0 grams cirium
0 grams flash dust
0 milliliters Cirium 2
0 milliliters Serum 854

THEY MOVE US from place to place—small camps of rebels
on the east side of the curtain. I'm asleep more times than
awake, but I'm aware of two things: air that smells of pine
whispering over my skin, and my father, speaking to me as he
tends my injuries, calling me back to myself. He says my name,
and it sounds different than it did before. Maybe because I am
different.

I squeeze his hand now. There's a question behind his words
that he's not asking. It's been there all along, but I haven't had
the strength to answer. Until now.

"Yes," I whisper.

"Orion?"

"Go to Alara." Not even my voice sounds the same. "Finish
the cure." The tech and equipment he needs are there. We don't

even have electricity, and we have to move constantly to evade the Congress.

He doesn't say anything, at least nothing I hear before I sleep again. Later, he kisses my head. I can't understand his soft words, but I know they mean good-bye.

He doesn't ask me to come. I don't tell him I'll see him in Alara.

I'm not sure I'm meant to live behind a shield.

———

Jameson stands beside a small hover outside the tent. He's dressed in his uniform, the civilized commissary I first met in Outpost Five. I've seen him conjure a tree from dirt, but what's even more astounding is his ability to conjure a different persona—one that the leaders of Congress haven't seen through.

I recognize the guards at his side—two that he trusts. But these men were not with him in the cordon. I wonder how many of his secrets they actually know.

I wonder how many of them *I* know.

"I can find a place for you both in Alara," he says. "Orion, you'd be close to your father."

"He's safe?" I ask.

"Safe as he can be developing the vaccine in secret. I have my best people working with him. As soon as it's ready, we'll take it to the cordons."

"He's happy," I murmur.

Jameson grins. "You should have seen his face when he saw the lab. When I left, he barely looked up from his microscope— just long enough to ask after you."

"When you see him next, tell him I'm happy too."

He hands Dram a narrow silver screencom. "Your father evaded capture and disappeared in the outlier regions. These are his last known communications."

Dram closes his fingers around the device. A possible link to his father.

"Thank you," he says softly.

Jameson's gaze shifts back to me. "So," he says. "Are you ready to go?"

He's offering us the protected city. Or what actually exists in place of the myth I've held in my mind all these years. Part of me still wonders what girls my age do in a place with clean air and a shield that keeps the storms at bay, but a bigger part of me doesn't care anymore.

I'm not that seventeen-year-old girl, and I never will be. A girl who had never endured a flash storm wouldn't have survived the cordons. A girl who didn't have to carry an axe and hunt for cirium would not have found the elements for a cure.

I look at Jameson. He watches me, waiting—even though he probably knows what I'm about to say.

"A Conjie once told me that the mountains are the only place you can still see the sunrise."

Jameson smiles. "True, but there's no electricity up there, no running water, no tech that can be tracked by the Congress." His smile dims. "The free Conjies are hunted, Orion. It's dangerous to associate with them."

Dangerous. I consider the word. It rides my nerves like tension in a climbing rope, but it doesn't fill me with fear. "I'm okay with dangerous."

Beside me, Dram laughs.

"What about you?" I ask him.

He looks toward the ridge of mountains. "No tunnels up there, but I'm pretty sure you still need me as your marker."

My smile matches his. "Mountains it is."

———

The free Conjies welcome us like their own. We celebrate with music and dancing and enough ale that it almost feels like Friday night at Outpost Five. Only we don't have to return to the tunnels anymore, and each choice we make is ours.

The idea is unfamiliar, but liberating—like the loose blouse and skirt I wear. A beaded scarf sways at my hips, a present from Dram on our special day. It's the purest shade of blue.

Like the sky, he said.

Like his eyes, I told him.

Dram takes my hand, and his new metal cuff brushes mine. We are not just scout and marker anymore. We were never just that, but now it's official. Well, as official as Conjies get, anyway.

"Bonding suits you," Bade says with a grin.

I watch him turn Aisla under his arm, thinking the same thing about him. She laughs at something he says, and the sound lifts on the wind like it's part of the music.

"I have something for you," Dram says.

"What did you steal?"

He smiles. "Not stolen. I promise."

"If you're showing me the inside of our tent, you're a little early."

His smile widens. "Not our tent, either." He loops a satchel across his chest and takes my arm. "Come with me. It's the perfect time."

He leads me away from the campfires, the raucous laughter

and the music. It fades until I hear only crickets and owls and the sounds of Dram's breath as we climb the path.

"Just a bit farther," he says.

We emerge through the trees, and I follow him up past the tree line, our steps silent over the pine needles that slowly give way to earth and stone. "Bade told me about this place."

We've made it to the top. I catch my breath, and Dram spreads out a blanket.

"It's better if you lie down," he says.

"Ah. Now I understand."

He grins. "*That* is not what I have in mind."

I lie back and set my head on the curve of his arm.

"Look," he says.

I lift my eyes. It's as if he threw my father's compound against a cloud of cirion gas. The stars shine that brightly. Brighter than I imagined as a child, listening to my mother's stories.

It robs me of breath. This far above the tree line, nothing hinders the view. The stars encompass the entire sky, illuminated like the shards of a cordon breach, only these are safely stowed far, far overhead.

"The North Star," Dram says, pointing. "Polaris. It's part of Ursa Minor. And if you follow it down"—he points to a grouping of stars—"you end up at the Big Dipper inside Ursa Major."

"Now—" He rises up, holding me close as he turns. "See those three stars in a row? They form—"

"A belt," I whisper, hearing my mother's voice from my memories. I know what he's going to say next. My heart races.

"That's Orion."

Tears burn the back of my throat. They blur the glimmering pinpricks of light stretched above me. I don't have any words so I just squeeze Dram's hand.

"Aisla said it's a constellation you can see from anywhere in the world," he says. "It contains two of the brightest stars in the sky." He catches me studying his face. "What?"

"Thank you," I whisper, leaning up and weaving my arms around his neck. He kisses me back, and I feel like I am falling across the sky, a blaze of light—one of the shooting stars my mother used to tell me about. We used to make wishes on stars we couldn't see.

Now I am the star, and our wishes spread before me, infinite and vast and unfolding inside me.

OTHERS HAVE STARTED leaving their marks in the rubble this side of the protected city. Sometimes notched in trees or doors, on roadways, even the bottoms of hovers: two vertical lines, angled. A simple cavers' mark that's now a symbol for something greater. The stories are spreading too fast for the Congress to contain. People have stopped believing the lies. They are who they believe themselves to be—and nothing less.

This wall says SUB—like the person was stopped before they could finish. I spray paint from a can, finishing the rebel's tag. SUBPAR. I stare at the word, thinking of our friends still trapped in Cordon Four.

"*Nos sumus fortunati,*" I whisper, touching the paint. We are the fortunate ones. Dram and I. But they are there—with those words on their sleeves.

"At least now they have hope, Orion," Dram says. "They know it's possible to break free."

Maybe we can give them more. "Let's go find your father."

He hasn't shown me the transmissions, but I know he's watched them countless times. He studies my face, looking for holes in my resolve.

"The outlier regions are lawless," he says. "Not even the Congress has maps for where he is."

"Then we'll make our own." I hand the paint to Dram. "Marker."

He grins and paints the lines. "Mark," he says, like he's just shot a light bolt into the stone.

We walk away, leaving behind a beacon.

Proof that there's a way out.

ACKNOWLEDGMENTS

Thank you to the amazing people who brought *Flashfall* to life with their talents and support:

To the best, most tenacious, forensically editing agent, Sarah Davies (who was once a caver herself!). You helped me get rid of "all the dodgy bits" so Orion's story could really shine. I'm so grateful to be part of the Greenhouse!

My wonderful editor, Kate Farrell, who believed in this book from the start and pushed and stretched me as a writer until the world was more dimensional and the characters so richly drawn they felt real. There's not a gift basket large enough to express my appreciation for your wisdom and guidance.

Everyone at Macmillan Children's Publishing, especially the talented team at Henry Holt, who worked tirelessly to bring *Flashfall* to new heights. I could not have asked for a more fantastic group of people to launch my debut, and I'm thrilled to continue the journey with you all on the next one!

To Mary Pearson and Aprilynne Pike, who have been very

special champions of this book. I cannot begin to tell you what your support means to me. I'm truly honored!

ALL THE LOVE to my family, friends, and fellow writers who supported, encouraged, and pushed me past the hurdles. I am grateful for each and every one of you.

Special thanks to my parents, Mary and Jim Brinda, who never set a limit on my dreams. When I wanted to fly, you pointed me toward the sky. And to my brother, Dave, who never stopped telling me to go for it.

To Jacob, who reminds me every day that teenage love is not only possible but quite spectacular, and to Caden, Landon, and Kai. You've taken this crazy journey right alongside me, and you make it all worth it.

And finally, to all the readers: none of this would be possible without you.

Nos Sumus Fortunati